ABOUT THE AUTHORS

Amy McGavin is the pen name of a Scottish wife-and-husband writing team whose real names are . . . Amy and Gavin.

The couple's contemporary romance novels are set in the Highlands. Each story is crafted with humour and heart, with a wee bit of heat thrown in.

The pair live in Glasgow with their daughter and very lively cocker spaniel. When they're not writing, they enjoy exploring Scotland's breathtaking hills, glens, and beaches, then treating themselves to coffee and cake afterwards.

To keep up to date with all their publishing news, and gain access to exclusive bonus content, join their newsletter by visiting amymcgavin.com.

Newsletter

Built for Love

AMY McGAVIN

GRUMPY GROUSE
PRESS

ISBN 978-1-916734-13-5

Cover character illustration by Ivanna Nashkolna

Cover design by Amy McGavin

Published by Grumpy Grouse Press

Built for Love

CHAPTER ONE

AINSLEY

"It smells like stinky socks in here!" Lily wrinkles her nose dramatically, her voice echoing off the bare walls of the empty salon.

"It just needs some fresh air," I tell her, flipping through my planner while Malcolm Walker jots something in his notepad.

"And new everything." Lily spins in a circle, her arms held out wide. "Can we paint it orange?"

"We're painting it blush pink and soft white, remember? You said you liked that."

"No. I like orange better now."

Of course she does. Four-year-olds are more fickle than a Highland forecast. "Pink is more sophisticated," I suggest.

"What's 'fisticated mean?"

"Sophisticated," I correct. "It means fancy."

"Oh." Another spin. "Can I be fancy?"

"You already are."

Malcolm chuckles and looks up from his notes. "She's a wee character, that one. My granddaughter, Isla, is the same. Seven going on seventeen, she is."

Lily's trainers squeak as she trots over to the front window, her brown pigtails bouncing. "Look! Someone painted the window so people can't see us." She smooshes her cheeks with both hands and blows a raspberry.

"Lily!"

"What? No one can see me, Mummy."

Malcolm chuckles. "The whitewash—the paint—is just so we can get on with the refurb in peace, Lily. Once it's done, I'll scrub it off for the grand reveal."

"Oh!" Lily turns around. "So we're keeping the salon secret till it's ready?"

"Exactly." I smile. "Now, how about you play quietly for a few minutes? Malcolm and I need to talk over everything that has to be done before opening day, okay?"

"Okay, Mummy." She strolls over to one of the old styling chairs and climbs up onto it. While she hums away to herself and spins around, Malcolm and I go over the plans again, confirming measurements and timelines.

As he talks, my gaze drifts around the room: the scuffed skirting boards, the cracked tiles by the back basin, the ghostly outlines where mirrors once hung. I picture it as it *will* be: fresh paint, new stations gleaming, sunlight spilling through clear glass instead of whitewash.

A bubble of nerves rises in my chest, mixed with something that feels suspiciously like excitement. This is my fresh start. No—I glance over at Lily, who's now holding her fingers like scissors and pretending to give herself a trim—*our* fresh start.

"Right," Malcolm says, pulling me back. He's scanning his notepad, pencil tapping lightly against the paper. "This should all be straightforward enough. My son, Struan, will be handling most of the work. He'll get started first thing Monday."

"Oh, your son's doing the renovation?" Hadn't realised that. Please let him be competent. A reliable tradesman who'll get the job done without drama.

"Aye, he's brilliant. Been working with me at Walker Builds since he left school. Actually, you're on Ardview Road, aren't you? Number twelve?"

"That's right. Well, I will be soon. I'm collecting the keys today."

"Ach, you'll be next door to him, then. He's at number fourteen."

"Handy," I say with a small laugh. "At least I'll know where to find him if anything goes wrong."

"Shouldn't be any problems," Malcolm assures me. "But aye, between the refurb and living next door to him, you'll be sick of the sight of him by the time this place opens." He winks at me.

"Mummy!" Lily jumps down from the chair. "Can we go see the new house now? I want to see my room!"

I check my phone. Eleven. The estate agent won't have the keys ready until noon at the earliest. "Soon, baby."

"You said that ages ago."

"Twenty minutes ago," I point out.

"That *is* ages ago!" She crosses her arms and her lower lip trembles. Oh God. We've had so many meltdowns lately, and I really can't handle one in front of Malcolm. "Tell you what, why don't we go to the soft play after we're done here? Would you like that?"

Her face transforms instantly. "Really? Can we?"

"If you let Mummy finish talking to Malcolm."

"Okay!" She smiles sweetly, the brewing tantrum forgotten.

"We're pretty much done here anyway." Malcolm tucks his pencil behind his ear. "I've got everything I need. This place will look great when it's done, and I'm sure it'll do well here in Ardmara. What brought you to town, if you don't mind me asking?"

The question catches me off-guard, and my chest constricts, just for a second. I smooth down a page in my planner, buying myself a moment. "Oh, I've always loved this part of the Highlands, and I've dreamed of having my own salon for years. When this one became available, it was a no-brainer." I keep my tone light, breezy. It's not a lie but it's not the whole truth either. Not even close. But I'm not about to tell him what I'm running from.

Malcolm nods, accepting the answer without question. "Right then, I think we're all sorted. Struan will be here Monday morning, eight thirty sharp. Should have you up and running in two weeks."

Two weeks. I glance around the tired salon again—water-stained ceiling tiles, walls that might have been white once, floors dulled by years of footsteps. Just two weeks until our fresh start officially begins.

Assuming nothing leaks, breaks, or bursts into flames before then.

CHAPTER TWO

STRUAN

"Arrr, first mate! There be sharks in these waters!" Isla bellows from somewhere ahead, her voice echoing through the plastic tubes.

I commando-crawl through the maze after her, my shoulders barely fitting through the kid-sized passages. "Aye, captain! Terrible beasties they are too. Did ye know sharks can smell a single drop of blood from three miles away?"

"That's not even true, Daddy."

"Course it is. And they've got a thousand teeth."

A dramatic sigh sounds from around a corner. "Most sharks only have fifty to three hundred teeth, Daddy. We learnt that at school."

"Well, these are special Scottish sharks. Highland sharks. They've evolved."

Her giggle bounces off the walls, and I catch a glimpse of her curls through one of those bubble windows. Seven years old and already too smart for my nonsense, but she still plays along. For now.

"Highland sharks aren't real!" she protests.

"Oh, they're real, captain. Vicious too. They swim up the rivers and into the lochs wearing wee kilts—"

"DADDY!"

"—playing bagpipes to lure unsuspecting pirates—"

"You're so weird." But I can hear the smile in her voice.

"Struan, mate!" Douglas's words cut through the plastic walls. "Your food's here."

"The crew be calling us to the galley, captain," I say to Isla.

"Can we finish the game after?"

"Aye, but only if ye promise not to make me walk the plank again."

We emerge from the tunnels like miners from a shaft, Isla pushing sweaty curls off her face while I unfold myself to my full height, joints protesting. Christ. Those things weren't built for someone six foot three.

The Pit—Ardmara Leisure Centre's soft-play area, to give it its proper name—assaults all five senses at once. Screaming kids, the smell of chlorine from the pool mixing with chips and stale coffee from the café, primary colours so bright they could trigger a migraine. We've been coming here for years, the Ardmara single dads and our wee ones, and somehow it never gets any more bearable. Just more familiar.

Our usual table is in the corner, as far from the speakers blasting kids' songs as we can get. Douglas looks ready to face-plant into his chips just to drown out his twins' squabbling. Logan and Rosie are arguing over who gets which juice carton. Lachlan, meanwhile, is wearing his usual expression, somewhere between stern and constipated, though it softens when Blair leans in to whisper something in his ear. I still find it weird seeing him actually smile. A few months ago, before Blair showed up to nanny Finn, I'd have bet good money his face would crack if he tried.

I pull out my phone as we sit down, opening the app linked to Isla's glucose monitor. The numbers are fine. I give her a small nod, and she reaches for a chip, already chattering to Finn about sharks with bagpipes.

"Here you go." The young server—Emma? Emily?—sets down another bowl of chips in front of me. She tucks a strand of hair behind her ear, not quite meeting my eyes. "We made too many."

She's . . . what, twenty? Twenty-one? Pretty enough, with a sweet face and big brown eyes. A bit young for me, though.

I give her a grin out of instinct—the easy, harmless kind I've been throwing at women for years—and she goes pink to the roots before skittering off.

Douglas stares at the bonus chips, then at me. "How come I didn't get extra? I'm the one raising twins."

"What can I say?" I lean back and stretch my arms behind my head. "Women love a single dad with a man bun. It's science."

"It's something," Lachlan mutters, but there's humour in it. The man's not *quite* as blunt as he once was. Blair's been good for him, rounded off his rough edges. Though if I pointed that out, he'd probably throw a chip at my head.

Hard to believe the grumpiest of us found love first. Means our wee single dads' club is down a member. Not that I'm looking for love, mind you. Right now I've got the best of both worlds: Isla at the weekends, peace during the week. Monday to Thursday, I can do what I want, see who I want . . . bring home who I want. Who'd rush to give that up?

"Da, look!" Rosie stands on her chair, a chip balanced on her nose.

"Rosie, sit down," Douglas says wearily.

"Logan dared me!"

"Did not!"

"Did too!"

And they're off, bickering at a volume that makes my ears ring. Douglas drops his head into his hands while across the table Finn picks up a chip, eyes it thoughtfully, and lifts it towards his nose—until Lachlan gives him a firm look. Finn grins sheepishly at his da and eats it instead.

Aye, a few days of this kind of stuff each week is quite enough, thank you very much. Not that Isla's like the twins. Nah, I've got to give it to her—she's normally very well behaved. Wise beyond her years too.

Something catches my eye. Across the room a woman threads her way through the chaos with a wee girl in tow, and Christ, she looks like she's walked into the wrong place. Everyone else here is in the usual soft-play uniform: hoodies, joggers, messy buns. But this woman's got glossy espresso-brown hair and a thick fringe so precise it probably required a spirit level. She wears a sharp jacket over fitted jeans and heeled boots.

She's small—petite, really—but with curves in all the right places and a walk that could make a bishop drop his Bible. There's something almost defiant about how polished she looks, like she's refusing to surrender to the soft-play dress code.

She's definitely not from around here. I'd remember her if I'd seen her before.

Wonder if she's single. Wait, no, I don't chase women at *soft play*, for crying out loud. If I did, Lachlan would never let me hear the end of it.

A burst of laughter snaps me back to the table. Not to be outdone by his sister, Logan is now proudly displaying a chip shoved halfway up his right nostril. The other three kids cackle while Douglas looks ready to move countries.

"Logan!" Blair says, her New York vowels cutting through the noise. "Get that out of there. Keep fooling around and we'll have to rethink having you and Rosie over on Monday."

Logan heaves an exaggerated sigh then yanks the chip from his nose. Of course, instead of disposing of it like a normal person, he waves it near Rosie's face. She shrieks and ducks under the table.

"Logan!" Douglas warns. "That's enough. Bin it—now."

He grins but obeys, hopping up to lob the chip into the bin then wiping his hands on his T-shirt like that makes him clean again.

"We're going to have pizza on Monday," Finn says excitedly. "And we can make a fort and play the floor is lava and . . ."

I catch the tiny furrow in Isla's brow. She won't be there on Monday.

"Of course, you're welcome to come too, Isla," Blair says quickly, clearly also clocking it. "It's just that I know you won't be around."

This happens sometimes. Weekend friends making weekday plans Isla can't join. It's just one of those things.

"It's fine," Isla says, forcing a smile. "I'll be in Bannock. Besides, I've got dancing on Mondays anyway."

A juice carton tips over into the middle of the table, prompting a chorus of groans as everyone scrambles for napkins. Isla giggles when Rosie insists it wasn't her fault, and just like that, the awkward moment passes. By the time the spill is sorted, everyone's laughing again, and before long our plates are cleared.

"Right then, Captain Isla," I say, pushing back from the table. "Shall we continue our adventure? I believe there were Highland sharks on the loose."

Isla shakes her head as she slides off her chair. "I want all the kids to play hide and seek instead."

Result. I wouldn't mind having a seat for a while longer. "Brilliant idea. Enjoy!"

"Oh, you have to play too, Daddy. You all hide. I'll count."

"Er, what about these three?" I gesture towards Douglas, Lachlan, and Blair. "Are they part of the game too?"

Douglas gives me a look that could freeze the North Sea. *Don't even think about dragging me into this*, it says.

"They're too old," Isla declares with the authority of someone who's decided thirty is basically deceased.

"*Too old?*" Blair exclaims. "Your dad is older than me!"

"Yes, but he's my dad. He has to play."

The logic is flawless, apparently.

"All right," Blair says, fighting back a smile. "Well, go on. We'll watch from here."

Traitors, the lot of them.

Isla covers her eyes and starts counting loudly. "One! Two! Three!"

The twins scatter like startled pigeons. Logan dives behind a padded cylinder while Rosie crawls into a tunnel. Finn, bless him, freezes until Lachlan hisses at him to hide.

Right, where the hell does a six-foot-three man hide in a soft play designed for people under four feet tall?

Hmm . . . the ball pit. It's my only option. Not that it's a particularly good one.

I head over and wade in. Sinking down, I arrange the balls

until I'm basically just a nose and a tuft of hair in a sea of garish colours.

"Seventeen! Eighteen! Nineteen!" Isla calls from the table.

From the top of the twisty slide, a woman's voice drifts down, calm and coaxing. "It's safe, Lily. I promise. Look, why don't I go first, okay?"

I shift, parting a few plastic balls to peek out, and glimpse her—the polished woman from earlier. Without her heeled boots, obviously. No shoes on the equipment.

She pushes off, disappearing into the yellow tube with an "Oh!" of surprise.

Done up like she's heading to a wine bar, but still happy to shoot down a slide just to show her wee girl it's safe? That shouldn't be attractive. And yet here we are.

The slide spits her out at the bottom, and she's just standing up, laughing and calling up, "See? Easy!"—when a small missile in pigtails shoots down after her.

"Wheeeee!"

The wee girl crashes straight into her mum's back, sending the woman stumbling forwards—and tumbling directly into my lap.

Balls fly everywhere. I sit up fast, hands instinctively catching her waist, steadying her. She lies across my legs, twisted just enough that I can see her face—wide-eyed and mortified.

"Well," I say, grinning down at her, "if this is your way of saying hello, I'm intrigued."

She scrambles off me like I'm electrified, but not before I catch a whiff of her scent—light and warm, gone too fast to name.

"Nope, I don't do meet-cutes in children's play areas." Her cheeks are flushed pink, and up close she's even prettier than I thought. Huge green eyes, accentuated with black liner and sooty lashes, and that perfect fringe somehow still intact despite the slide. Subtle streaks of caramel run through her hair.

Christ, she's gorgeous—all polished edges but with fire in her eyes.

She looks at me like I'm trouble. Fair. "Why exactly is a grown man sitting in a ball pit by himself?"

"Excellent question," I admit. "I'm playing hide and seek with my daughter. She's around here somewhere . . ."

I glance around but can't see Isla anywhere. Brilliant.

The woman's wee girl peers at me with open curiosity. "Why is your hair so long? Do you ever wear it in pigtails like me?"

I chuckle. "Not usually, no. Think it'd suit me?"

She tilts her head, thinking this over. "No. Boys look better with short hair."

Ouch.

"*Daddy!*" Isla appears at the edge of the ball pit, hands on hips. "Why aren't you hiding?"

"I *was* hiding. Then I got a visitor." I gesture to the woman, who's now climbing out of the pit. "By the way, I'm Str—"

Her phone rings, cutting me off, which is probably for the best. I was starting to sound like a man trying too hard.

She fumbles for it, answering quickly. "Hello?" A short pause, then: "The keys are ready? Great. We'll be right there."

She grabs her daughter's hand. "Come on, Lily. Time to go."

"But Mummy, I want to play a bit more!"

"We'll come back another time. For now, let's go see your new room."

And with that, the woman strides off, her wee girl trotting to keep up. No goodbye, no "sorry for landing on you", not even a glance back over her shoulder. Just a view of her retreating figure, that impossibly shiny hair swishing with each step.

Bloody hell, she's something else.

"Who was that?" Isla asks.

"No idea," I say. But I watch her like an eejit all the way to the exit anyway.

Wouldn't mind if fate shoved *her* into my lap again.

CHAPTER THREE

AINSLEY

The old stone houses of Ardview Road rise up the hill like a staircase, each one perched a little higher than the last. My hands tighten on the wheel as I coax the car up the incline.

All right, new house, new life. A clean slate. No complications.

Naturally, that's when a man's face pops straight into my head—wide grin, messy man bun, big hands catching my waist as I tumbled straight into his lap. The kind of man who charms you senseless then leaves chaos in his wake. The kind of man I moved to Ardmara to get away from.

"There it is!" Lily exclaims, pulling me back to the present. She bounces in her seat, pointing. "Number twelve! Our new house!"

It sits near the top of the hill, its grey walls mellowed by years of Highland weather. It's nothing fancy—just solid, dependable Scottish architecture with white-framed windows and a small front garden that's more weeds than anything else. It's semi-detached, joined on the right to number fourteen, with a low hedge separating the two gardens. So that's where Malcolm's son lives, the one who'll be doing up the salon. His side is tidier, with neat window boxes and a freshly painted door.

I pull in behind Da's ancient Volvo, which is already parked outside, and kill the engine. Climbing out, I glance back down the hill. The view steals my breath, just as it did the first time I saw it: the harbour spread below, fishing boats bobbing in their berths, a white ferry pulling away from the terminal. The September sun breaks through the clouds, catching the water and making it sparkle.

Lily knocks impatiently on her window. I round the car and open her door, and she jumps down, having already unbuckled herself.

"There's my wee angel!" Mum calls as she steps out of the Volvo.

Lily races towards her, and Mum drops to a crouch for a proper cuddle, covering Lily's face with kisses while she giggles and squirms.

"Granny, that's enough! I need to go see my room!"

Da gets out the car too and shoots me a grin. "Right, let's get you two settled in your new place, eh?"

I fish the keys from my pocket and unlock the front door. It opens on a narrow hall with stairs leading up. The walls are magnolia—safe but bland—with beige carpet to match. Not my style, but it's clean and reasonably well maintained. Once the salon is up and running, I'll make this place properly ours. Paint these walls something with personality, put down flooring that can cope with Lily's inevitable spills. For now, though, it'll do.

Lily darts through the doorway to my right. "Oh! This is the living room." A few moments later: "And this is the kitchen! My room must be upstairs." She whizzes past me and thunders up the stairs.

"Careful!" I call after her.

"I'll start unloading the cars," Da says, already heading back outside.

"I'll help," Mum adds. "It's tomorrow the removal van is coming, yes?"

"Aye, sometime in the morning," I confirm.

Most of my furniture is in storage, ready to be delivered tomorrow. The essentials are packed in the cars, though, including Lily's bed, which I dismantled this morning. My own bed won't be arriving until later in the week because I ordered a new one. Couldn't face taking the old one, not after sharing it with . . . well, with *him*. Too many bad memories soaked into that mattress.

I head out to help and am halfway to my car when Lily's voice bellows from upstairs: "This is going to be my room!"

Mum smiles and shakes her head. "You'd better check she's found the right one. Just in case she's claiming yours."

"You're right. I'll be back in a minute." I huff a small laugh and head up the stairs. I find Lily in the smaller bedroom to the left, spinning in circles, arms outstretched, hair flying.

"Yes," I say. "This *is* your room." It's as bare as the rest, but her joy fills it anyway. "We'll make it cosy," I promise her. "We'll get all your furniture in, maybe put up some fairy lights—"

"Mummy, lift me up!" She's stopped spinning and is now bouncing in place, trying to see through the window. "I want to see outside!"

I scoop her up, her small body warm and solid in my arms.

"Wow! I can see the sea from my room. I love it!"

"It is a special view," I agree. The extra height lets us peek over the neighbours' rooftops, giving us a wide sweep of the harbour, more sprawling and vivid than it looked from down on the street.

"Come see my room," I say, carrying her across the landing and to my window. "I've got the same view."

"Oh!" Lily breathes, pressing her hands to the glass. "You can see the boats from here too. Can we watch them every day?"

"Of course, if you want."

"I do."

I let out a slow breath. She's completely on board with this move. There's no "I want to go home", no "I miss Daddy." No questions about when she'll see Danny again. Just pure excitement about our new adventure. Maybe she understands, in that way children sometimes do, that this is better. That we both deserve better than what we had.

"Ainsley?" Mum's voice floats up from downstairs. "That's me taken in your kettle, and I packed some biscuits from our house. Why don't we all have a cuppa before we start unloading properly?"

I smile to myself. That's so Mum—suggesting a tea break before the work's even begun. She just can't bear the thought of anyone ever going unfed.

"Biscuits!" Lily wriggles out of my arms and bolts for the stairs.

"Lily, please *walk* down the stairs!" I call after her, but she's already halfway down them, giggling away.

I follow at a more sensible pace, shaking my head. By the time I reach the kitchen, the kettle's boiling and Mum's laid out a few mugs and a packet of biscuits. Lily's sitting cross-legged on the floor, happily demolishing a chocolate digestive and scattering crumbs everywhere.

Mum pours the tea and hands me a mug. We lean against the worktop to drink.

"Next time you come over, I'll have actual chairs," I say.

Mum smiles warmly. "There's no rush. You'll get the furniture sorted soon enough." She looks around the bare kitchen. "Turning a house into a home takes time, but I think you're going to be happy in Ardmara. I think we all are."

It's not just Lily and me who've moved to Ardmara—Mum and Da have too. They got their keys a week ago, and Lily and I have been squashed into their spare room since then. It'll be nice to have our own space again, but I'm so grateful for everything they've done: coming with me to this new town, supporting me, after everything that happened. After I couldn't bear to show my face anymore in the village where I grew up, where everyone knew what Danny did to me.

"You know," Mum says, "I've joined a knitting club in town. Meets Mondays at the community centre."

"Er, Mum, can you even knit?"

She waves away my concern. "I'll pick it up. It's more for the blether anyway. It'll be nice to make some friends around town. I'm sure you'll be making some soon too."

I'm less sure of that. It's going to take me a while to trust anyone again outside of the people in this room—and Da, of course. Speaking of Da . . .

"Where's Da got to?"

"Murdo!" Mum calls. "Where are you? Your tea is here and it's going cold."

"Just trying to fix this light, Pauline," Da's voice carries back. "I'll only be a minute."

Mum and I exchange a look of horror. Da and DIY do *not* go together.

"Da, leave it!" I hurry out of the kitchen and find him just outside the front door, peering up at the exterior light fitting with the determined expression of a man about to make things worse.

"I'm perfectly capable of changing a lightbulb, Ainsley," he says, not looking away from his target.

I open my mouth to argue but Mum beats me to it. "Remember the kitchen tap?" She crosses her arms. "Or the bathroom fan? Or that time with the—"

"Those were different." His ears go pink. "This is just a bulb."

"Honestly, Da, I'll sort it later. You've both already done so much for me. If you can just help unload the cars, that's all I need today. For now, Mum's right: have your tea while it's still hot."

He considers, then sighs. "Oh, all right. I suppose I could do with a cuppa."

We head back to the kitchen, where Lily has clearly helped herself to another biscuit and is trying to look innocent. I don't have the heart to tell her off.

Mum takes a sip of tea. "We might not be much use with DIY, but you do know we'll help out however we can, don't you, Ainsley?"

I swallow hard. "Mum, seriously, I don't think you and Da *could* help any more than you already have."

And it's true. They've done everything—relocated their lives for my fresh start, invested their savings in the salon, lent me the deposit for this house. I owe them more than I'll ever be able to give back.

The weight of it sits heavy on my shoulders. Exciting though this all is, the whole venture terrifies me. Because it *has* to work. For my parents, so I can pay them back one day. For Lily, who deserves stability and happiness. And for me, because I need to stand on my own two feet again after being knocked down and humiliated by the man who should've loved us both.

But I won't let my parents see that fear. Not today, when everything's supposed to be about new beginnings.

So I grab a chocolate bickie, dunk it in my tea, and take a bite.

◆ ◆ ◆

It's just gone six, and for the last wee while it's just been me and Lily. My parents left a while ago, after both cars had been emptied.

Lily's bed has been reassembled in her new room—took me the better part of an hour to remember which bit went where—and she's up there now, arranging her cuddly toys in order of importance. My room, meanwhile, boasts nothing but boxes and an air mattress in the corner. Not exactly a glamorous fresh start, but it'll do for a few nights until my proper bed arrives.

"Mummy!" Lily calls down. "Mr Flops wants to know when we're having dinner."

"Tell Mr Flops we had fish and chips earlier, remember? That *was* dinner."

"But that was ages ago!"

I glance at my phone. We ate less than an hour ago. "You can have some milk and a snack before bed if you're still hungry."

"Okay!"

I open the front door and look up at the light fixture, the one Mum and I stopped Da from meddling with earlier. When Lily and I nipped out for our fish supper, I grabbed a new bulb. Might as well pop it in and see if that fixes the problem. It'd be nice to tick one more thing off the to-do list.

I grab a folding chair—the only seat we have until the furniture arrives tomorrow—and position it beneath the light. Then, screwdriver in hand, I climb up. The fixture is just a bit too high. Even standing on the chair, I still have to stretch.

The cover is held on by two small screws. Balancing on tiptoes, my calves trembling, I try to work the first screw loose. "Come on, you wee—"

The chair wobbles, just a bit, but enough. My balance goes. I flail, arms windmilling wildly, the screwdriver slipping from my hand and clattering somewhere behind me. My stomach drops, the world tilts, and then I'm falling backwards, a gasp tearing out of me—

But I don't hit the ground. Strong arms catch me, and suddenly I'm cradled against a warm, solid chest. My breath catches as my eyes lock with a pair of golden-brown ones.

Oh no. No, no, no. I recognise those eyes. Because they've already looked down at me once today.

Of all the people in this town, why did I have to be caught by the man whose lap I fell into this morning? The man I mentally filed under *avoid at all costs*.

And now he's got me scooped up princess-style. Of course. Humiliation bingo: full house.

Heat, masculine scent, the press of muscle . . .

I catch myself. "Put me down!" I snap, cheeks burning with a mix of indignation and pure mortification.

He sets me on my feet gently, his hands lingering at my waist for just a second as if to make sure I'm steady. "You all right?"

"Fine." I step back, putting space between us, and smooth down my top. "I had it under control."

His lips twitch. "Aye, looked like it."

"I don't need—" I stop. Force myself to take a breath. He did just save me from a nasty fall. "Thank you."

"No problem." He extends a hand. "I'm Struan, by the way.

Your next-door neighbour." He nods to number fourteen. "Your joiner too. For the salon renovation?"

You have *got* to be kidding me.

This man? This man with the stupid tawny curls that look like they tousle themselves, and cheekbones you could slice cheese with? This man who screams trouble with a capital T?

He's Malcolm's son? My new neighbour and joiner? Clearly, the universe is having a laugh at my expense.

I stare at his outstretched hand for a beat too long before reluctantly taking it. His grip is warm and firm, calluses rough against my palm. And I don't know what's wrong with me, but a bloody zing shoots up my arm.

I pull my hand back quickly. Swallow. "Ainsley."

"And *this*," Struan says, gesturing to the curly-haired girl who's appeared behind him, "is my daughter, Isla. We didn't get a proper chance to introduce ourselves earlier. You left rather quickly."

I don't take the bait. Instead, I force a smile I don't quite feel and keep my eyes firmly on Isla, not her father. "Hello, Isla."

Summoned by our voices, Lily comes pattering down the stairs. "Oh!" She points at the girl. "I know you! You were at soft play earlier. I'm Lily. What's your name?"

Isla glances at her father, then smiles. "I'm Isla."

"That's a pretty name," I say, keeping my tone polite. "What year are you in at school, Isla?"

"Primary three."

"At Ardmara Primary? Lily here has just started at the nursery."

"No, I go to school in Bannock. That's where my mum lives."

Ah. So he's divorced, or separated. Not that it matters. Not that I care about his relationship status in the slightest.

"Do you want to see my room?" Lily asks Isla, bouncing on her toes. "It's got a view of the sea and everything!"

Isla looks at Struan again, who shrugs. "If Ainsley doesn't mind?"

"Of course not," I say lightly, even though I badly need a moment to get my breathing under control.

The girls disappear upstairs, Lily chattering away as they go, not shy of the older girl in the slightest. Which leaves me alone with Struan.

He glances up at the light fixture. "Want me to sort that for you?"

"I can manage," I insist.

But he's already grabbed the screwdriver from where it fell and is reaching up, not even needing the chair. He pops off the light cover with ease, the movement casual, effortless. His shirt rides up as he stretches, revealing a strip of lean, toned stomach and that stupid V at his hips—the one no man has any business flaunting. And then there's the thin trail of golden hair leading down from his navel. My eyes follow it before I can stop myself. I jerk my gaze away, heat prickling my neck.

Nope, Ainsley. Absolutely not.

He removes the current bulb then holds out a hand to me. "The replacement?"

I pass him the bulb I picked up earlier and he holds it up, comparing it to the original. A slight smirk tugs at the corner of his mouth. "I think I see a problem here. The connections are different. The original is a bayonet bulb, but this new one is a screw cap. That's not going to work."

"Right," I say, embarrassed and a little annoyed. I grabbed the same kind I used to get for my old place. Figured it'd be the same here. "Easy mistake."

"No worries. Think I've got one next door. Give me a sec."

Before I can tell him not to bother, he's heading for his house. I stand there on my doorstep like an eejit, arms crossed, listening to Lily and Isla's giggles drifting down from upstairs.

He's back in under a minute, the correct bulb in hand. Again he reaches up, and again that flash of stomach.

Fuck's sake, Ainsley. Eyes up.

Within seconds the new bulb is in place.

"All right, want to try it?"

I step inside, flick the switch by the door, and the light comes on.

"There you go." He gives me an easy smile. "Next time, maybe don't climb wobbly furniture. You can borrow my stepladder anytime. Or just ask me to do it."

"Thank you," I say crisply, "but I've already ordered my own stepladder."

Of course, I haven't. But the thought of needing to ask him for help, of knocking on his door like some damsel in distress, makes my skin crawl. This fresh start is supposed to be about Lily and me standing on our own feet.

"And next time I'll know to buy a bulb with a bayonet fitting," I add, my tone clipped. "Every day's a school day."

His grin widens and he nods. "Fair enough. But if you need anything else—boxes moved, shelves put up, furniture assembled—I'm just next door."

"We're fine."

"Course you are." There's something about the way he says it, not quite mocking but not quite serious either. "Well, if ever you change your mind, you know where to find me. Anyway, Isla!" he calls up the stairs. "Time for dinner!"

Small feet race across the landing, then both girls appear at the top of the stairs.

"Does Isla have to go already?" Lily says. "I've not even introduced her to all my toys yet."

"Maybe she'll get to meet the rest of them another time," Struan says. "But for now Isla needs to come with me and have her dinner. C'mon, princess!"

Isla traipses down the stairs, and Struan glances at me. "I'll see you Monday morning at the salon. If we don't run into each other before then." He winks, then he and his daughter head around the dividing hedge and disappear into their house.

A *wink*? Just who does he think he is? I close the door and let myself exhale, long and slow, willing the flutter in my stomach to bugger off.

"Mummy, Isla's really nice," Lily says, tugging on my top.

"Mmm."

"Can she come around again?"

"Maybe."

Lily sighs. "That means no."

"It means maybe, Lily. Now, come on, let's get you some supper."

As I lead Lily into the kitchen, I shake away the memory of how easily Struan held me, like I weighed nothing at all. Because I've got no business thinking about that. I didn't come here to fall into the arms of my next-door neighbour.

Even if I've somehow managed to do it twice in one day.

CHAPTER FOUR

STRUAN

The sound hits me before I even open the salon door—high-pitched wailing mixed with words I can't quite make out. I pause, hand on the handle, wondering if I should come back in five minutes. But then I hear Ainsley's voice, stretched thin as wire, and curiosity wins.

I push inside to find Lily flat on her back on the floor, face tomato-red, fists balled at her sides. Full-blown tantrum mode. Ainsley's crouched beside her in fitted jeans that do excellent things for her arse—not that I'm looking—trying to reason with a four-year-old who's gone nuclear.

"Lily, nursery lunch is lovely. It's baked potatoes today. You like potatoes."

"No! They're yucky!" Lily's legs kick against the floor. "I want a packed lunch!"

"I've not had time to do a proper shop. We've only just moved in, remember? I promise I'll get you a packed lunch sorted for tomo—"

"I want it TODAY!"

Ainsley's shoulders slump. Then she glances behind her and

spots me in the doorway. For a second I see it all—the exhaustion, the frustration, the embarrassment. Then her walls slam back up, shoulders tightening, chin lifting.

"Oh, Struan." She straightens. "Sorry about this. We'll be out of your way in a minute. I need to drop this one off at nursery."

I set down my toolbox and crouch down by Lily. "Hey there, Lily. What's all this about?"

Ainsley stiffens—a flicker of tension I can't quite read.

"I don't have a packed lunch and nursery lunch is *horrible*," Lily announces, still lying flat on her back, delivering her grievances to the ceiling.

"Oh dear, now that *is* a problem," I say, keeping my tone gentle. I unzip my rucksack and pull out my lunch bag. "Tell you what, how about you have mine? It's just a cheese sandwich, nothing fancy. Oh, and an apple too."

Lily sits up so fast she nearly headbutts me. "Really?"

"Course."

She snatches the bag out of my hand before I can change my mind, then peers inside like it contains treasure. "Mmm! This is a good lunch!"

I glance at Ainsley. She's staring at me, lips slightly parted in . . . relief? Or annoyance? Hard to tell with her. She's a puzzle I haven't worked out yet. Whatever it is, she quickly schools her expression, forcing on a polite smile—all surface, no warmth. "Lily, what do you say to Struan?"

"Thank you, Stwuan!" Lily beams up at me, tears already drying on her cheeks. Crisis averted, just like that.

I stand, and Ainsley smooths down her top—that same nervous gesture from the other day. "You didn't have to do that," she says.

"It's just a sandwich." I shrug. "I can pick myself up something from the Lighthouse Café instead."

"Even so . . . thanks. Really." Her voice is tight, like thanking me is the last thing she wants to do. Strange. I'm not used to women being this frosty with me. Maybe she's just proud. Or private. Or both.

"No bother."

Lily peers up at me. "Where's Isla?"

"She's with her mummy, getting ready for school."

"Oh." Lily's brow furrows. "You don't live with her mummy, do you?"

Ainsley winces. "Sorry, she's four. There's no filter."

"It's all right," I say with a smile. "And no, I don't live with Isla's mummy."

"I don't see my daddy. Mummy says he's a bloody b—"

Ainsley clamps a hand over Lily's mouth. "Lily! We don't repeat grown-up words, remember?"

I press my lips together, fighting back a laugh. Lily's eyes sparkle with mischief above her mum's fingers.

"Right," Ainsley says, releasing Lily's mouth and grabbing her hand instead. "We need to go. Nursery drop-off, then I've got a few errands to run." She looks at me, all business now. "You know what you're doing here? You and your da went over everything?"

"Aye, all sorted. First, I'll remove the old fixtures, then I'll start sanding, patching, and prepping the walls. Actually, I should get your number."

Her eyes narrow. "My number?" The suspicion in her voice could curdle milk.

"In case anything comes up I need to run by you. Don't worry, professional purposes only."

She watches me for a long moment, like she's weighing up whether this is some line. Then she exhales and recites the digits like she's handing over state secrets.

"Let me just check I entered that right." I hit call, and Ainsley's back pocket erupts with the sound of ducks quacking. Loud, enthusiastic quacking.

I can't help it—I quack back. Lily dissolves into giggles.

"Lily chose it," Ainsley says a little defensively.

"It's brilliant." I save the number. "Good choice, Lily."

"*Anyway*," Ainsley says, "I'll be back later."

"Yes, boss."

Her mouth tightens—she doesn't love that—but she lets it go. She steers Lily towards the door, though Lily turns back and waves before she leaves. "Bye, Stwuan!"

That little lisp on my name—Christ, it's adorable. "Bye, Lily. Enjoy the sandwich."

The door closes behind them, and I'm left in the sudden quiet of the empty salon. I should get straight to work—there's plenty to do—but I hover a moment longer, replaying that interaction. Ainsley's a hard one to read, all edges and defences, but there have been a couple of times now when I thought something else was about to crack through.

And then the walls came back up again.

I shake my head and grab my tools.

Focus, Walker. She's your neighbour. Your boss for this refurb. And she's clearly dealing with some shite involving her ex.

But as I set to dismantling the first of the old styling stations, my mind drifts back to Saturday. How she felt in my arms when I caught her—both times. There had been this spark . . . this pull.

Or at least, I thought there had been. Seems I was the only one feeling it.

Yesterday I'd kept finding excuses to be in the back garden with Isla, hoping to catch a glimpse of Ainsley. Pathetic, really. She and Lily didn't make an appearance, though I did hear them through an open window at one point—Ainsley doing silly voices while she and Lily played some game, both of them laughing. In those moments she sounded very different to the woman who keeps me at arm's length with clipped words and cool stares.

Aye, she's a bit of an enigma, my new neighbour.

Professional, I remind myself, attacking a stubborn screw with more force than necessary. *Keep it professional, Walker.*

◆ ◆ ◆

When Ainsley returns just before noon, I'm crouched by the far wall, attacking years of neglect with sandpaper, sweat making my T-shirt stick to my back. My forearms burn from the repetitive motion, but it's good, honest work.

I turn to greet her only to notice her blinking once, twice, then jerking her gaze away from me. Interesting. Maybe the attraction between us *isn't* one-way. She smooths down her top then strides towards me with a paper bag in hand.

"Replacement sandwich." She thrusts it at me like she's paying off a debt she desperately wants cleared. "From the Lighthouse Café."

I stand and wipe my hands on my jeans. "You didn't have to do that."

"Aye, well, you shouldn't go hungry because of Lily." Her words are to the point but not unkind. "Cheese and pickle. Hope that's fine."

"Perfect. Thanks."

She nods once—transaction complete—and looks around the

salon, taking in the bare walls and the empty spaces where the old stations used to be. "You've cracked on, I see."

"Aye." I bob my head towards the street. "Already loaded the van with all the old fittings and furniture for the skip."

"Good." She pulls out her phone and angles it for a selfie—even her closed smile is professional. "For the salon's socials," she explains, then disappears into the small kitchenette at the back.

I follow with my sandwich. "Mind if I sit at the bar for lunch?"

A pause. Just long enough to be noticeable.

"Oh. Aye, sure." She sits on a stool, eyes on her phone. "I'll mostly be working, though."

Translation: don't expect conversation. Don't expect friendliness. Don't expect anything.

Jesus. I'm going to be here for two weeks. We don't need to be pals, but a bit less frost wouldn't hurt.

I settle beside her at the cramped breakfast bar. She immediately shifts a few inches further along, creating whatever space she can between us. Even so, I catch a glimpse of her phone, open on her Instagram profile, "The Lily Room".

"Nice," I say. "You're naming this place after your wee girl?"

She glances up, and for once there's no guard, no walls. A real smile lights her face—and wow, it's a good one. She really is stunning.

"Aye. She drives me up the wall sometimes, but she's my world. Felt right to name the salon after her."

I nod, the corners of my own mouth lifting. Finally, we're getting somewhere. "And how are you settling in?" I ask, keen to keep the conversation going. "Ardmara treating you well so far?"

"It's fine." Her smile dims slightly. "Different from where I was before, but that's not a bad thing."

"Where were you—"

"Sorry, I've got things to do." Her tone returns to arctic in a heartbeat. She takes out her laptop, opens it, and angles both it and herself away from me, radiating a quiet but unmistakable "don't talk to me" energy.

Bloody hell. Seriously, what did I do to this woman? With no further hopes of conversation, I pull out my phone and scroll through the news while I eat, but my attention keeps drifting. Ainsley is close enough that I catch hints of her perfume—something warm and sophisticated, like vanilla mixed with something spicy. Expensive-smelling. The kind of scent that makes you want to lean in closer, find out exactly where she's dabbed it on her skin.

Keep it professional, I remind myself.

I try to focus on the sports article I'm reading, but when Ainsley lets out a small noise of frustration, I glance up. She's chewing her bottom lip, completely absorbed in whatever's on her screen. For a moment I can't help but stare, drawn in by the way she unconsciously nibbles and sucks on that pouty lip.

Christ, Walker. Behave. Don't be a creep.

Needing a distraction, I fire off a quick message to Sophie, Isla's mum.

STRUAN

Isla left her water bottle at mine yesterday. I can swing by with it later, if you like

SOPHIE

LOL, you don't have to drive forty minutes here and forty minutes back to drop off a water bottle. I had a spare. She took that to school today. It's fine

Right. Of course it's fine. Aye, I was hardly going to drive eighty bloody minutes to return a water bottle. I just . . . wouldn't have minded seeing my wee girl for five minutes. Which is ridiculous, given I saw her only yesterday.

Mei is Sophie's girlfriend. She's great. I mean, sure, it took me a *wee* while to get used to it when things between them got more serious. It shifted the dynamic a bit. But we've settled into a decent routine now.

I finish my sandwich. "Right, I'm going to head back to work. Mind if I put some music on?"

Ainsley waves a hand without looking up. "Whatever you like."

I connect my phone to my portable speaker and queue up some Fleetwood Mac. "Dreams" fills the space, mellow and familiar. Ainsley doesn't object, which I take as a win.

The afternoon settles into a rhythm. Sand, wipe, check for rough spots, repeat. Ainsley types and clicks and occasionally makes these tiny frustrated sounds she probably doesn't realise she's making. Once, passing the kitchenette, I catch her tapping her foot to "Go Your Own Way".

"Would you like a cup of tea?" she asks after a while, peering out from the back. Her voice is polite but formal, like she's ticking a box rather than offering an olive branch.

"Aye, please. Milk, one sugar."

She nods and disappears again. A minute later she returns, coming over to pass me the mug. She rotates it just so, making sure I take the handle, as if determined our fingers won't brush. I accept it with a nod of thanks and we go back to our separate tasks.

We don't speak. The atmosphere isn't *frosty*, but it isn't exactly companionable either. Just . . . focused.

The peace holds for another hour. Then—

"Fuck's sake!"

I'm working on the wall closest to the kitchenette. I look over and spot her scowling at her laptop screen.

"Everything all right?"

"Just a supplier being a pain in the arse." She grabs her phone. "Give me a sec."

I keep my eyes on the wall as I continue to work, but it's impossible not to overhear the call, at least her half of it.

"Hi, yes, this is Ainsley Reid from the Lily Room . . . Right, about that delivery date we agreed . . . No, that's not what we discussed . . ."

A pause, then—her voice as sharp as cut glass—"I'm not your 'darling'. Now, about the delivery. We agreed on the eighteenth. I have it in writing . . . Yes, I'm sure you're very busy, but so am I, and I need that stock in for my opening . . ."

Something tightens low in my gut—anger at whoever's on the other end not taking her seriously. But Christ, the way she handles him, not raising her voice but not backing down either. It's impressive. Pretty damn hot too.

"I'll expect confirmation by email within the hour," she finishes, and sets the phone down.

"You handled that well," I comment.

She glances at me, and I catch a flicker of something—embarrassment, maybe, that I heard the whole thing. But she schools her expression fast and, without further comment, packs up her laptop. "I need to go collect Lily now." She pulls a key from her pocket. "Here. A spare, so you can lock up when you're done."

I take it then she strides for the door. My gaze drops, unhelpfully, to the sway of her hips, the way those jeans hug her curves, before I drag my eyes back up.

Christ, Walker. Get a grip.

The door clicks shut behind her, leaving me alone with mellow seventies rock drifting from the speaker and the faint trace of Ainsley's perfume hanging in the air.

I scrub a hand through my hair, probably spreading sawdust everywhere.

She's my neighbour. My temporary boss. And clearly not interested in anything beyond professional distance. I should *not* be drawn to her.

And yet . . . she's hard not to notice.

CHAPTER FIVE

AINSLEY

"I don't *want* Granny and Grandpa to pick me up!" Lily's declaration rings across the nursery playground, and I know—just know—we're about to have a repeat of yesterday's packed lunch meltdown. She's clutching Mr Flops so tight I'm honestly worried the poor rabbit might lose an ear.

I crouch down, keeping my voice even despite the exhaustion already creeping in at quarter to nine in the morning. "But you love Granny and Grandpa. You always have fun with them."

Her bottom lip starts its warning wobble. "I want to play Barbies with you after nursery. Like last night."

I hold back a sigh. I'd planned to work late at the salon today. There's so much to sort before opening—hundreds of tiny details that'll eat up hours. I need time to get everything organised.

"You can play Barbies at Granny and Grandpa's house," I try.

"Nobody plays them right except you, Mummy!" The wail that follows could strip paint. Several parents turn to stare, and outside the playground a dog barks. I glance over my shoulder. A golden retriever stands at the railings, tail wagging, its owner watching with open curiosity as she passes by with a boy on her way to the primary school next door.

God, can I not even do a nursery drop-off without becoming a spectacle?

Lily's volume increases. "I WANT YOU TO GET ME! I WANT TO PLAY BARBIES!"

More heads turn. I can feel their eyes—some sympathetic, some judging. My chest tightens. I spent months being whispered about back home. I've no wish to be the centre of attention here too.

"Okay," I cave, hating myself for it. "*I'll* pick you up."

The transformation is instant. Tears evaporate, wailing stops, and she beams at me like I've just promised her a pony. "Really?"

"Really."

She flings her arms around my neck and plants a wet kiss on my cheek. Then she swans into nursery like the picture of innocence. Bloody hell, I was just thoroughly outmanoeuvred by someone who still needs help putting on her shoes.

On my way out, I text Mum.

AINSLEY

Change of plans. I'll get Lily this afternoon x

MUM

No worries, love. Everything okay?

AINSLEY

Grand x

It's not, though. I'd thought Lily was coping well with the move, but maybe these tantrums tell a different story. Back in our old village, Lily loved nursery, practically dragged me there each morning. But that was before her world got turned upside down.

Maybe these meltdowns over seemingly small things—lunch, pickup arrangements—are her way of processing everything. New house, new nursery, not seeing her daddy. Not that Danny was much of a father even when he was around.

Christ, can I really blame Lily for the odd tantrum? Sometimes I wouldn't mind lying on the ground myself, and having a good thrash and scream about everything that's happened.

Out on the street, I'm passing the school gates when a gentle touch on my arm stops me.

"I'm so sorry for staring." It's the woman with the dog and the boy, though the boy has now disappeared into the school. Her accent is unmistakably American, bright and quick. "That was incredibly rude. I'm Blair."

Something about her directness disarms me. "With a kid screeching like that, who wouldn't look?" I say. "I'm Ainsley."

"The new hairdresser, right?" Her face lights up. "I heard you were young and stylish with a cute little girl. The description fits."

My cheeks warm. "News travels fast here."

"Like wildfire." She grins. "I'm not used to it either. Only been here a few months."

"Oh? Did you and your son come over from the States?"

"Just me. The boy you saw, Finn, isn't my son, though I was his nanny over the summer. Then his dad and I . . . well, long story short, we're together now."

"Wow. New town, new man, a wee boy, and a dog thrown into the bargain?" I bend to greet the golden retriever. "Hello, gorgeous. What's your name?"

Delighted, he noses my palm, tail wagging wildly.

"That's Gus," Blair says with a laugh. "He has absolutely no concept of personal space."

"Neither does my daughter. Maybe they'd get on."

"They probably would." Blair smiles. "So, what brought you to Ardmara?"

Oof.

Smile, keep it light, don't let anything show.

I slip into my practised spiel. "I've always loved this part of the Highlands, and I've always wanted my own salon. It came up at the perfect time."

Blair nods, though the faint furrow in her brow tells me she senses there's more. But she doesn't push, and I'm grateful.

"Speaking of the salon," she says, "I *desperately* need a haircut. These bangs are getting out of control."

Business mode kicks in—safer territory. I pull out my phone and swipe to my portfolio. "What kind of style were you thinking?" I show her some before-and-afters, warming to my subject as she makes appreciative noises.

"These are incredible! I'd love to book an appointment for opening week. Also, if you fancy, we could grab a drink sometime? Compare notes on being newcomers in a town where everyone's known each other since they were in diapers. Us fresh arrivals need to stick together, right?"

My stomach knots. Drinks means talking. Sharing. Potentially letting my guard down. And after what happened back home . . .

"That's lovely of you, but childcare's a bit tricky for me." A white lie, given my parents literally moved here with me, but hopefully Blair doesn't know that.

She doesn't look offended. "Well, the offer stands if you change your mind."

♦　♦　♦

I walk along the waterfront, the sharp salt air catching in my lungs as gulls wheel overhead. My nerves are still jangling from Lily's nursery meltdown, but the moment the salon's white-washed windows come into view, something inside me settles. This is mine, my fresh start. And in two short weeks, it'll be open for business.

The salon sits between a fashionable boutique bursting with Harris Tweed and a tiny antiques shop crammed with old treasures. It's a good spot. A hopeful one.

My gaze lands on the Walker Builds van parked outside, and my calm evaporates.

Of course he's already here.

The sight of the van is enough to trigger yesterday's memory reel: Struan's sweat-damp T-shirt clinging to him, that easy grin, the way his forearms flexed as he worked . . .

I exhale hard. Why, in the name of all that's holy, does my neighbour-slash-joiner have to be hot?

Maybe once upon a time I'd have fallen for his sexy man bun and the lazy grin. Flirted back. Enjoyed the attention. But not now. Not after Danny. I didn't move to Ardmara to get tangled up with another charming man who'll mess me around. My priority now is Lily and building a stable life. Full stop.

Inside, the salon is empty. No sign of him.

Good. Maybe he's nipped out. Gives me space to breathe.

I glance around, and the transformation from yesterday stops me short. The main wall, where the mirrors will hang, gleams with new plaster. The others are already primed white, and the sharp smell of paint fills my nose. It's starting to look like something real, something mine.

The steady sound of sawing drifts from the back. I follow it past the toilet and kitchenette to the fire door, which stands slightly ajar. I push it open—then stop dead.

Struan's set up a makeshift workshop from old pallets in the small courtyard. His back's to me and he's bent over a plank of wood, sawing with steady, practised movements.

And he's shirtless.

For fuck's sake. Of course he is.

His back muscles, broad and defined, ripple with each push of the saw. Sweat tracks down his spine despite the cool September morning, making his skin glisten.

A tiny, ridiculous sound escapes me, half gasp, half . . . something.

Mortification floods hot through my cheeks. Brilliant. Did I actually just make a noise?

He straightens and turns. And now I get the full view. His chest is lean and sculpted, abs carved from real work, not hours in a gym. They taper down into that maddening V that disappears into jeans slung low enough to reveal the waistband of his boxers. Dark blue, if anyone's asking. Not that I'm looking. Much.

He shoots me his easy grin, like being half-naked at work is the most normal thing in the world. "Morning."

"Hi." My voice comes out higher than intended. I clear my throat, forcing myself to focus on his face. Except loose strands have escaped his man bun, curling against his neck in a way that's so effortlessly, infuriatingly attractive I want to throw something at him. Or maybe at the universe for dangling this walking, talking, man-bun-wearing piece of forbidden fruit in front of me.

"Looking good," I say, then immediately wince. *Great start, Ainsley.* "Inside, I mean! The walls. They look good."

"Aye, got most of them done yesterday. Came in early to skim the big one." He sets down the saw and wipes his forehead with the back of his hand. "Just working on the bench while it dries. With any luck, might have some colour on the walls by tomorrow."

The morning sun catches his face, lighting up the gold in his eyes, and I'm distracted all over again.

For God's sake, Ainsley. Stop it. This man is clearly another Danny—all charm and no follow-through. Remember that.

"I, er . . . right. Anyway, I've got a to-do list the length of my arm." I wave vaguely towards the door. "So I'll . . . leave you to it."

One corner of his mouth twitches, like he's fighting a smile.

Brilliant. He's noticed I've turned into a complete idiot.

"Sure thing," he says.

I retreat at a frankly undignified speed and slip back inside.

Honestly, Ainsley. You came here to escape men like him, but then he takes his top off and you can barely string a sentence together? Pathetic.

I set up my laptop in the kitchenette and stare at my daunting list for today. Outside, the sawing resumes, rhythmic and steady. I can still picture him out there, all that skin and muscle and—

"Focus, Ainsley," I mutter. "You've got a hundred things to get through, and drooling over your joiner isn't one of them."

But an hour and a half later, I'm still stuck on item one—and not because I'm distracted by Struan. No, the booking system keeps throwing error messages about "third-party cookies" that might as well be written in ancient Gaelic for all I understand them.

"Oh, for fuck's sake!" I glare at the screen. "You absolute piece of shite software. Just bloody work, would you?"

"You okay?" Struan appears in the doorway, dusting wood shavings from his hands. He's pulled on a shirt, thank God.

Before I can stop him, he's behind me, one hand on the back of my chair as he leans over to see the screen. The scent of sawdust and fresh sweat surrounds me, and I have to fight not to squirm in my seat. Jesus, why does his mere proximity turn my bones to jelly?

"Third-party cookies," he reads. "Right. I'm good with my hands but useless with technology." He straightens, and I can breathe again. "My sister works in IT in London. Want me to give her a ring? She's brilliant with this stuff."

"No, it's fine. Thanks."

"You sure?"

"Aye. I'll figure it out."

He nods and starts to turn away—

"I think I'm just having one of those days." The words tumble out before I even realise what I'm saying. Why am I telling *him* this?

He turns back. "Oh?"

I hesitate, then admit, "Lily had another meltdown this morning. Demanded I pick her up instead of my parents, so now I've got to leave early. And I've got no Wi-Fi at home until next week."

"Ah. Isla didn't tantrum often as a wee one, but when she did? Epic. Once lay down in the middle of Tesco and screamed because I wouldn't buy her a whole watermelon."

I can't hold back a smile. "A whole watermelon?"

"She was three. Logic wasn't her strong suit." He tilts his head. "Tell you what, use my Wi-Fi for now. Should reach through the wall between our houses."

"I couldn't—"

"Course you can. Password's PrettyFlyForAWiFi."

A laugh escapes me before I can stop it. He grins and shrugs.

"Right, well . . ." I gesture to my laptop. "I'd best get back to it. But thanks for the password."

"No bother. Just shout if you need anything else."

The moment he's gone, I blow out a breath.

Really, Ainsley? Laughing at his lame Wi-Fi pun? Get it together.

CHAPTER SIX

STRUAN

The Ferryman's Rest is doing decent Tuesday night business—not rammed, but busy enough that nobody notices one bloke nursing a pint alone. The low rumble of conversation mixes with the clink of cutlery and occasional burst of laughter from the group of lads by the fruit machine. Pre-match rugby commentary drones from the TV above the bar, though nobody's properly watching yet.

I check my phone again. Douglas should be here any minute. Dinner and the Scotland match—just two guys escaping reality for a few hours.

My mind drifts to earlier, to Ainsley, to the moment she caught me working shirtless out back. The wee noise she made, and then the look on her face, like . . . well, like she wanted to lick the sweat off my chest or something.

She clamped down on it instantly, all icy composure again. She'd deny it—no question—but she liked what she saw. I know she did.

Ha. She's too cute.

Still, I shouldn't be this pleased about it. And maybe I *should* keep my clothes on in future, even when I'm roasting and think I'm alone.

I rub a hand over my face. Christ, I need to think about something else.

I lift my phone. A good dose of my wee girl is exactly the distraction I need. I video-call Isla, and she answers after a few rings.

"Hey, princess."

Her face appears pixelated for a second before the connection steadies. "Daddy!" She's still in her school uniform, navy cardigan slightly askew. "Guess what happened at school today?"

"What?"

"Mrs Henderson told me I'm going to join primary four for reading time! Just reading, not maths or anything else. But still!"

Pride swells in my chest. "That's brilliant, Isla! Primary four already? You're getting too clever for your old da."

She rolls her eyes but she's beaming. "I'm not *that* clever. But I did learn something really cool today about octopuses. Did you know they have three hearts?"

"Three hearts? That's mental."

"I know! And if they lose an arm, it grows back. Like magic but real."

Sophie's voice drifts from somewhere off-screen: "Isla, Mei is looking for her sous chef!"

"Oh!" Isla perks up. "Mei and I are making homemade pizzas tonight. She lets me choose all my own toppings, even pineapple, and Mummy doesn't even complain."

Sophie appears behind Isla, her dark-blonde hair tucked behind one ear and a quick, tired smile on her face. "Oh, hi, Struan. Did Isla tell you about the reading group?"

"Aye, just now. That's amazing."

"I know, we're really proud. Sorry, but we're about to have dinner. Would it be okay if Isla calls you back after?"

"But we're playing rummy after dinner!" Isla says.

"True, but you can still give your da a quick call."

I smile. "It's fine. I'll check in with you tomorrow, okay? Enjoy your pizzas."

"Will do." Isla grins. "Byeee!"

The screen goes black before I can get another word in.

I set my phone down, reach for my pint, and take a long sip. Rummy, eh? That used to be our game. Started teaching Isla when she was five, using Maltesers as stakes. She'd concentrate so hard, wee brow furrowed, determined to beat her dad.

I huff out a laugh, shaking my head at myself.

Christ, Walker. You're a grown man. You're way too old to get jealous over a game. Sort yourself out.

Still, things *have* been different since Mei came onto the scene. It used to be that I'd drive to Bannock every Wednesday for dinner—me, Sophie, and Isla. We always said it was important for Isla to see her parents getting along—which we do. But now those nights are once a month, if that. And, aye, Mei's usually there.

Which is fine. Of course it's fine. It's just . . . different, that's all.

My phone pings, saving me from the world's saddest pity party. For about three seconds.

DOUGLAS

Mate, disaster. Rosie's just projectile vomited all over the living room. My folks were meant to be watching the twins tonight but I can't risk them getting whatever this is. Sorry. Rain check?

A flicker of disappointment hits—daft, considering it's only a pint—but I brush it off and shoot him a message back.

STRUAN

> No worries. Hope she feels better soon and you and Logan avoid it ✌️

DOUGLAS

> Cheers. Though Logan's already complaining that his tummy hurts so not looking likely . . . 🤢

Poor bastard. Douglas's situation is almost the complete opposite of mine. While Sophie and I have found a decent rhythm, Douglas is basically raising the twins solo. Their mum, Leah, pops back every few months, plays happy families for a week or two, then buggers off again. No warning, no explanation. Just gone. The twins are too young to understand why she comes and goes, and Douglas is left picking up the pieces every time.

The man's knackered, but at least he gets those wee moments every day—bedtime hugs, morning chaos, all that stuff.

Not that I'm complaining. Nah, my setup's grand.

Mostly.

Christ, if anyone could hear the monologue in my head tonight, they'd be laughing their arses off. I'm meant to be Mr Laid-Back, not . . . whatever this is.

I glance around the pub. The table nearest the window has a family of five, the youngest maybe Lily's age. She's carefully colouring on the paper place mat while her siblings squabble about something. At another table a grandfather is helping a wee boy cut up his fish while the grandmother wipes ketchup off a girl's chin.

Christ, this place is crawling with kids tonight. Not exactly the vibe I'm after.

I drain my pint and eye the specials board. Slow-cooked lamb shank. Pan-seared sea bass. Venison burger. All sound good, but the thought of sitting here by myself, surrounded by families while I eat dinner alone . . .

No. Not tonight.

Through the window, I see the sky is still bright enough—September evenings holding onto their light. The waves are decent. Not huge, but enough to get the blood pumping. And the wind's dropped since this afternoon.

Only one thing for it, then.

I stand and head for the door. A ten-minute drive, and then I can be out on the water.

"Heading off already, Struan?" Alan calls from behind the bar.

"Aye," I say with a grin. "Waves are calling. Be rude not to."

"At this time? You're mental."

"Wouldn't be the first time I've been called that."

I push through the door and into the evening air.

Sometimes the only way to clear your head is to throw yourself at something that demands every bit of your attention. And the Atlantic? That definitely qualifies.

◆　◆　◆

The sun's sliding towards the horizon by the time I reach the cove, painting the sea bronze and copper. I love this quiet sandy stretch. Here it's just me and the Atlantic having it out.

The first duck dive shocks the air from my lungs, September water cold enough to make my teeth ache. Salt stings my eyes, my hands numb for a moment before the burn kicks in. But that's what I need, something sharp enough to cut through all the noise in my head.

I reach the break, and by the third wave, my body remembers what to do. Paddle, pop up, ride. The surfboard hums beneath my feet; spray hits my shins. My shoulders burn, forearms screaming, but it's the good kind of pain. The kind that reminds you you're alive.

Out here, there's no room for thinking about daft shite, like Isla playing cards with Sophie and Mei, or me nursing a pint by myself, or women with perfect fringes who make tiny gasping sounds when they see you shirtless. There's just the next wave, the balance, the break. And for now, that's enough.

The lights of Corraig flicker to life across the water as the sky deepens. I catch one last wave, a beauty that carries me almost to shore, then paddle in with my arms feeling like wet noodles and my head finally, blissfully quiet.

I drop onto the towel I threw over the driver's seat earlier, wetsuit dripping everywhere despite my best efforts, and crank up the heating. I love getting out on the water, but man, this is the bit I don't like: when the fun's over and I'm just cold. I swear my balls have retreated so far north they're practically saying hello to my liver. And my cock? It's gone into full hibernation mode. September surfing in Scotland—not exactly a *Baywatch* moment.

I shift in the seat, trying to coax some warmth back into places that have fully given up on life. "Sorry, lads," I mutter. "I promise we'll have a hot shower as soon as we're home."

I start the engine and set off. The radio plays something folksy I don't recognise, but I hum along anyway as I navigate back towards Ardmara.

The sky's doing that September thing where it can't decide if it's pink or purple or gold, colours bleeding out over the water. It's stupid how beautiful it is. Makes the drive home feel quieter somehow.

As Ardmara's lights come into view—scattered along the seafront like someone shook a box of fairy lights—my mind, of course, drifts back to Ainsley. Seems that even cold-water shrinkage can't keep me from thinking of her. When am I going to get the message? She's complicated. Guarded. And I'm working for her. I should really keep my distance—at least until the salon refurb is over.

After that, it'd no longer be unprofessional, so . . . different story.

The van protests as I turn up Ardview Road, engine whining about the incline. House windows glow warm against the darkening sky. The McNairs haven't drawn their curtains yet, and I can see them on their sofa watching the rugby match I'm missing. Their living room flickers green from the massive telly Andy bought last year, despite Kim insisting it was too big.

My own house sits dark and still at the top of the hill. God, the place looks dead. Maybe I need to get a dog or something. It'd be nice to have someone to greet me when I get home.

I pull into my drive, kill the engine, grab my board, and head round the back of the house.

"Are you Batman?"

Jesus Christ. I nearly jump out of my skin.

A small figure stands by the fence between my back garden and Ainsley's, peering through a gap in it. Lily, wearing a nightie covered in tiny stars. She's studying my wetsuit with curiosity.

"What do you think?" I ask, playing along.

She tilts her head, considering. "You're Stwuan. Unless . . ."

Her eyes narrow. "Unless Stwuan *is* Batman. But where's your mask? And your cape?"

"Well"—I lean in conspiratorially—"I really am Batman but it's a secret. Can't go wearing the cape all the time or everyone would know. What are you doing out here so late?"

"Spying," she says solemnly. "And looking for fairies. They like gardens."

She reaches her wee hand through the fence and picks up a stone, peering underneath it with obvious hope. Her wee face falls when she finds nothing but dirt.

"Lily?" Ainsley's voice drifts from inside their house. "Where have you got to?"

"Wait there," I tell Lily. I duck into my shed, stash my board, and rummage until I find what I'm looking for—a short length of bamboo. "Here," I say, handing it through the fence. "It's a fairy-spotting telescope. Works best in daylight, but only if you hum to it first."

Her eyes go wide as saucers. She snatches the bamboo and bolts for her back door without another word. "Mummy! Mummy! Look what Batman gave me!"

"*Batman?* Lily, what are you—"

"He said it's for spotting fairies but I have to hum first!"

Chuckling, I head inside.

Honestly? That wee kid's got better chat than some adults I know.

CHAPTER SEVEN

AINSLEY

The morning sun filters through the whitewashed windows, casting the salon in soft, diffused light. Struan's clearly been hard at work since I was last here two days ago. Things are starting to take shape.

"The colour makes such a difference," I say as he walks me through his progress. The rose-gold feature wall glows at the far end, warm and inviting, while the other walls—a softer, toned-down blush—balance it out perfectly. It's exactly how I pictured it when I picked the colours from tiny sample cards.

"Glad you like it." Struan flashes a smile that probably gets him free coffee all over town.

Ugh. No, I'm here to inspect walls, not grins that belong in a toothpaste advert. If there's something pleasant about his smile, that's completely irrelevant.

"Thanks for the Wi-Fi, by the way," I say, keeping my tone brisk. "Got a lot done. Anyway, I should—"

"Here, I've got a few more things to show you."

His tone is warm—annoyingly warm. This is exactly the kind of charm that got me into trouble before. Easy smiles, helpful gestures, making me feel like I'm centre stage and everyone else is scenery. I know how this story ends.

He flips a switch, and instead of the old harsh spotlights, soft white bulbs bathe the space in a relaxing glow, the kind that'll make clients look good even before I've touched their hair.

"Less dentist, more salon?" he suggests.

"They look great," I admit, and a little thrill runs through me that has *nothing* to do with the man standing beside me. Because this is actually happening. My salon is coming together, piece by piece.

I pull out my phone and snap a quick selfie in front of the feature wall, captioning it "transformation in progress!" before uploading it to Instagram.

"And now for the big reveal." Struan strides to the front of the salon where something large sits under a tarpaulin. He whips it off with a flourish, the movement pulling his jeans tight across his arse, and for a moment I'm embarrassingly distracted by—

"What do you think?"

My eyes snap up, heat flooding my cheeks. Oh God, he caught me staring at his—

But no, he's looking at the bench. The gorgeous custom-built waiting bench he's made, all smooth lines and elegant curves.

For God's sake, Ainsley. Get a grip.

I dig my nails into my palm, using the small sting to pull myself together. I didn't come to Ardmara to ogle joiners. I came here to build something stable for Lily and me. *Not* to make the same stupid mistakes all over again.

"It's . . ." I clear my throat. "You've done a brilliant job. Really."

"Glad you think so." He gives the bench a once-over. "Won't fix it in place until the flooring's sorted, of course."

I fish my planner from my bag, grateful to have something to do with my hands. "And the new flooring's going down when?"

"First thing Monday." He glances at the tired vinyl tiles. "Da's helping, so we should have it done by Tuesday afternoon at the latest. Then I can start assembling the rest of the furniture."

I jot the details down and make a mental note to double-check the furniture delivery dates. I can feel his gaze on me as I write, and when I glance up, he's looking at my hair.

I wore it down today, curled at the ends in soft, bouncy spirals. It took me forty-five minutes this morning—an indulgence I can rarely afford with a four-year-old. I didn't do it for *him*, obviously. No, I need to look the part if I'm going to convince this town to trust me with their hair. It's branding. Professionalism.

His gaze lingers a heartbeat too long, warm enough to make my stomach tighten, and that just irritates me more. I don't want to react to him. I don't want to feel *anything* when he looks at me.

Then the door opens, pulling Struan's focus from me.

"Cooey!" Mum bustles in, carrying a stack of flyers. "Oh, this place looks great!"

"You must be Mrs Reid." Struan extends his hand. "Pleased to meet you. I'm Struan."

Mum beams at him. "So polite. And handsome too! Lucky you, Ainsley, having him live next door."

Oh God. Could she be any more embarrassing?

"We should get going," I say. "Lots of ground to cover today."

"Of course." Struan's lips twitch. "Well, I'll just be here, working on your salon and being handsome."

Mum actually giggles. Giggles! Like she's sixteen instead of sixty-two.

Kill me now.

I grab her arm and steer her towards the door before she can mortify me any further. "Thanks for the update, Struan. See you later."

As soon as we're safely outside, I release Mum's arm and round on her. "You're terrible!"

"What? He *is* handsome. I tell you, if I were thirty years younger and single—"

"Mum! Does it not occur to you that he's exactly like Danny was? All grins and patter. How did that work out for me?"

Mum's expression softens. "Sorry, love. Honestly, I was just being friendly."

I blow out. Maybe I'm overreacting. But the wound is still too raw, and Struan's particular brand of casual confidence hits too close to home.

"Anyway, where first?" Mum asks, wisely changing the subject.

We start with the boutique next door. The bell above the door chimes as we step inside, the scent of expensive wool and lavender potpourri wrapping around us. My stomach flutters—this is it, my first real pitch to the locals—but I push my shoulders back and paste on my brightest smile.

A woman behind the counter looks up, her faded blonde bob tucked neatly behind her ears.

"Hi," I say. "I'm Ainsley Reid. I'm opening the new salon next—"

"Oh, fantastic!" She brightens. "I'm Moira. So you're taking over Maggie's old place, eh? She did my hair for years, and I always went for the same thing. But honestly, I've been thinking for a while it's time for a change. What would you do with this?" She gestures to her bob.

My stylist brain switches on instantly. I take in the colour, the texture, the way it frames her face.

"I'd add some lowlights for dimension, maybe a bit of honey to warm it up, and for the cut . . ." I tilt my head, visualising. "A graduated bob, slightly shorter at the back, would give you more volume and frame your face beautifully."

Her eyes light up. "Sold! Book me in. For opening day, if you've got a slot."

"I do." I pull out my phone and bring up the booking app. "How's ten o'clock?"

"Perfect."

By the time we leave, Moira's got a handful of flyers and has promised to put one in her window. I walk out feeling lighter, a spark of confidence flaring in my chest.

See? I *can* do this.

We continue along the seafront, popping into the bakery, where the owner promises to mention me to her regulars, then the Lighthouse Café, where I leave a stack of flyers by the till. With each friendly chat, my confidence builds.

Outside the corner shop, a group of older women stand chatting. They listen politely as I tell them about the salon, but when one flips the flyer over and scans the price list, her eyebrows shoot up.

"Maggie never charged anything close to this," she says. "And this is *with* your opening discount?"

"Well, the services are quite different," I explain, keeping my voice pleasant. "I specialise in modern cutting techniques, balayage, colour correction—"

The women exchange a look, the kind that needs no translation. As Mum and I walk on, fragments of their conversation drift after us:

"... daylight robbery ..."

"... Maggie did my hair for twenty years ..."

"... she won't get customers with those prices ..."

And just like that, my fragile confidence takes a hit. Because what if they're right? What if I've completely misjudged this? I don't just *want* this business to succeed, I *need* it to. There's too much at stake for it to fail.

"Don't take it to heart," Mum says, patting my shoulder. "Folk can be resistant to change, especially the older generation. But they'll come round when they see how fabulous you are."

I want to believe her but doubt is already nibbling away at my resolve.

We're down to our last few flyers when a voice calls, "Ainsley! Hi!" Blair appears with Gus trotting beside her, his tail wagging enthusiastically.

"Hello, Gus." I give him a pat. "And hi, Blair. This is my mum, Pauline. Mum, this is Blair."

"Lovely to meet you," Mum says warmly.

"You too."

We fall into easy small talk, about the salon, Mum's first impressions of Ardmara, the mischief Gus got up to this morning. Then Blair asks, "Have you had any luck figuring out childcare? For that drink we talked about?"

I open my mouth to make my excuses, but Mum jumps in before I can speak.

"Oh, I'll babysit! Tonight, if you like. Lily and I can have a wee girls' night. Paint our nails, watch some cartoons, drink hot chocolate."

I bite back the urge to tell Mum to stay out of this. Blair, though, is already running with the idea.

"Really? That would be amazing. Eight o'clock at the Ferry-man's Rest?"

And just like that, I'm trapped. "Er . . . okay, sure. Eight o'clock." I manage a smile, pretending I'm a normal woman with a normal past who knows how to make friends.

"Awesome! See you then." She heads off with Gus, leaving me to give Mum a pointed look.

"Thanks, Mum. I've got *so* much to do at the moment. Going out for drinks wasn't on the agenda."

"A night out will be good for you. And it's a chance to meet new people, make new friends."

"Hmm." It's one thing putting on a professional smile to drum up business. Quite another to sit in a pub with someone I barely know and let them see past the polished surface.

"Look," Mum says, "I know how hard this has been for you, but you've got to see Ardmara as a fresh start. Not every man you meet will be like Danny. And not every woman will be like Rachel."

Hearing their names is like pressing on a bruise that hasn't healed. I'm saved from having to answer when a couple rounds the corner. I paste on a smile and hand them a flyer. "Hi! I'm opening a new hair salon on the seafront . . ."

CHAPTER EIGHT

AINSLEY

Blair sets two glasses of white wine on our tiny table, one of the last free ones, tucked against the old stone wall where the din dips from deafening to merely chaotic. The place is heaving: crowded but cosy, voices layered over one another, the whole pub buzzing with laughter, clinking glasses, and the kind of debates that sound fierce but are really just friendly noise.

"I'm so glad you came out." Blair slips into her chair. "I mean, I've got a few friends here now, but I'm still fairly new myself. Figured us newbies should stick together." She lifts her glass in a toast.

I clink mine against hers. "Aye, of course."

It's just a drink, I remind myself. *No big deal.*

The wine is cool and sharp on my tongue, exactly what I need after a long day of smiling at strangers and trying to look like I've got everything under control.

"You look amazing, by the way." Blair gestures at my outfit. "That dress is gorgeous."

I smooth a hand over the soft fabric, a deep plum wrap dress that sits just above my knees. "Thanks. I do like to dress up, but I don't get many chances these days."

Even though Mum basically volunteered me for this, I did enjoy getting ready. Same soft-glam make-up I always wear, just dialled up a notch. Dress instead of jeans. Ankle boots with a heel.

Maybe a bit fancy for the Ferryman's Rest, but it feels like armour. Like I'm still the version of myself who had her shit together before everything fell apart.

"So," I say, leaning forwards, "the other day you mentioned falling for your boss. Sounds like there's a story there."

Blair arches an eyebrow. "SparkNotes or novel version?"

"Novel. Definitely novel."

She launches into it—losing her gran, breaking up with her ex, and getting pushed out of her dream job in children's publishing, all within a year. Heavy stuff, but she tells it with a wry tilt to her mouth, like she's learnt to make peace with the wreckage.

"So," she says, "I decided to come to Scotland to escape everything for a while. I took a nanny job to get back on my feet and found myself working for a *very* grumpy single dad. At least there wasn't any danger of me catching feelings. Or so I thought."

I laugh. "Let me guess, behind the grumpiness, he's not so bad after all?"

"Oh, Lachlan can be stubborn and infuriating, but he's a decent man. And gorgeous. He's got a good heart. And . . ." She shrugs, a little sheepish. "He's just . . . him. Rough edges and all. But everyone's got them, right?"

I snort. "I'm practically made of them."

"I don't believe that for a second." Blair reaches across the table and squeezes my hand, giving me a wee smile. "Anyway, what about you? Is Lily's dad—"

"He's not on the scene."

The familiar tightness grips my chest—that hot, prickling sensation I get whenever anyone gets close to the topic. I should steer us somewhere else. Ask more about Lachlan. Comment on the wine. Anything.

But Blair's been so open about her own life . . .

"Oh, I'm sorry," Blair says. "We don't need to talk about that. We can—"

"He was hooking up with my best friend behind my back."

The words come out blunt. Graceless. Like I've coughed them up rather than chosen to say them. Blair's eyes widen.

"That's the real reason I came to Ardmara." I exhale, my fingers tightening around my wine glass. Seeing as I've already told her the headline, I might as well tell her the rest. "Everyone back home knew. I couldn't go to the shops without getting pitying looks or hearing whispers."

And now I've told someone here, I realise. But it feels good to have said it out loud, if a wee bit terrifying too.

"Oh my God, Ainsley, that's awful. I'm so sorry. Listen, you don't have to talk about it if you don't want to. But if you *do*, I'm right here."

I let out a shaky breath. "And if I'm dragging down the mood too much, just tell me to shut up." I try for a smile. "But honestly? I wouldn't mind getting some of it off my chest. It's easier talking to someone who doesn't know the whole cast list."

Blair nods, her expression soft.

"Danny—Lily's dad—and I were always on-again, off-again. That didn't change during the pregnancy, and it didn't change after Lily was born. Some weeks he'd stay with us, others he wouldn't. He never really settled into being a dad, but I kept telling myself that some kind of father was better for Lily than none.”

I trace the rim of my glass with my fingertip, the old humiliation crawling up my neck. “Then, during what I thought was an ‘on’ period, I caught him in bed with Rachel, my best friend since primary school. And in the argument that followed, I discovered it had been going on for months.”

“Jesus.” Blair shakes her head. “Lily’s father and your best friend . . . that’s a double betrayal.”

“So when this opportunity came up . . .”

“You ran.”

“I relocated,” I correct, though we both know she’s right. I swirl my wine. “I haven’t spoken to him since I told him I was leaving. He didn’t fight it.” A humourless laugh escapes me. “Looked relieved, actually.”

“For what it’s worth, they both sound like assholes who didn’t deserve you.”

This time, a genuine laugh slips out. “That’s one way to put it. I’d appreciate it if you kept this to yourself. Not for me, but for Lily. She doesn’t understand what happened, and I don’t want her overhearing something that might upset her.”

“I won’t say a word,” Blair promises. “Not even to Lachlan.”

“Thanks.”

The sound of instruments tuning pulls my attention to the small stage area. I do a double take—because Struan’s there, guitar in hand, sitting between a woman with a fiddle and an older man with an accordion.

For the love of . . . he’s everywhere! Working in my salon, living next door to me, sitting in ball pits, catching me when I fall off chairs. And he plays guitar in a band too?

“That’s the Celtic Kicks,” Blair says, following my gaze. “The fiddler, Ellie, is a friend. Works at the library." She catches my expression. "Oh, you're not into folk music? I totally forgot to say they'd be playing."

"No, I'm just . . . surprised." I tilt my head towards Struan. "Had no idea he played. He's doing my salon refurb. And he's my neighbour."

Blair smiles. "I know him a little from 'soft play' meet-ups, as you Brits call it. Lachlan, Struan, and another dad—Douglas—go most Saturdays. Actually, those three don't even call it soft play. They call it 'the Pit'." She makes air quotes. "You know, because it's the pits."

I can't help smirking. As a mum who's spent her share of hours in soft-play hell, it's a pretty accurate name.

Struan's laugh carries across the room—rich and deep, cutting through the general noise. My eyes find him again before I can stop myself. He's leaning towards Ellie, head tipped as he adjusts his guitar, chuckling at something she's said.

"So, Struan and Ellie, are they . . . ?" I wave my hand vaguely, trying for casual.

"No, no. They're definitely just friends."

Right. Just friends. Figures. Men like him never limit their charm to one woman.

"I'm going to run to the bathroom before they start," Blair says. "Be right back."

Left alone, my gaze drifts straight back to Struan. I really shouldn't look, but I've had wine and he's right *there*.

His work jeans have been traded for . . . another pair of equally worn jeans. He's in a faded checked shirt over a white T-shirt, and his hair's in a half-up ponytail—deliberately messy, firmly in *sexy* territory. He looks completely at ease, legs stretched out, guitar resting on his lap.

He adjusts the tuning pegs with practised ease, a strand of hair falling across his face, his long fingers moving with hypnotic precision.

Ugh. Could this man love himself any more?

He taps the mic. "Evening, folks. For those of you new here . . ." His gaze sweeps the crowd and lands squarely on me. Heat flickers up my neck before I can stop it. Of course he's seen me. Of course.

I raise an eyebrow at him, my best "I'm not impressed" look.

His smile widens.

"We're the Celtic Kicks. I'm Struan on guitar, this is Ellie on fiddle, and Rab here is on the box."

A wolf whistle rings out from the bar. "Looking good, Rapunzel!"

Laughter ripples through the room. Struan tips his head and gives his hair a mock toss.

God, he soaks up the pub's attention like it's his birthright. While the rest of us go through life riddled with anxieties, everything is sunny and rosy in the world of Struan Walker. Meanwhile, I can barely hand out flyers without panicking about people whispering behind my back.

"Right, then. Tonight's a bit of a mix—plenty of folk, and we'll throw in a few ceilidh reels too. If you've got a favourite, keep it in mind and shout at us near the end."

The first song kicks in—Ellie's fiddle bright and soaring, the accordion weaving through, Struan's guitar providing a warm, steady foundation. The rhythm is infectious, impossible not to move to.

Much to my annoyance.

"They're catchy, right?" Blair says, sliding back into her seat.

"Aye," I admit grudgingly. Only then do I notice my traitorous fingers are tapping against the table.

We try to continue our conversation over the music, but my attention keeps drifting to the stage. To the way Struan's fingers move over the strings—smooth, confident. By the second song, we give up on talking altogether, both of us bobbing along to the beat. A few couples link arms and spin in the limited open space. Others bounce in place, pints sloshing dangerously.

The third song is fast and playful, a duel between Ellie's bow and Struan's fretting hand. Halfway through, he rises to his feet, legs braced wide as his fingers fly over the strings.

Oh, *come on*! Does he think he's performing at the Hydro?

And yet, those hands . . . I can't look away from them. The same ones that fixed my light, that caught me when I fell.

It's the wine. Definitely the wine.

For a split second, entirely uninvited, I imagine those fingers skimming over my skin instead of the guitar. Starting at my collarbone, trailing lower . . . lower . . .

Oh God.

I glance up and catch him watching me watching him. He grins.

I flush and grab my wine, draining what's left.

Wait. Was drinking more wine a good idea or a bad one?

Either way, when I risk another look, his attention is mercifully elsewhere.

During the next reel, Struan throws in what can only be described as a cheeky jig, deliberately hamming it up. More wolf whistles. The whole pub's laughing now, feet stamping, hands clapping. There's a sheen of sweat at his temple and his cheeks are flushed, but his grin is pure mischief.

Blair starts clapping and shoots me a smile. I join in, reluctant at first, but the mood is infectious. The music thrums through the floorboards, vibrates in my chest. Before I know it, I'm laughing along with everyone else, experiencing a kind of carefree abandon I haven't felt in months.

Struan's eyes find mine again—and he winks.

I stop clapping. Glare. Look away.

Blair notices but turns back to the music without comment.

God, he actually winked. Does he think he's some kind of rock star?

I reach for my glass but it's empty. So is Blair's. I'm just standing to get us another round when the song ends and Struan speaks into the mic.

"Right, this next one's a wee vocal piece. 'Mo Nighean Donn'."

I sink back down. He sings too? And in Gaelic?

The drinks can wait a few minutes.

The instruments fall silent. Struan closes his eyes and his voice fills the space—deep, melodic, threaded with something bittersweet. The hairs on the back of my neck rise. The whole room goes still, like we're all afraid to breathe and break the spell. Even the clatter from the bar seems to hush.

At this point, I'm not even surprised. Of course he can sing. I just hate that it gives me goosebumps.

When he finishes, the silence is almost startling.

Then he cracks one eye open, grins, and his playful self slides back into place. "All right! Back to being lively. On your feet, grab a partner—there's not much room, but on-the-spot dancing will do just fine."

The crowd surges with laughter and movement as the fastest reel of the night bursts into life.

"Come on!" Blair tugs at my arm.

"I'm not sure..."

"I'm American! You have to show me what to do."

I let her pull me to my feet, hesitant at first. But the music's relentless, impossible to fight against, and Blair's enthusiasm is contagious. We laugh our way through the rhythm, dancing in place with everyone else, my dress swishing around my knees like it's been waiting for this moment.

When the music ends, the cheers are deafening. Blair and I high-five, both of us breathless and grinning.

Despite being *way* too full of himself, I'll give Struan this—the man can put on a show.

◆ ◆ ◆

I'm at the bar, waiting to order more drinks for Blair and me. The band have finished their set, and I'm fanning myself with a beer mat, hot from all the dancing.

A short way to my left, Struan is surrounded by a small crowd. They're all laughing at something he's said, hanging on his every word like he's some kind of celebrity rather than just a bloke who can play a bit of guitar. An attractive blonde—maybe ten years older than him, and with perfect lipstick—actually twirls a strand of hair around her finger as she gazes at him.

Ugh. Obvious much?

I catch myself and frown. What does it matter if women flirt with Struan? It's nothing to do with me. The man can charm whoever he wants with his guitar and his stupid man bun and his—

I shake my head, trying to dislodge whatever this is.

Get a hold of yourself, Ainsley.

"What can I get you?" The barman's voice cuts through my thoughts.

"Two white wines, please."

While he pours, I pull out my phone to check for messages. There's one from Mum sent twenty minutes ago—a photo of Lily mid-Barbie drama, dolls scattered across the living room floor. At least she looks happy. Though Mum better be getting her ready for bed soon or tomorrow morning will be rough.

Anyway, *this* is what matters. My wee girl. Not some charmer with a man bun.

I switch to Instagram. My post from earlier today, showing the salon's new walls, has got a decent bit of engagement. The first three comments are locals excited about the opening. One's from Mum, which hardly counts, but I'll take it. The fourth comment, though, makes me pause.

Who's the hottie in the background? I might need to come to Ardmara just to see him 🐷

I peer at the photo. Shit. Struan photobombed it, looking straight at the camera with that cheeky, gorgeous grin on his face. I didn't even notice when I uploaded it. I was so busy making sure *I* looked presentable I missed him lurking in the background.

It seems even some random stranger on the internet can't help themselves. Struan bloody Walker: stealing the spotlight everywhere he goes, even in a post that was supposed to be about my salon.

A warm presence looms at my back, and I catch that scent of his—warm and earthy and deeply, unmistakably male.

"Am I the hottie?"

I turn, already frowning, one hand moving to my hip. "It's rude to read people's messages."

"That's not a message, it's a public comment." His mouth

curves into a cocky, infuriatingly adorable smirk. "And if I'm understanding correctly, they mean me."

"Modest, aren't you?"

He shrugs, unbothered. "Who else is in the background?"

"Want me to delete it?"

"Nah." He waggles his eyebrows. "Might drum up more business for you."

I roll my eyes. This man is impossible.

The barman sets two glasses of wine in front of me. I tap my phone against the card reader to pay, ready to escape back to Blair, but Struan leans against the bar, one leg crossed over the other, clearly in no hurry to let me go.

"What did you think of the Celtic Kicks?"

"Not bad." I pick up the wines.

"Not bad?" He lifts a brow. "Looked like you were enjoying yourself, dancing with Blair."

"Would've been rude not to teach the American a bit of our traditional dance." Even to my own ears, I sound surly.

"Do you always make a habit of downplaying your enjoyment?"

My pulse skips, irritation and something else—something warmer—tangling in my chest. "Do you always make a habit of winking at your neighbours and clients?"

"Only the bonny ones."

The words land like a spark on dry kindling. Part of me wants to throw the wine in his face for the presumption. Another part—a part I'm trying very hard to smother with common sense—reacts to the warmth in his voice in ways I absolutely refuse to examine.

This is the wine, I tell myself firmly. *And the dancing. Nothing more.*

His gaze travels from my boots up to my face, unhurried. "You are particularly bonny tonight."

Heat floods my cheeks. My mouth opens for some cutting retort, but nothing comes. The way he's looking at me—not leering, just . . . *appreciating*—scrambles my brain completely.

I pivot on my heel and head back to the table, wine sloshing dangerously close to the rim of the glasses. I can feel his eyes on me the whole way, hot on my back as my dress sways with each step.

CHAPTER NINE

STRUAN

The van rattles along the winding road to Bannock, and I drum my fingers on the steering wheel in time with the radio. Friday afternoon—best part of the working week. Not just because I get a break from sanding and painting, but because I'm about to collect my wee girl.

A tractor lumbers out of a farm track ahead, trailer stacked high with hay bales that wobble precariously with each pothole. I drop down a gear, biding my time until the road straightens, then swing out and overtake. The farmer raises a hand from the wheel in that universal countryside greeting, and I return the gesture.

Nancy Sinatra's voice crackles through the speakers: "These Boots Are Made for Walkin'". I find myself grinning like an eejit. Christ, this song. It's pure Ainsley Reid energy—all sass and sting, ready to crush a man under those wee heeled boots she wore last night.

God, the way she'd watched me play, those green eyes tracking my every move across the strings. And when she'd danced with Blair, that plum dress clinging to her thighs, swishing around her legs with every spin . . .

She'd *smiled*—not that she'd aimed it at me. Nah, too busy pretending she's not interested. But I saw the way her cheeks flushed when I called her bonny—the prettiest shade of pink. She can play ice queen all she likes, but I know attraction when I see it.

I shift in my seat, willing my body to calm the fuck down. Because nothing says "responsible father" like getting a semi thinking about your neighbour on the way to pick up your kid.

Still. Only one more week of the refurb, then I'm no longer her builder. After that? All bets are off. We'll see if those walls of hers stay up.

A thought niggles as I navigate another bend. Maybe it'd be smarter to find a tourist for a one-night reset. Rather than the woman I live next door to. The woman I'll see every bloody day whether things go well or spectacularly sideways.

Aye. That *would* be smarter. But not as fun.

Bannock's Main Street opens out ahead of me, its stone buildings bathed in late-afternoon light. Flower boxes run along the pavement, bright against the grey stone. I pass the pub—the Pheasant—then Morag's Bakery, which I'm keen to visit since the cakes are supposed to be amazing, but it's always shut by the time I get here.

I turn right onto the narrow side street that runs alongside the River Garve. I've got to give it to her, Sophie picked a cracking spot to live. Old stone cottages, doors and window frames all painted in bright colours, wee tidy gardens full of flowers, and back gardens backing right onto the water. Dead-end street too, so barely any traffic.

As I pull up outside her place, a wee girl darts across the lane, giggling, a blond guy a few years older than me chasing after her. "Callie!" he calls, laughing. "Come back here, you wee menace!"

I can't help smiling, remembering when Isla used to be that small—about the same age as Ainsley's wee girl, Lily, come to think of it.

And there I go, straight back to Ainsley again. Christ. What is it about her? Is it just that she tells me to bugger off when everyone else laughs along?

I get out the van and walk up the short path to Sophie's bright yellow door. I knock then try the handle and, as usual, am able to let myself in. Sophie's philosophy: in a place like Bannock, what's the point of locking your door? Used to make me nervous, but her house, her rules.

The smell hits me first—onions, mushrooms, something creamy. I follow my nose to the kitchen, where Sophie is stirring a pot, her dark-blonde hair twisted up in a messy bun.

"What you making? Smells almost edible."

She starts then turns, wooden spoon in hand. "Struan! Didn't hear you come in. It's mushroom stroganoff, and it smells better than edible, thank you very much."

"Aye, well, I'll be balancing out all your veggie meals by letting Isla eat her body weight in sausages over the weekend." I wink at her. "Might even teach her how to grill a steak rare enough to moo."

Sophie shakes her head but smiles and pulls me in for a quick hug. "Honestly, Struan, you never change."

"Aye, well, one of us had to stay predictable."

She laughs then calls up the stairs, "Isla! Your da's here!"

"Hi, Da!" Isla shouts back. "Be down in a minute! Just finishing packing."

I remember when she was smaller and the second I walked through that door, she'd come thundering down the stairs and launch herself at me. Now it's "be down in a minute". Growing up, I suppose.

"She was a wee bit upset earlier," Sophie says, turning back to her cooking. "Katie and Freya are having a sleepover tonight."

"Ah." I lean against the worktop. "And she can't go cause I've got her."

"Aye, but these things happen. It's not the first time and it won't be the last. She knows that. But she was still disappointed."

"You should've texted me, Soph. I could've picked her up tomorrow morning instead."

She glances over her shoulder. "I didn't want to cut into your time with her. You already have her for less of the week than I do."

"I'm not a monster, Soph. I do let her have pals." I grin. "If something like this comes up again, just give me a shout. It's not a big deal."

"You sure? Because . . . well, I *was* thinking we could do a sleepover here at some point and invite Katie and Freya over. But it'd need to be at the weekend—a school night just wouldn't work."

"Course I'm sure." But even as I say it, there's a wee flicker in my gut at the thought of losing a night with my girl.

Christ, Walker, you're a grown man. You can cope with losing one Friday evening so Isla can have a sleepover with her mates.

"Great, I'll check with the other mums. Maybe next weekend?"

I shoot her a smile. "Works for me."

"You can tell her in the van, if you like. Might cheer her up."

"Aye, will do."

Sophie nods, then takes a breath. "Actually, while we've got a minute . . . Mei's coming for dinner tonight, and . . . I'm going to ask her to move in."

My stomach does a weird little drop. Mei, here permanently, part of Isla's everyday life in a way I'm not—

And then I catch myself.

What's wrong with me? I *like* Mei. Besides, Sophie deserves this and Isla adores her. I really need to get it together.

I pull Sophie into a hug. "That's brilliant news. She'd be daft to say no."

Sophie relaxes against me. "You sure you're okay with it?"

"Course I am. Mei's great." And I mean it. Between the two of them, Isla's going to be fed, loved, and fussed over to within an inch of her life. That's a good thing.

"Don't say anything to Isla yet," Sophie says after I let her go. "Not until Mei's given me her answer. And I'd like to be the one to tell her."

"My lips are sealed."

Footsteps on the stairs pull both our gazes to the doorway. Isla appears, rucksack slung over one shoulder, curls escaping from her ponytail.

"You've grown again, wee yin," I say, opening my arms.

She walks into the hug, but it's quieter than usual—no full-body tackle today. Sophie's straight in checking Isla's bag, then her Dexcom, then rattling off reminders to me about sensors and hypo snacks and logging carbs and all the usual diabetes stuff.

"Got it all, Soph," I say, smiling so she knows I'm not annoyed. "We go through this every Friday." I nudge Isla with my elbow. "You'd think she'd trust me by now, eh?"

She gives a small smile. "She likes to fuss, doesn't she?"

"Can't help it," Sophie says. "Habit. Right then, have a good evening, both of you."

"Bye, Mum." Isla gives her a quick squeeze before slipping her hand into mine.

As we head for the door, I glance back at Sophie, give her a small nod, and mouth, "Good luck."

◆ ◆ ◆

"So," I say to Isla as we leave Bannock behind us, "tell me about this primary four reading group, then. You showing those older kids how it's done?"

"It's fine." She looks out the van window.

"Just fine? Come on, you must be reading some good stuff. What have they got you on? *War and Peace*? The complete works of Shakespeare?"

A tiny smile tugs at her mouth. "We're doing *Charlotte's Web*."

"Ah, the spider book. Classic. Though personally, I always thought Wilbur was a bit of a drama queen."

"Da." She rolls her eyes, but the smile's still there.

"What? He was! 'Oh no, I'm going to be bacon!' Meanwhile, Charlotte's out there writing actual words in a web, and does she get any credit?"

She giggles, shaking her head like I'm the daftest person alive. Good. That's better.

"Listen, princess, your mum said you were a bit upset earlier. About the sleepover?"

Her smile falters. She nods.

"Tell you what," I say, like the idea's just occurred to me, "how about you have your own sleepover? At your mum's place. Next weekend, if it suits Katie and Freya."

She turns to me, eyes brightening. "Really?"

"Course. I'll pick you up Saturday morning instead of Friday night. Give you the whole evening with your pals."

"Can we have pizza? And watch films? And make friendship bracelets?"

She's already planning the whole thing out. There's no "but that means one night less with you, Da!" Not that I expected it. Besides, her grin right now is worth trading a Friday evening for.

"Sounds good to me, and I'm sure your mum'll be fine with all of that."

She pulls a wee notebook from her rucksack—because of course she packed a notebook—and starts scribbling. "We'll need snacks. Good ones, not healthy ones. And maybe we could do makeovers? Oh, and ghost stories!"

I chuckle. There's my girl.

"Can we go to the shop tomorrow? To get crisps and sweets?"

"Absolutely."

She beams at me, a proper smile this time. "Thanks, Da."

"Anything for you, princess." I nod towards a sign for Duntreath. "Fancy stopping at that restaurant you like? The one that does the ice cream sundaes?"

"Yes!" She actually bounces in her seat. "Can I get the one with the sparklers?"

"If you eat some actual food first."

"Deal!"

CHAPTER TEN

AINSLEY

"Argh! Ya cheap pile of shite!" The words echo off my bedroom walls as the bed frame collapses. Again.

I glare at the instruction manual spread open on the carpet. The diagrams look like they were drawn by someone who's never seen a bed, let alone built one. Connect A and B? Okay, sure. Except the wee holes on B don't bloody line up with A.

The gentle music of *In the Night Garden* drifts up through the floorboards, all soothing and dreamy. At least Lily's happy, curled on the sofa with her bedtime milk, completely oblivious to her mother's DIY disaster zone upstairs.

I managed to put together Lily's bed last week, so surely I should be able to manage this one? Mind you, Lily's bed was smaller and simpler, with fewer pieces. Oh, and it was a whole lot lighter.

I try again, lining up the headboard with the side bit, but the pre-drilled holes just don't match. I flip it. Then flip it again. Finally I get a bolt in. I feel a flicker of hope, then shift the frame to grab the next piece and—

It all crashes down, the headboard narrowly missing my foot.

"Oh, come ON!"

Right. That's it. I'm done.

I snatch up the instruction manual, storm to the window, yank it open, and hurl the useless thing straight out of it. Good riddance.

I flop onto the carpet and throw my arms over my face. Why, oh why, did I think assembling furniture on a Friday night was a good idea? I'm knackered. Half my day was spent drowning in salon admin, the other half catering to a four-year-old's every whim.

At least I have a proper mattress now. Still wrapped in plastic and propped against the wall, but it's here. If all else fails, I can just sleep on that on the floor. Better than the air mattress anyway. Who even really needs a bed frame?

The doorbell rings.

I groan. Who the hell turns up at someone's door on a Friday night? I'm so not in the mood for visitors.

Dragging myself to my feet, I trudge downstairs, navigating the boxes still cluttering the hall. I've tried to make the place feel more like home—hung a couple of photos—but it's still very much a work in progress.

I peek into the living room, where Lily's transfixed by Igglepiggle's antics, then swing open the front door.

Struan stands there with that infuriating grin of his, Isla at his side. He's in khakis and a navy jumper, hair pulled into its usual messy bun, a few strands escaping to frame his face. Meanwhile, I'm in my rattiest hoodie, joggers that have seen better days, and not a scrap of make-up.

For a split second, I feel a flicker of self-consciousness—then I squash it flat. No, this look is fine. Because I don't care what this man thinks of my appearance. Not one bit.

"Er . . . hi?" I say, keeping my voice cool. Isla's presence stops me from being outright rude, but only just. "Is there something I can help you with?"

Struan holds up some crumpled papers. The instruction manual. "This came flying out your window as we pulled in."

My cheeks warm before I can stop them. Brilliant. Now I'm embarrassed *and* annoyed.

"Oh, er . . . thanks. I was chasing a fly out the window and that . . . fell out of my hand." Never in my life have I sounded less convincing.

Struan's grin widens. He knows I'm talking rubbish.

Before he can call me out, Lily appears beside me, and her face lights up. "Isla!" She bounces on her toes. "Come see my kitchen—it's in the kitchen!"

Isla frowns, clearly confused.

"She means her toy kitchen set," I explain. "She keeps it beside the real oven so she can 'cook' beside me."

"Oh!" Understanding dawns on Isla's face. She looks at me hopefully.

I hesitate. Inviting Isla in means Struan lingers on my doorstep longer. But Lily's already tugging at my arm, and I can't exactly say no with both girls looking at me like that.

"Go on, then," I say to Isla, summoning a smile. "Lily can show you."

Lily wastes no time, dragging Isla away and chattering about making pretend cakes.

Struan watches them go then waves the manual, one eyebrow raised. "So . . . a fly, aye?"

I hold his gaze. "A very aggressive fly. The thing was huge."

"Uh-huh." He's not buying it.

I last about three more seconds before I cave. "Fine. I lobbed it. Bloody thing deserved it. It's been no help whatsoever. I've been at it for ages and my bed's still in pieces."

"Want me to take a look?"

My shoulders stiffen. Definitely not inviting him into my bedroom. "No, thanks. I'll manage."

"Okay, but . . ." His lips twitch. "Will you, though?"

"I'll have to. I can't pay you. I have *no* spare money right now."

"Ainsley, I'm not after payment. Just being neighbourly."

My eyes narrow. "Neighbourly, eh? Or are you trying to get on my good side in hopes I'll . . ." I lower my voice ". . . drop my knickers out of gratitude?"

He nearly chokes on a laugh. "Jesus, woman. No. I'm working for you—it wouldn't be professional."

"Oh, really?" I fold my arms. "Because last night at the pub, you were laying it on thicker than plaster."

He flashes me a cocky, lopsided smile. "Was I?"

"Aye. You were."

"Fair enough." He shrugs. "I *was* being flirty, but it was just a bit of banter. I promise, right now I'm only here offering to be a good neighbour. But if you'd rather I left you to it . . ."

He trails off, and I picture the carnage upstairs. The collapsed frame. The mattress still wrapped in plastic.

My pride wages war with practicality. Practicality wins.

"Fine," I sigh. "Maybe I would appreciate a hand."

"All right, then." He steps inside, and suddenly the narrow hall feels even smaller. Up close, he's so tall I have to tilt my head back to look at him properly. Without my heels, he's more than a foot taller than me.

"After you," I say, stepping aside. No way am I walking up the stairs in front of him and putting my arse at his eye level.

Which means I follow him up instead, his arse at my eye level.

Don't look, I tell myself firmly. *Do not look.*

I look.

And what an arse it is. Tight, perfectly shaped, unfairly good in those khakis.

Fantastic. You're meant to be keeping your distance, and here you are eyeing up his backside. Pull yourself together, Ainsley.

"So, just to check," he calls over his shoulder as we near the top. My eyes snap up guiltily. "You didn't lob any actual bed parts out the window, did you? Or was it just the manual?"

"Just the manual," I grumble.

He steps into my bedroom and stops, taking in the chaos. Bed pieces scattered across the floor like someone's detonated a flat-pack bomb. He presses his lips together, clearly trying not to laugh.

I hover in the doorway, suddenly hyper-aware that this is my *bedroom*. And he's standing in it. It feels too intimate, too personal, having him here among my things.

It's just a room, I remind myself. *And he's just fixing a bed. Nothing more.*

"All right." He crouches to examine the pieces. "Aye, here's your issue. This bit's the left side, not the right. You need to swap these pieces over."

"Oh." Irritation flickers through me—at myself, mostly, for not spotting something so obvious. And maybe a tiny bit at him for making it look so easy. "Well, DIY really isn't my thing."

He picks up the headboard from the carpet, tests its weight, then rests it against the wall. "Is this where you want the bed? Against this wall?"

"Yes, please."

He glances at the wall, then back at me, a glint in his eye. "You know, my room's a mirror of yours. Bed's in the same spot. Means we'll be sleeping with just brick and mortar between us."

My stomach does a stupid little flip. This man—honestly. So much for the whole "just being neighbourly" routine.

I open my mouth to ask where the hell else I'm meant to put the thing in a room this size, but before I can, he turns his back to me and tugs off his jumper. His T-shirt rides up, revealing a strip of toned lower back and the waistband of his boxers. Red today, for what it's worth.

My throat goes dry.

Oh, for crying out loud. I tear my gaze away, annoyed at myself. I *really* need to stop staring every time this man shows a bit of skin. It's been months since I've been intimate with anyone—that's the only explanation for why I'm reacting like this. My body's just . . . confused. Starved of attention. It doesn't mean anything.

I clear my throat. "I'll probably just be a hindrance. So I'll, er, leave you to it. I'll . . . oh, I'll make tea."

I escape downstairs before he can respond, my pulse fluttering ridiculously.

◆　◆　◆

Five minutes later, I'm back upstairs again with a mug of tea in one hand and a plate of chocolate digestives in the other. I've got my composure back. Mostly.

Before facing Struan again, I pause outside Lily's room. She and Isla migrated up here when I started busying about in the kitchen. Apparently, I was cramping their style.

Through a crack in the door, I see Lily thrust a plastic dog into Isla's hands. "You be the dog. I'll be the vet."

"Okay." Isla settles onto her knees. "What's my name?"

"Kayla," Lily replies with absolute confidence. "She's got babies in her tummy." Lily proceeds to stuff three plastic puppies through the flap in the toy dog's belly. They all came together as part of a play set. After rummaging in her toy box, Lily adds, "And a kitten. And a hamster."

Isla blinks. "But dogs don't have kittens or hamsters—"

"Just pretend!" Lily cuts her off, dismissing science with a flap of her hand. "Also, Kayla talks."

"Okay . . ." Isla grins, giving in. She whines dramatically in her best dog voice: "My tummy's all wriggly, but I don't know why."

"Lie down, Kayla. I'll look in your tummy with my magic wand."

I bite back a laugh. This girl is too sassy for her own good, but watching her so delighted—and Isla going along with it all—melts something in my chest. Technically, it's past Lily's bedtime, and she had a late night yesterday too, with Mum letting her stay up late while I was at the pub. Even so, I don't mind. Not when she's getting on so well with the older girl from next door.

Right. Time to face Struan again.

I carry the tea and biscuits into my bedroom and stop dead. Because somehow Struan has *already* created order from my chaos. The frame is taking shape, solid and sturdy.

"Jesus," I say. "You're making quick work of it."

"Och, it's a simple frame." He glances up, catches my expression, and his mouth curves. "What I mean is, flat pack is easier for someone who builds things for a living."

I arch a brow. "Nice save."

He stands and accepts the tea. He takes a biscuit too, dunks it, then pops it in his mouth. God, even the way he eats is attractive. Manly somehow.

Seriously? You're turned on by biscuit-eating now? What's wrong with you?

"Thanks for doing this." I make a conscious effort to soften my tone. He *is* helping me out, after all. In his own time. For free. "After sleeping on an air mattress for the last week, it'll be nice to have a proper bed."

"No problem. Besides, I'm always happy to be rewarded with biscuits."

"Should I offer Isla one?"

He shakes his head. "Nah, she's not long eaten, and she had a sundae as a treat. A biscuit would just throw her numbers off. I'll give her some supper when we're back."

"Oh, of course. I noticed Isla has that . . ." I tap my arm, searching for the word.

"CGM," Struan supplies. "Continuous glucose monitor. Helps us keep an eye on her blood sugars."

"Right. Diabetes?"

He nods.

"Does it take a lot of planning?"

He leans back against the chest of drawers. "Bit of a steep learning curve at first. It wasn't in either of our families, so me and Soph had to figure it all out from scratch. Soph is Isla's mum, by the way. Anyway, once we found the rhythm of it, it got easier. As long as we plan ahead, Isla can do pretty much everything other kids do. Maybe with a bit of extra thought, but close enough she doesn't feel left out."

His smile turns wry. "At least, not because of her diabetes. Having to come to Ardmara at weekends when her pals are having sleepovers in Bannock? That's a whole other story."

"Ah," I say. "There was drama tonight?"

"Och, nothing major. She was a wee bit put out, but we've got a plan now. She's going to host her own sleepover, next weekend hopefully. Crisis averted." He drains his tea and sets the mug down. "Anyway, back to it."

"Is there anything I can do? I promise I won't undo your hard work."

That earns me a half-smile. "I'm almost done, but if you like, you can take the wrapping off the mattress."

So I do. We work in comfortable silence, him turning the Allen key with practised ease, me wrestling with industrial-strength plastic. My mind wanders—to "Soph". He said her name so casually, like they're still a good team. Clearly better co-parents than me and Danny ever managed. Which isn't saying much.

A stupid knot twists in my stomach. Envy, maybe. Not of Soph specifically—I couldn't care less about Struan's romantic history—but of what they've managed to build. A functional partnership. Two parents who actually show up for their kid.

"That's the frame done," Struan announces, pulling me from my thoughts.

Together we hoist the mattress onto it. As soon as it's in place, I flop down onto the bed with a grateful sigh, stretching my arms wide.

"God, this feels amazing. *So* much better than that air mattress."

The words are barely out of my mouth before I realise what I've done. I'm lying sprawled across a bed, Struan Walker standing over me.

What the hell is wrong with you, Ainsley?

I scramble upright, smoothing down my hoodie like that'll restore some dignity. "Thank you, Struan. Really." I gesture at the bed. "If it wasn't for you, this would still be in pieces. Or out the window."

He smiles that disarming half-smile. "No problem."

I think he's going to go. But instead, he steps closer.

My pulse stutters.

"You've got something in your hair."

His fingers brush my temple, gentle as he plucks free a bit of polystyrene packaging caught in the strands. He flicks it aside.

But he doesn't step back.

His eyes meet mine, and the air between us thickens. Shifts. Warmth spreads through me, a prickling awareness that starts at my scalp and travels down my spine.

Step back, I tell myself. *Step back right now.*

But I don't move.

Why am I not moving?

His gaze drops to my mouth, and for a moment, just a moment, I think he's going to—

Peals of laughter echo from across the landing.

I jolt backwards, the spell shattered. Coming to my senses, I snatch up his jumper and thrust it at him.

"Here," I blurt, my voice far too high. "You should—I need to start Lily's bedtime routine."

Struan takes the jumper, something unreadable flickering across his face before his usual easy expression slides back into place. "Aye, of course. I'll grab Isla." He pulls the jumper on and heads for the door, pausing at the threshold. "Night, Ainsley. Sleep well."

"Night," I manage.

I listen to his footsteps sound across the landing, hear him coax Isla away from the game, hear the front door open and close.

I let out a long breath.

What the hell just happened?

CHAPTER ELEVEN

STRUAN

The knocking is insistent, urgent, dragging me from sleep. Huh? What . . . ? Who . . . ?

I stumble out of bed and yank open my bedroom door.

Ainsley.

She's barefoot in a tiny nightie that barely covers her thighs, her hair rumpled and wild, like she's been tossing and turning on the other side of my bedroom wall.

"Ainsley? What—"

She doesn't answer. Just reaches up, grips my face with both hands, and pulls me down to her mouth.

For a heartbeat I'm frozen, my brain trying to catch up. How did she even get in the house? But then her tongue slides against mine and, Christ, I'm gone. I haul her against me, one hand tangling in her hair, the other splayed across her back. She makes this tiny sound—half gasp, half moan—and it spears straight through me.

Her hands slide down to grip my arse, pulling me tighter against her, and fuck, there's no way she doesn't feel exactly what she's doing to me. The thin cotton of her nightie doesn't hide a thing—not from her, not from me. She's all heat and soft curves, fitting against me like she belongs right here.

I get my hands under her thighs and lift them, and she wraps her legs around my waist. We stumble back towards the bed, her mouth hot and demanding on mine, teeth nipping at my bottom lip.

"Struan," she breathes, and the sound of my name ripples through me—soft, needful, impossible.

Too impossible.

I jolt awake, my heart hammering against my ribs like I've just been slammed off my board by a monster wave.

Sunlight pours through a gap in my curtains. I'm alone. Completely and utterly alone in my bed with a raging hard-on.

"Jesus fucking Christ." I scrub both hands over my face.

A dream. Of course it was a dream. Because Ainsley Reid would never show up at my door in a nightie demanding to be kissed senseless.

I lift the duvet and peer down at my enthusiastic morning situation. "Really? We're doing this now?" I mutter. "I'm working for her for another week, you eejit. Think you can behave yourself till the job's done, at least?"

My cock, predictably, has no response except to remain stubbornly, achingly hard.

I groan. Brilliant. Now I'm having sex dreams about her. About the woman who's literally on the other side of this wall, probably still asleep in that bed I built for her, dark hair spread across the pillows—

Stop. Stop right there, Walker.

But Christ, I can still feel dream-Ainsley's mouth on mine. The weight of her in my arms. The way she said my name . . .

It's not like I haven't had the odd hook-up with a client over the years. But it's always been *them* that's made the first move, not me. I've enough sense to know *I* shouldn't be initiating anything with someone who's paying me to do a job.

But then, last night in her bedroom . . . I'd stepped closer to get that bit of packaging from her hair, and a pulse of want hit me, clear and unmistakable. I was *this close* to—

"Get a grip," I mutter. "You can manage one more week without trying to snog her on that brand-new bed."

Cold shower it is, then.

I drag myself out of bed and pad to the bathroom, turning the water to arctic. The shock of it against my skin makes me hiss through my teeth, but it does the job. By the time I'm done, I'm shivering and my cock's gone from proud soldier to deserter.

Back in my room I pull on shorts and a T-shirt, then I check on Isla. Still fast asleep, curls spread across her pillow. I wake the Dexcom receiver on her bedside table—5.8 mmol/L, nice and steady. My phone would've alerted me if her blood sugar went wonky in the night, but I always double-check anyway.

I head downstairs, glancing at my phone. There's a message from Sophie.

SOPHIE

Mei said yes to moving in 🤍

Something tightens in my chest—just for a second—before I shake it off. Not my house, not my life. And this is good news. Great news, actually.

STRUAN

Congratulations 🎉

When's it happening?

Two weeks? Christ, that's soon.

I catch myself. What's wrong with me? This is *good news*.

I shake my head, smiling. What is she like? I may play the relaxed, fun dad, but when it comes to Isla's health, I don't mess about. Sophie knows that.

I shoot her another thumbs-up emoji, then set my phone down on the kitchen worktop and grab the eggs to make French toast. Isla's favourite.

I crack them into a bowl, whisking as my mind wanders. Mei moving in—it *is* a good thing. Sophie deserves to be happy, and Isla adores Mei. Besides, it's not like anything's *really* changing. Mei's already there most evenings anyway.

Lost in thought, I fumble one of the eggs. It slips from my fingers and splats on the floor.

Smooth, Walker.

Right. Focus. Happy thoughts. French toast. Weekend with my girl.

I'm cleaning up the mess when my phone buzzes. I expect it to be Sophie again, but it's the Dadventurers chat, a group I'm in with Lachlan and Douglas.

LACHLAN

How about a beach BBQ at my place instead of a Pit meetup? Weather's meant to be good this afternoon

DOUGLAS

I'm out. Logan's sick now too. Living the dream 🤢

STRUAN

Oof, unlucky mate. Two sick kids is rough

But a BBQ? Aye aye, captain. What can I bring? 🍔🌭🍺

LACHLAN

We'll sort the food. Blair's invited Ainsley. She's bringing soft drinks. Can you bring wine and beer?

Ainsley will be there? A grin spreads across my face before I can stop it, and my mind unhelpfully flashes back to this morning's dream. The nightie. The way she'd—

Walker, it's a beach barbecue with kids present, not a wet dream sequel. Keep it in your pants.

STRUAN

👍

DOUGLAS

Ainsley?

LACHLAN

New friend of Blair's. Single mum. Took over
the old hair salon

STRUAN

Which I'm refurbing for her. Also happens to
be my new neighbour. And the same lass who
fell into my lap at soft play

DOUGLAS

Oh, HER. If I remember right, she was easy
on the eye

STRUAN

Aye. Could've done worse for a new boss and
neighbour 😊

LACHLAN

Right . . . anyway. See you this afternoon,
lover boy

Lover boy. If only he knew what my subconscious had been
up to earlier. Christ.

◆ ◆ ◆

I'm loading beer into the cool bag when there's a knock at the
front door. I open it, and for a split second my brain short-
circuits.

Ainsley and Lily stand on my doorstep, both dressed in
denim—Ainsley in a dress that shows off her legs, Lily in a wee
playsuit. In the afternoon sunlight, Ainsley's hair gleams with those
caramel streaks, and her green eyes are bright behind her fringe.

After the dream I had this morning, seeing her actually here is
doing things to my head.

"Er, hi," she says, looking slightly awkward. "Lily heard Isla was going to the barbecue and insisted we all walk together."

"Ah. Aye, that's fine." I try to sound casual, like I haven't been dreaming about her showing up here in considerably less clothing.

"Also," she admits, "I'm not entirely sure where Lachlan's house is. According to my maps app, it's in the sea."

I laugh. "Near the sea, not in it. Edge of town by the pebble beach."

"Awww." Lily's face falls and her shoulders droop. "I wanted it to be underwater. Like a mermaid house."

Isla appears at my side, grinning. "Lily, houses can't go underwater. Only submarines can."

"Then I want a submarine house!"

The two of them dissolve into giggles at this, no idea why. Ainsley gives me this small, helpless smile, which is . . . disarming. I'm more used to seeing her sharp-edged.

"Right, Isla, pop your shoes on," I say. Then, to Ainsley, "Let me just go grab the booze."

A minute later we're good to go. I lock up then hold out a hand to Ainsley, who's carrying a bag of soft drinks. "Here, I'll take that."

"I can manage—"

"I know you can." I take it anyway, our fingers brushing in the exchange. Just a touch, nothing more. Still, my stupid body notices. "My mum would skelp me if she saw me letting you carry it when I've got two hands."

I notice Lily's holding a small tote. "Want me to carry that too, Lily?"

"No! These are my Barbies. For the Barbie-cue."

"Once again, Lily," Ainsley says in a resigned tone, "barbecues have nothing to do with Barbie."

Lily pulls a face, then we set off down the street towards the seafront, the girls skipping ahead. Ainsley walks beside me, the pavement so narrow our arms nearly brush.

Don't think about the dream, Walker. Don't look at her legs. Don't wonder what she's wearing under that dress. Definitely don't imagine peeling it off her.

"Sleep well in the new bed?" I ask, then wince internally.

Smooth. Now you're picturing her in bed.

"Actually, yes." She smiles, and it's easier, warmer than usual. "First morning in ages I've not woken with a sore back. Thanks again."

"Any more flat-pack disasters, you know where to find me."

"Next week you might regret saying that. Wait till you see how many salon pieces I've ordered."

There's something different about her today. Lighter. Less guarded. Like maybe a good night's sleep on a decent bed has done her some good. Or maybe it's something else.

"Ach, all in a day's work."

When the girls reach the bottom of the street, they stop to wait for us. Lily points at the ferry pulling away from the harbour.

"That goes to Corraig, the island you can see out there," I hear Isla explaining importantly. "And Lachlan—whose house we're going to—he drives it during the week."

"He's the captain," I say with a grin.

Isla launches into facts about whales and dolphins, and I catch Ainsley watching her with amusement.

"You could double as a tour guide," she says as we head along the seafront towards Lachlan's.

"I like facts. Also, Mei knows *so* much. She works in conservation and knows loads about animals. She can tell which bird's which just by the sound. She also knows how to tell if a seal's sick just from the way it lies on the rocks."

"Wow," Ainsley says. "And, er, who's Mei?"

"Mum's girlfriend."

"Oh. Well, she sounds very knowledgeable."

"Mm-hmm," I say, shooting Ainsley a look. "She does, doesn't she?"

Ainsley smiles, and there's understanding in it. Like she gets it without me having to explain.

The girls hurry ahead again, then stop to rummage through Lily's Barbie bag. After a few moments, they whisper to each other then burst into fits of laughter.

"What's so funny?" Ainsley calls to them.

They exchange a look, then Isla holds up a doll. "Look, Da! This Barbie's just like you. She's even got a bun!"

I squint at it. The hair's roughly my colour and is indeed in a bun. More than that, though, she's dressed almost exactly like me. Tan shorts, plain T-shirt. Christ.

"Well, would you look at that," Ainsley says, grinning.

"'Splorer Barbie's new name is Stwuan!" Lily declares.

Everyone laughs, even me. And something about Ainsley's laugh—real and unguarded for once—catches me off-guard. Makes me want to hear it again.

We reach the pebble beach and spot the gang gathered just down from Lachlan's place, the barbecue already smoking away beside them. The sea breeze carries charcoal and cooking meat to us. I joked to Sophie about feeding Isla plenty of meat this weekend. Seems I'm actually following through.

Gus spots us first and comes charging over, all golden fur and boundless energy.

"Hiya, boy," I say, crouching to greet him.

But the traitor throws himself at Ainsley's feet instead. She laughs and pats him. "Good boy," she croons. Gus practically melts.

"Really?" I complain. "I've known you for years, and *she* gets the hero's welcome?"

Ainsley just smiles, scratching behind Gus's ears as he gazes up at her adoringly.

Can't say I blame the daft mutt, though. Something about her gets me too.

CHAPTER TWELVE

AINSLEY

Blair and I sit in camping chairs on the pebble beach, shades on, glasses of wine in hand. The afternoon sun glints off the sea, and for once, I'm not thinking about getting the salon up and running or bracing for Lily's next meltdown. Down by the water, Finn, Isla, and Lily take turns throwing sticks for Gus, their laughter carrying on the breeze.

Blair's phone buzzes. She checks it and groans. "Aw, Ellie's pulled out. I was looking forward to you meeting her properly."

"Ellie?" I take a sip of wine. "Oh, she was the fiddler the other night, wasn't she?"

"That's right."

I remember her vaguely—frizzy light-brown hair, oversized jumper, sleeves bunched up at her elbows as she played. If I'm honest, my attention had been much more firmly fixed on the guitarist with the half-up ponytail and the voice that could melt butter.

Of course, it really shouldn't have been. Temporary insanity brought on by the music and dim lighting. That's my excuse and I'm sticking to it.

Blair glances around then leans in conspiratorially. "You know how you confided a secret in me the other night? Maybe I can confide one in you. There's no way in hell Ellie would've pulled out if Douglas had been coming."

"Douglas?"

"Big red-haired dad? Has twins who are little chaos gremlins? Let's just say Ellie's into him. In a big way." She wiggles her brows. "Entirely unrequited, though. The man is oblivious."

"Oh." I've not been in Ardmara long, but it seems I'm already being initiated into the town gossip.

"Anyway," Blair says, settling back in her chair. "How about those two, huh?" She nods to where Lachlan and Struan stand chatting while Lachlan prods at the grill. "Men and fire. An ancient, irresistible pull."

I thump my chest and intone, "Man . . . need . . . make . . . fire."

Blair snorts into her wine. "Accurate."

The breeze ruffles my hair and I let out a long, contented sigh. Aye, this is exactly what I needed today.

I set my glass on the trestle table, which is *reasonably* steady on the pebbles, then lean back and lace my hands behind my head. "Sun, sea, and"—I nudge a pebble with my toe—"well, not sand, but close enough. This is the life."

"It really is," Blair agrees, smiling.

A knot inside me loosens. Maybe it's the wine, maybe the good weather, or maybe the simple bliss of not being needed by anyone for five blessed minutes. Whatever it is, I feel something I haven't in a long time: relaxed.

Then a low, warm laugh drifts over from the grill, and my treacherous gaze slides back to Struan before I can stop it. The sunglasses give me the perfect cover to look without getting caught, and apparently I have zero self-control today because I take full advantage.

He's in shorts, all long legs and easy confidence, the sun catching on the gold hairs on his strong calves. His T-shirt stretches over broad shoulders and a chest that's burned into my brain, thanks to the shirtless courtyard incident earlier in the week.

If we were at a beach barbecue somewhere warmer, there's a good chance he'd have his top off right now and I'd be able to—

Stop it.

I give myself a firm mental shake. I didn't come to Ardmara to drool over toned chests and sun-kissed calves, no matter how distractingly well-assembled the package.

But then a memory flashes into my head. Last night. Struan in my bedroom, standing inches from me, his gaze dropping to my mouth.

My pulse trips. So much for relaxed. Now I'm getting hot and bothered, which is not ideal. At all.

I wrench my attention away and take a long sip of wine, determined to focus on literally anything that isn't Struan Walker. My eyes land on Isla instead, laughing as she chases Gus along the shoreline. Sweet kid.

So . . . her mum's partner is a woman.

A flicker of curiosity sparks. Was that why things with Sophie and Struan never worked out? Did she realise she preferred women? Or did they simply grow apart?

None of your business, Ainsley Reid. Absolutely none.

And yet my eyes, far too nosy for their own good, drift right back to Struan. Of course they do.

As if sensing my gaze, he glances over, and despite my sunglasses, I swear he knows I'm staring. My cheeks flush and I look away fast, pretending the sea is the most fascinating thing I've ever seen.

Too late. He's already walking over.

"How long till the food's ready?" Blair asks as I hide behind my wine glass, taking another sip for good measure.

"About ten minutes."

Out of the corner of my eye, I see him bend and pull two beers from the cool bag.

"Ainsley?"

"Hmm?"

"Lachlan wants to know if you're veggie?"

He untwists one bottle cap with his bare hand, then the other, the muscles in his forearm flexing with the movement. Incredibly—and annoyingly—sexy.

It's a bottle cap, Ainsley. Not a striptease. Get a hold of yourself!

"Oh my God." Blair sits up. "I should've asked you that when I invited you! Who invites someone to a barbecue without checking if they're vegetarian?"

"Oh, no, I like to eat meat," I say.

I like to eat meat.

Why. Did. I. Say. It. Like. That.

"I'm not veggie" would've worked just fine. Or literally any combination of words that didn't sound like a come-on. But no. *I like to eat meat.* In front of *him.* Kill me now.

Struan's mouth twitches. "That's . . . good to know." He takes a swig of beer, eyes still on me, then strolls back to the barbecue.

As soon as he's out of earshot, Blair pushes her sunglasses up. "Okay, I know Struan's naturally flirty, but *that*? That was something. He's definitely interested in you, Ainsley."

I scoff. "Nah. Just banter."

"Banter? I could practically smell the pheromones coming off him."

I wave her off. "Even if he is, I'm not interested in him."

Blair gives me a look that suggests she doesn't believe me.

I take another sip of wine and stare very pointedly at the sea.

I'm not interested in him. I'm *not*.

◆ ◆ ◆

My patience is fraying fast. A slight wind has picked up and the sun's hiding behind clouds, making it cooler. But Lily is flat out refusing to put a cardigan on. We're over by the rocks—because she ran off the second I mentioned the word "cardigan".

So much for my relaxed, wine-soft mood. I should've known better than to let my guard down for five minutes.

"Come on, Lily," I say, holding out the cardigan and trying to keep my voice calm. "Just pop it on for me."

She folds her arms, scowls, and stamps her foot. "It's itchy."

I feel the first stirrings of a headache—or maybe that's the two glasses of wine catching up with me. "Lily, you might catch a chill if you don't put it on."

She stamps her foot again. "No!"

I exhale sharply. A short way away, Finn and Isla are sitting like angels by the table, chatting away. Both put their hoodies on without a fuss. Why can't Lily be like that—just once?

"Lily," I warn, "if you don't put the cardigan on, we'll have to go home and there'll be no toasted marshmallows later."

The reaction is instant. Lily lets out a shriek that makes Blair, Lachlan, and everyone else look over. Gus pauses from where he's splashing in the shallows. A family further along the beach turn to stare. I want the pebbles to swallow me whole.

Struan jogs over, Barbie doll in hand—the one Isla and Lily said looked like him. "Hey," he says, crouching beside us, "this Barbie's getting cold." I notice he's picked out a tiny jacket from Lily's Barbie bag. "Think you could show her how to put on her jacket by putting yours on too?"

Lily takes the cardigan from me. "Like this, Stwuan Barbie!" she says, proudly putting her arm in one sleeve, tantrum apparently abandoned.

I blink.

"Perfect," Struan says, putting the doll's jacket on. "Oh, wow, she feels warmer already."

While he keeps Lily distracted with the Barbie, I help her with the rest of the cardigan and button it.

Finn runs over and flashes a gap-toothed smile. "Blair's going to show us how to make s'mores. Want to help, Lily?"

"What's s'mores?" she asks, eyes wide.

"Chocolate and marshmallows sandwiched between biscuits, all gooey together."

Lily gasps and holds out her hand for Finn's. He takes it and they run off towards the others.

I let out a breath then turn to Struan, who's still holding the Barbie. "Thank you," I say. "That's twice now you've managed to defuse a tantrum."

Part of me is genuinely grateful. But another part—the prickly, stubborn part—is slightly irritated that *he* can calm *my* daughter down so easily when I'm the one who's been doing this for four years. What's his secret? A cocky grin and a stupid man bun?

He shrugs. "No bother. She's a wee firecracker, that's all. Strong-willed." His mouth curves. "Wonder where she gets that from, eh?" He winks at me.

Ugh. This man, honestly. Of course he had to wink. Can't just help out quietly, can he? No, he has to go and be . . . *him.*

♦ ♦ ♦

I sit with Lachlan on the camping chairs while Blair and Struan, over by the barbecue, assemble s'mores for the grown-ups. The kids, having devoured theirs earlier, are now running riot by the sea, Gus darting between them.

I sip my Diet Coke, feeling my earlier headache start to fade. Tantrums and wine-induced dehydration—never a winning combination.

I glance at Lachlan. Tall and broad-shouldered, dark hair touched with silver at the temples, eyes a striking green. Put this man in a captain's uniform, and I can see why Blair fell for him while nannying his kid. He seems solid. Dependable. The kind of man who wouldn't wink at you after defusing your daughter's meltdown.

Take notes, Ainsley. When you finally brave the dating scene again, this *is the sort of man you should go for. Steady. Sensible. No cocky grins or stupid man buns in sight.*

I look to the island on the horizon. "So, Lachlan, I hear you sail to Corraig?"

"Aye," he says. "Twice a day, weather permitting."

"I'll need to do the crossing with Lily at some point."

"When you do, pop into the wheelhouse," he offers. "She can see how everything works."

"Really?" I smile. "She'd love that."

Talk turns to the salon. Lachlan asks if Struan's pulling his weight or slacking off.

"I can hear you, you know," Struan calls from the barbecue,

mock offended. "And for the record, I did your en suite last year, mate. There were no complaints then."

I take a sip of my Coke. "I've no complaints about his craftsmanship," I say to Lachlan like Struan hasn't spoken. "His work ethic seems solid too. Though . . . he might try keeping his shirt on occasionally."

Blair's head snaps up. "I'm sorry—*what* now?"

Struan laughs and holds up his hands. "I was out the back! Doing intense work. I didn't know she was going to appear out of nowhere."

"I didn't *appear out of nowhere*," I say. "I walked out the back door of my own salon."

Blair is grinning like she's just been handed the juiciest piece of gossip in a decade. Lachlan shakes his head, the corner of his mouth lifting.

"Oh, would you look at that," Struan says, rapidly changing the subject. "The s'mores are ready. Time to tuck in!"

Blair—still smiling from ear to ear—carries over the tray, and Struan hands the paper plates round. The chocolate oozes; the marshmallows are toasted to perfection.

I take a bite and forget myself entirely. "Dear God, Blair, that's *orgasmic*."

Lachlan chokes on his s'more. Blair's eyebrows shoot up. And Struan, who hasn't taken a bite yet, turns to look at me with a slow, deeply entertained smile.

Oh no.

No, no, no.

Heat floods my face. First "I like to eat meat", and now *this*? What's wrong with me today? It's like my mouth has completely disconnected from my brain.

"Orgasmic, eh?" Struan nudges Blair. "That's high praise."

Then he bites into his own s'more and lets out this low, appreciative groan—and it's ridiculous how the sound makes my insides go soft.

Fantastic. Really, just brilliant. Now I'm reacting to a man eating melted marshmallow.

Oh God.

◆ ◆ ◆

The trestle table has been cleared, and I sit alone beside it while Blair and Lachlan head up to the house to take things in and make coffee. Struan and I are keeping an eye on the kids, although his approach is a bit more hands-on. He's down by the water with them, crouched among the pebbles. They seem to be hunting for something—shells or smooth stones, maybe. Whatever it is, Lily's using Barbie's hands to scoop pebbles into a pile, her face scrunched in concentration.

A tightness tugs in my chest. My wee girl, slotting herself in with the others, so intent on her task.

Isla rushes up to Struan, proudly holding out a shell she's found. He takes it and turns it thoughtfully between his fingers. She pulls him towards the rocks to show him where she found it, and soon they're crouched together, heads bent, completely absorbed.

He could be up here, I realise. Chatting away to me while Blair and Lachlan are away. Turning on that charm of his. But he's not. He's down there with the kids, giving them his full attention.

He's . . . good at the dad stuff. Really good.

I've been telling myself for weeks that it doesn't matter that Lily doesn't have her da around. Plenty of kids grow up in single-parent homes and turn out brilliant. And anyway, Lily's got my parents, who adore her. They uprooted their whole lives to be here with us.

But watching this—watching Struan's attentiveness, the way Isla glows under it—I can't help wondering what it might have been like for Lily to have this. An energetic father who actually *wants* to be with her. Who dotes on her the way Struan clearly dotes on Isla.

Danny was never like this. Not even close.

I push the thought away. No point dwelling on what Lily doesn't have. We're doing just fine.

Movement catches my eye—a slim blonde woman jogging along the shoreline from the direction of town, in leggings and a fitted long-sleeved top. I wince just looking at her. That cannot be a fun run on pebbles.

The woman slows and lifts a hand. "Struan!"

He returns the wave, says something to Isla, and straightens, dusting off his hands. The jogger stops beside him, breathless and smiling. Recognition prickles at me. I saw this woman at the pub the other night—after the Celtic Kicks finished their set, when people were crowding round Struan at the bar. She was twirling her hair around her finger, making her interest painfully obvious.

From here, I can't make out much of their conversation—just the odd word carried on the breeze—but I can see enough. The smiles. The way she tucks her hair behind her ear and laughs at something he says.

Then she pulls out her phone. Struan does the same.

Are they . . . swapping numbers?

My stomach does something uncomfortable. I tell it to behave.

Maybe she needs a joiner. Plenty of people need joiners. And if it's not about joinery? If it's for a date?

Then it's none of my business. Absolutely none.

The woman slips her phone back into her pocket, gives Struan one last smile—and a quick arm squeeze—then jogs off the way she came. Struan watches her go for a moment before turning back to Isla.

Aye, none of my business.

And yet the thought of Struan taking this woman out for drinks—or dinner, or whatever—sits in my chest like a splinter. Which is ridiculous. I don't care who Struan Walker dates. I don't.

In fact, if he starts seeing someone, maybe he'll finally stop flirting with me. That would be a *good* thing. A relief, even.

Aye. A relief.

Mm-hmm.

CHAPTER THIRTEEN

STRUAN

Dinner's long gone, but my parents' kitchen still smells of roast beef and gravy. I'm at the sink with Mum, sleeves rolled to my elbows, scrubbing while she dries. The rhythm's familiar—we've been doing this since I was tall enough to reach the taps.

From the living room, a giggle floats through, followed by Isla's bossy wee voice: "Grandpa, you can't move your rook like that! It only goes straight, remember?"

Mum shoots me an amused look. "She certainly keeps your da on his toes."

"Aye. Keeps everyone on their toes."

Mum hangs up a mug then reaches for the next one to dry. "I was on the phone to your sister this morning."

"Oh? All good in London?"

"Seems to be. She's busy as ever. We were chatting about your friend Lachlan, actually. About how he got together with that American lass." She pauses. "Got us to talking about you, son."

I suppress a sigh and attack a stubborn bit of dried gravy on the pot I'm cleaning. Doesn't take a genius to figure out where this is heading.

"We think it'd be good for you to find yourself a girl like Lachlan did. We worry you might be . . . lonely."

I scoff. "Mum, I've got Isla at the weekends, a busy job, the band, surfing. Not exactly the schedule of a man pining for company." I flash her a grin. "I'm a happy bachelor. Absolutely *not* lonely."

Does the house get a bit quiet mid-week? Sure, but that doesn't mean I'm *lonely*.

Mum studies me for a moment but lets it drop. Instead she asks after Sophie.

"Aye, she's fine. The usual." I do have news, of course—that Mei's moving in—but I've got to keep quiet about that until Sophie tells Isla. She'll probably do that tonight when I drop Isla off.

"And the refurb of the old salon? How's that coming along?"

"Also fine."

"Good. I've already booked myself in for a trim on opening day. The whole town's talking about the place." Mum gives me a not-so-subtle sideways glance. "As well as its bonny new owner."

"Hmm." I set the clean pot aside and reach for the roasting tin, keeping my expression carefully blank.

"And it's funny, isn't it," she goes on, "that she's both your neighbour *and* you're doing up her salon. Must be seeing quite a bit of each other?"

My mum is about as subtle as a fire alarm in a library.

"Pauline, Ainsley's mum, has started coming to knitting club," she continues.

"Aye?"

"And, well . . . you know how we like to blether at knitting club." Mum lowers her voice. "It seems Ainsley's ex left her utterly heartbroken, the poor soul. Pauline wouldn't say more than that, but isn't that just awful?"

I frown down at a bit of caramelised carrot, scrubbing harder than necessary. "You know, maybe Ainsley doesn't want her mum sharing that with the knitting club. She strikes me as a pretty private person."

Mum pauses, then nods slowly. "Fair enough. Point taken."

Mum's as fond of a blether as anyone in this town, but hope-fully she—and the rest of the natter-knitters, as Da calls them—won't be passing the story round. Though Ardmara's hardly famous for its tight lips.

Still. Food for thought. If Ainsley's ex did a number on her, I bet the last thing she wants is me winking at her like some daft eejit every five minutes. Probably explains the whole ice-queen routine. Maybe I need to dial it back a bit.

"Son, you'll take the shine clean off that thing if you keep at it."

I blink. The metal scourer's squeaking over a surface that's already spotless.

"Daddy, come see! I beat Grandpa!" Isla's triumphant shout rings from the living room.

Winking at Mum, I put the roasting tin on the rack then quickly dry my hands and head through. Da's sitting back in his armchair with a look of theatrical defeat, while Isla beams at the chessboard like she's just conquered a small nation.

"Good lass!" I crouch down to inspect the board. "Brutal. Absolutely brutal. He never stood a chance." I ruffle her hair. "Well done, princess. But now that game's done, I reckon it's time to get you back to Bannock, eh? You've got school tomor-row. Let's get your things together and say goodbye to Gran and Grandpa."

The drive to Bannock is quiet. Isla's half-asleep by the time we pull up outside Sophie's cottage, the chess victory and a full Sunday roast having done their work.

I grab her overnight bag and walk her to the door, her small hand warm in mine. Before I can knock, it swings open. Sophie stands there, Mei just behind her.

"Hey, you!" Sophie pulls Isla into a hug. "Good weekend?"

"I beat Grandpa at chess," Isla says, rubbing her eyes.

Mei grins. "Future grandmaster, this one."

"Aye," I agree, "and in the not-too-distant future at this rate." I hand the bag over to Sophie. "Dexcom's charged. Front pocket."

"Cheers, Struan." Sophie shifts the bag to her shoulder. "Come on in, sweetheart. We've got some news to tell you."

Isla perks up, sleepiness falling away. She glances back at me.

"On you go. I'll see you next weekend, aye? On Saturday morning. Enjoy the sleepover." Sophie messaged me earlier to confirm Friday works for the other girls, so the sleepover is on.

Isla nods. "Bye, Daddy. Love you." She disappears inside, then the door clicks shut behind her.

I stand there for a moment, on the step, breathing in the cool evening air.

Right, then.

I'm halfway to the van when something makes me glance back. Warm light spills from the living room window, and inside Isla bounces on her toes—before flinging her arms around both Sophie and Mei.

So she's taken the news well, then. Good.

The three of them stay like that for a beat, wrapped up together.

I watch for a second longer, then turn and climb into the van.

The drive back to Ardmara is even quieter than the drive here. Just me and the radio and the dark hills rolling past.

CHAPTER FOURTEEN

STRUAN

The salon's coming together nicely, if I do say so myself.

Da and I are on our knees working on a shelving unit that'll display styling products once Ainsley's up and running.

We finished the flooring Monday and Tuesday, and now it's just fittings and the small jobs that pull everything together. Another few days and we'll be out of Ainsley's hair. Another job in the bag.

At the front counter, a young web designer—can't be more than twenty-two, twenty-three—is hunched over Ainsley's laptop, walking her through some technical fixes. Ainsley's leaning in, brow furrowed in concentration, nodding along as he explains something.

"—so if you clear the cache and refresh, that'll force it to pull the updated style sheet," he says.

"Right, right." Ainsley tucks a strand of hair behind her ear. "And that should fix the layout problem?"

"Yes, exactly." His eyes drift from the screen to her face. Then lower. Then back to the screen again.

If he's trying to be subtle, he's failing.

"Struan." Da's voice cuts through. "You listening, lad?"

I blink. "What?"

He gestures at the backboard lying on the dust sheet, a sturdier bit of MDF I cut earlier to replace the flimsy fibreboard panel the flat pack came with. "Pass that over."

"Right. Aye. Sorry."

Christ. What am I doing, getting distracted by some kid making eyes at Ainsley? Not like she's mine to get territorial over.

We position the board against the back of the unit, which is lying horizontal on the floor. I brace it while Da starts securing it with panel pins—quick, precise taps of the hammer.

"By the way," I say, "I'll be heading out later to give Lindsey McVey a quote for a new bathroom."

"Lindsey McVey . . ." Da pauses, thinking. "That the lady who just got divorced?"

"Aye. Bumped into her at the pub last week, then again at the beach when she was out for a jog. She's bought a new place and needs some work done."

"I can come with you," he offers, reaching for another pin.

"Nah, don't worry about it. You've got that fence repair to do."

He grunts. "Aye, well, make sure you get a decent price for it."

"Don't I always?"

As Da drives in another pin, my eyes flick to the counter. The web designer is pointing at something on Ainsley's laptop, his shoulder practically brushing hers as he leans in.

Does he really need to stand *that* close?

Ainsley shifts back a touch and gives a polite little nod, but I get the impression she's done listening. Or maybe that's just me hoping.

"—and if you ever need help with anything else," the lad goes on, lowering his voice into what he probably thinks is a smooth register, "website stuff, social media strategy, whatever—I'm always happy to help."

"I'll bear that in mind," Ainsley replies, crisp and polished.

"Actually, I was wondering . . ." He hesitates, then pushes on. "Do you have a personal Instagram account? Maybe we could follow one another?"

My jaw tightens.

"Thanks for all your help, but I really am quite busy just now." Translation: jog on, Romeo.

A flicker of satisfaction warms my chest.

Steady on, Walker. You don't get to be smug. You've no claim on her.

The lad deflates. "Aye, sure. Well, good luck with the opening."

The bell above the door chimes as he leaves, and Da gives the backboard one last tap before nodding. Together we lift the finished unit, stand it upright, and carry it to its spot against the wall.

"Ainsley?" Da calls over. "Come take a look at this, would you?"

She crosses the salon, heels clicking on the new vinyl plank flooring.

"What do you think?" Da asks. "More to the left?"

"No, that looks good there." She steps closer to the unit, and as she does, that warm vanilla-and-spice scent of hers drifts over. My stupid pulse reacts. She raps her knuckles lightly against the new backboard and nods with approval. "The new panel's a big step up from that bit of cardboard it came with." She smiles at Da. "It was a clever idea replacing it."

"Och, it was Struan's idea, actually."

Ainsley's gaze flicks to mine, and her warmth drains instantly. "Mmm. Well, good job," she says flatly.

She turns back to Da. "I'm about to put the kettle on. Fancy a cuppa, Malcolm?"

"Aye, please."

"Struan?" she all but sighs.

"Er . . . no, thanks."

She turns on her heel and click-clacks towards the kitchenette.

"Christ, Struan," Da mutters the moment she's out of earshot. "What did you do to annoy her?"

"Nothing." I keep my voice low. "Nothing that I know of anyway."

I scratch my chin and frown. Aye, I did lay it on a bit thick at first, but I thought she'd thawed a touch recently—first when I helped her with her bed, then again at the barbecue.

But that chill just now? That was a whole new level of ice queen.

"Maybe she's just stressed about the opening," Da suggests.

"Aye. Maybe."

But the niggle in my gut says it's something else. I just don't know what.

◆ ◆ ◆

Lindsey McVey's cottage sits just up from the harbour, bright blue door, tidy wee garden.

I knock twice and wait. Footsteps approach, then the door swings open and Lindsey beams at me.

"Struan! Come on in."

She's dressed in a silky blouse and fitted trousers, hair done up. Bit dressy for a quote visit, but maybe she's off somewhere afterwards.

I step into the hall, which is just as tidy as outside. The place smells of fresh paint.

"Thanks for coming."

"No bother."

"Bathroom's this way." She smiles again and leads me down the hall. She shows me in then stays by the door, giving me space to move around the small room. I tap the walls, run a thumb along the old sealant, run the taps. The place isn't in bad nick— functional, just dated. A bit tired round the edges.

"You mentioned you were thinking of replacing the whole suite?" I say as I examine the pipework.

"That's right." She leans against the doorframe. "New tiling, different layout, maybe underfloor heating if the budget stretches. I want it to feel like mine, you know? Fresh start and all that."

"Aye, I get that." I pull my tape measure from my back pocket and start working out the dimensions. She talks me through her vision while I measure. Sleek wall tiles, brighter lighting, a rainfall shower. Her tone is polite and businesslike, but every so often I catch wee glimmers of something else. A flick of her gaze when I stretch for a measurement. The way she tucks her hair behind her ear whenever I look her way.

Could be nothing. But also . . . could be something.

I jot the final numbers in my notebook then snap it shut. "Right. I'll get a quote to you by the end of the day."

"Perfect." She smiles but doesn't move from the doorway. "Coffee before you go?"

"Thanks, but I'm good." I step forwards, expecting her to shift aside. She doesn't.

"Something stronger, maybe?" She lifts an eyebrow playfully. "Wine?"

Ah. So I wasn't imagining it.

"At this hour? You'll ruin my reputation."

"Oh, I doubt that." She steps closer, her fingertips brushing my forearm. Light, but deliberate. "This is a little bold of me—okay, *very* bold—but I've heard it said you're . . . well, known for being up for a bit of fun from time to time."

I give a wee smirk but don't bite. She's not wrong.

"I know you're single, and now that I am too, I thought maybe we could . . . you know. See where it goes."

The words hang in the air.

Temptation flickers. Lindsey's lovely. Friendly, attractive, confident enough to make the first move. It'd be so easy. A lean forward, a kiss, whatever might follow.

But a pair of sharp green eyes flashes into my mind.

Really? Of all moments, my brain chooses *now* to conjure Ainsley Reid? When another woman is literally standing in front of me and putting herself out there?

For fuck's sake.

I try to focus on what's right in front of me, but Ainsley's face keeps swimming back, stubborn as the woman herself.

"Lindsey," I say, exhaling, "that's really flattering. But I don't think I can."

Bloody hell. When did I become the guy who turns down perfectly good fun?

She gives a small, nervous laugh. "Because . . . I'm older?"

"No," I say quickly. "You're gorgeous. It's not that." I hesitate, knowing I sound like an eejit. "I've just . . . got a bit of a thing for someone else at the moment."

A bit of a thing? Christ. When did I start talking like a fourteen-year-old?

Lindsey's cheeks flush but she takes it gracefully. "Lucky girl, whoever she is." She steps back, giving me space. "And fair enough. But you can't blame a girl for trying, right?"

I smile, hoping to take the sting out of the rejection. "For what it's worth, I bet there are plenty of men in Ardmara who'd queue up for a chance to date you."

"That's sweet of you to say." She looks down and bites her lip.

A beat of silence stretches—awkward, but not terrible.

Right. Time to make a clean exit.

I clear my throat. "I'll get that quote to you tonight, aye?"

CHAPTER FIFTEEN

AINSLEY

Two days. In two days this place opens.

I stand behind the counter with Sheila and Ruby, the stylists I've hired, running them through the till system while trying not to let my nerves show. The Lily Room is finally taking shape, my vision materialising into something real and tangible. The rose-gold feature wall gleams behind the styling stations. Our saddle stools sit ready in their spots. The whole space feels bright, sharp, ready to shine.

"Right," I say, tapping the screen to bring up the payment options. "The card machine's synced, so you just hit this button for contactless."

Sheila nods. Early fifties, neatly cut dark hair, calm and capable. The kind of stylist clients trust with both their hair and their secrets. She worked at the old salon before it closed, and I'm hoping most of her clients follow her here. Strategic hire, that one.

Ruby, meanwhile, practically vibrates beside her. Nineteen, freshly qualified, coppery waves tumbling past her shoulders.

She's been bouncing on her toes since she arrived this morning, all flushed cheeks and breathless enthusiasm.

"Got it," she says. "Contactless. Easy."

Across the room, a soft metallic scrape draws my attention. Struan's crouched by one of the new saddle stools, tightening bolts with an Allen key, sleeves rolled up past his elbows. He's been quiet today, the occasional tap of a hammer or clatter of tools a steady reminder he's there, but otherwise he's kept to himself.

Good. That's exactly how I want it.

I've worked hard to keep things strictly businesslike between us lately. Brisk, professional, no room for misinterpretation. And to his credit, he's dialled down the charm. The easy grins are still there when I *have* to speak to him, but the winks have stopped. And the flirty remarks. And the lingering gazes.

Well, the lingering gazes have *mostly* stopped.

Earlier, while I was peeling the protective film off the mirrors—God, that was satisfying—I caught his reflection watching me. Not openly. Not boldly. Just . . . there.

Even so, it made my skin prickle. And I *really* didn't like that.

Tomorrow he'll be finished here, and things will be simpler. No more long days breathing the same air. No more catching that smell of sawdust and soap and *male* every time he passes within three feet of me. We'll be neighbours who wave politely over the hedge and nothing more.

"Okay," I say, flipping open my planner and focusing on the task at hand. "Opening day, Saturday. We've got a few pre-booked clients in the morning, then it'll mostly be walk-ins after that. I want everyone who steps through that door to feel pampered. Fizz, music, nibbles—the works."

Ruby claps her hands together. "I'm so excited! My first

proper hairdressing job, and it's at a brand-new salon. How lucky is that?"

I can't help but smile. Her enthusiasm is infectious. "We're lucky to have you."

"Are we getting matching tunics?" Her eyes are bright. "Like, with the salon name embroidered on them?"

"No uniforms," I say. "Wear what makes you feel comfortable—tidy and professional, aye? Nothing too low-cut, and no builders' bums on display." I catch Ruby tugging self-consciously at her neckline. "You're fine. Just . . . keep it classy."

She grins. "Classy. Got it."

We move to the waiting bench to run through Saturday's schedule, making sure we're all clear on our roles. Everything's going smoothly, the three of us settling into an easy rhythm, until a soft *click-hiss* pulls my attention sideways.

Struan's perched on the saddle stool now, testing the hydraulic lever, long legs braced wide as he pumps it up and down. The seat rises, then lowers again, and the movement shouldn't be remotely interesting, except his jeans are pulling taut over strong thighs, and his forearm is flexing with each pump, and—

Oh, for God's sake.

Heat prickles the back of my neck. I jerk my gaze back to my planner, pulse skittering.

He's checking a lever, Ainsley. A lever. Not performing a Magic Mike routine. Get a grip on yourself.

"—so Sheila, you'll coordinate walk-ins if I'm tied up with a booking," I say, forcing my voice to stay steady. "Sound okay?"

Sheila nods, unfazed. "No bother. Done it a thousand times."

"You okay, boss?" Ruby asks. "You've gone a bit pink."

"Fine. It's just warm in here. Anyway, Ruby, stay on top of socials. Photos early in the day while everything's fresh, aye?"

"Of course!" She beams. "We're going to smash it. Oh, and I'm still doing the deep-conditioner treatments, right?"

"Yes, those are yours."

I pull out my phone to check on the delivery status of the shampoos and conditioners that were supposed to arrive this morning. The same shipment I had to argue about on the phone last week, when that patronising arse of a supplier talked over me three times before finally agreeing to dispatch on schedule.

Shipment delayed. New estimated arrival: tomorrow.

My stomach dips. Of course. Of bloody course.

I exhale slowly through my nose. Tomorrow is fine. Tight, but fine. As long as they don't delay again, or send the wrong products, or—

No. Positive thoughts. No spiralling.

I force a bright smile and explain the situation to Sheila and Ruby. "Bit annoying, but it'll be here before we open. Let's just hope that's our only hiccup."

"Sorry to interrupt, ladies." Struan walks over, toolbox in hand. There's a smudge of something dark across his forearm— grease, probably, from the stool mechanism. "That's the last of the furniture built. I'll head to the toilet next and put up that shelf, so let me know if any of you need in before I start."

"I'm fine," Sheila says.

"All good here," Ruby adds brightly.

I keep my tone brisk. "Aye. We're fine, thanks."

He nods once and disappears towards the back of the salon.

The moment he's out of earshot, Ruby leans in, voice dropping to a conspiratorial whisper. "God, he's fit, isn't he?"

Sheila hums knowingly. "Och, he's a charmer, that one. Keeps the tourists busy in summer, if you know what I mean."

My stomach tightens. "Aye, I got that vibe."

I picture the blonde runner from the beach last weekend. The one who'd casually touched Struan's arm and exchanged numbers with him.

I overheard enough of Malcolm and Struan's conversation yesterday to know that Struan went to her house for an appointment. Seemed pretty keen that his dad did *not* go with him.

No prizes for guessing why.

It really shouldn't bother me. In fact, it's a good thing. Because it reminds me who he is.

There'd been moments at the barbecue—and that night he helped me with my bed—when I'd started letting Struan's charm slip past my defences. Started softening towards him.

Talk about not learning from my mistakes.

After Danny, I really should know better. Men like that are all sparkle and no substance. They make you feel special right up until you realise you're not the only one they're making feel that way.

So yes. It's a *good* thing I've come to my senses.

I just wish it *felt* good.

◆ ◆ ◆

The sign is up.

I stand on the pavement with Mum, Da, and Lily, tilting my head back to take it in. THE LILY ROOM, spelled out in elegant rose-gold lettering against a soft blush background, with a delicate water lily to the right of the words. It's exactly what I envisioned when I sketched it out months ago, back when this whole thing was just a desperate dream scribbled in a notebook.

"Well?" I crouch down to Lily's level. "What do you think, baby?"

She scrunches her nose. "Where's my face?"

"Your face?"

"It's the Lily Room. Shouldn't my face be on it?"

I blink. "What? No, that was never the plan. But look—it *says* Lily, and there's a pretty water lily. See?"

Lily considers this for approximately half a second. "It'd look better with my face on it."

Mum stifles a laugh behind her hand. Da doesn't bother hiding his.

Despite my daughter's less-than-enthusiastic reaction, I pull out my phone and snap a selfie in front of the sign, angling to catch the lettering behind me. I tap out a quick caption and post it to social media.

Signage installed! It's official: the Lily Room is ready to bloom ❁

"Right," I say, pocketing my phone. "Who wants the grand tour?"

Da's face lights up. Mum and I have been keeping him away from the salon during the renovation. Officially because we wanted him to see the finished product without "spoilers". Unofficially because we were worried he might try to step in and "help". Da and tools just do not go together, no matter how good his intentions are.

"Lead the way," he says.

I head in first, holding Lily's hand. There's a moment of quiet as Mum and Da take it in.

"Oh, Ainsley." Mum presses a hand to her chest. "It's

gorgeous."

"It really is something, love," Da agrees, turning slowly, his eyes roaming over every detail. "You should be proud."

Warmth spreads through my chest. "Thanks, Da."

Lily, apparently over her signage grievance, lets go of my hand and clambers up onto one of the styling chairs. "Can I have my hair cut here, Mummy?"

"Maybe. If you're good."

"I'm *always* good."

Mum and I exchange a look, but neither of us contradicts her.

The sound of a drill whirs from the back, and a moment later Struan emerges, wiping his hands on a rag. He gives Lily a high-five then flashes my parents a friendly, lopsided smile. "Afternoon. Here for a look around?"

"We are indeed." Mum beams at him. "And I must say, Struan, you've done a wonderful job. Hasn't he, Murdo?"

Da nods appreciatively, running his hand along the edge of the waiting bench. "Aye, this is quality work."

Mum huffs a laugh then says to Struan, "Not that Murdo would know where to begin with something like this. He once tried to put up a shelf and drilled right into the airing cupboard."

"It was an honest mistake," Da mutters.

"Ach, anyone can do this stuff with the right tools and a bit of practice." Struan gestures Da over to the back shelving he's been working on. "Here, want to see how these fixings work? You can help me out with one, if you like."

Da hesitates for a second, unused to being invited rather than warned off. Then he ambles after Struan, keen to get involved.

Curiosity gets the better of me. I take a few steps after them and watch as Struan patiently demonstrates something about wall anchors, Da nodding along and asking questions. Struan doesn't talk down to him, doesn't dismiss him the way I've seen other tradespeople do. He just . . . explains. Like Da's curiosity matters.

Something in my chest loosens, just a fraction.

Stop it.

I clamp the feeling down. Hard. Because so what if he knows how to make my da feel included rather than useless? So what if he's good with kids? So what if he's handy with a drill?

None of that changes who he is. A man with charm on tap. Trouble waiting to happen.

I know his type. All too well.

I show Mum and Lily around the salon, pointing out a few of my favourite details. After a while I say, "Right, we should probably let Struan get on. He's got a lot to finish before tomorrow."

"Come on, Murdo," Mum calls. "Let the man work."

Da reluctantly tears himself away from the shelving demonstration. "Thanks for showing me that, son. Might have to pick your brain again sometime."

"Anytime," Struan says easily.

I shepherd my family towards the door, but at the threshold I pause and turn back. Struan's watching me, that familiar half-smile playing at the corner of his mouth.

"Everything *will* be finished tomorrow, won't it?" I ask. The words come out more pointed than I mean them to. Or maybe just as pointed as I mean them to. "Before the opening?"

If he's bothered by my tone, he doesn't show it. "Aye, everything's on schedule. Just finishing touches now."

I give a brief nod then leave before he can say anything else.

CHAPTER SIXTEEN

STRUAN

The salon's quiet save for the faint squeak of a small roller. I'm on my knees, touching up a scuffed patch by the skirting, when the front door opens.

I glance up, expecting Ainsley's usual crisp entrance—heels clicking, planner in hand, ready to tick the final items off her list. Instead she slips inside like she's trying not to be noticed.

No make-up. Hair scraped back in a messy ponytail. Eyes that look like they didn't get much sleep last night.

She barely glances my way. "Morning."

"Morning," I reply, straightening, but she doesn't slow. She heads straight for the kitchenette.

I frown. That was . . . unusual. Ainsley Reid doesn't do *dishevelled*. Something's off.

I give it a minute. Two. The kettle doesn't click on. No cupboard doors opening and closing. Just silence.

Right.

I dust off my knees then head through to the back. At the door to the kitchenette, I say, "Mind if I grab some water?"

Ainsley's standing at the breakfast bar, bag open in front of her, her hands rifling through it with jerky, agitated movements. She doesn't look up. "Help yourself."

I don't move. Just watch as she pulls out her phone, her keys, a packet of tissues, then a lipstick.

"Where is it?" she mutters. "Where the hell is it?"

"What are you looking for?"

"My planner." Her voice is tight now. Fraying. "It's got everything in it. The schedule for tomorrow, the checklist, the—"

Her breath catches—a horrible, hitching sound that makes my chest tighten.

"Hey." I step closer. "Ainsley, what's going on?"

She shakes her head, jaw tight like she's physically trying to hold herself together. But her eyes are glassy, and when she finally looks at me, there's none of the usual sharpness there. Just exhaustion. And something that looks a lot like defeat.

"Everything's fine," she says.

Unconvincing as hell.

"Doesn't look that way."

She lets out a breathy huff that's almost a laugh then sinks down onto a stool. "No," she admits quietly. "You're right. Everything's not fine."

She drags in a breath. "I just—" She stops. Shakes her head. Tries again. "I'm so tired."

I wait. Don't push.

"Lily just won't settle at night, but she's still up at the crack of dawn every bloody morning. I swear I'm knackered before I've even dropped her off at nursery. And *that's* not getting any easier. Today she clung to me. *Screamed.* I had to peel her off me while everyone was watching."

She swallows hard, eyes fixed on the breakfast bar. "Sorry. I didn't mean—this is ridiculous. Ignore me."

"That sounds brutal." A beat. "Plus you've got the salon opening tomorrow."

"And the products . . ."

I shift a little closer. "Aye?"

She presses the heels of her hands against her eyes. "The shampoos and conditioners I need for tomorrow. They were supposed to arrive yesterday. Then today. And now the company's saying they can't deliver until tomorrow afternoon, but by then—"

Her voice cracks.

Christ.

I've never been good with crying women. It's my kryptonite. Always has been. Something about tears just bypasses every rational circuit in my brain and goes straight to *fix it, fix it now*.

But this isn't just any woman crying. This is Ainsley—normally so sharp, composed, in control. And now she's falling apart in front of me.

Instinct screams at me to cross the small space between us and pull her into my arms. But I hold back. She's barely tolerated me lately. The last thing she needs is me overstepping.

Instead I flick the kettle on and tug a tissue from the packet she dropped earlier. I press it into her hand.

"Here."

She takes it without looking at me. Dabs at her eyes. "Sorry. I never do this."

"Do what? Have feelings?"

A wet laugh escapes her. "I'm used to clients unloading on me. Not—" She gestures vaguely. "This."

"Maybe it needed out."

The kettle rumbles to a boil. I make her a tea and set the mug in front of her. She wraps her hands around it like it's a lifeline.

For a while neither of us speaks. Just the quiet hum of the fridge and the distant cry of gulls outside.

Then, softer now: "The nursery pulled me aside this morning."

"Oh?"

"They suggested I bring Lily in a bit later. When it's calmer. Fewer parents around." She stares into her tea. "Also, apparently she's been . . . unsettled. Acting out a bit with the other kids."

"She's four," I say. "Sounds fairly standard."

"You're probably right. But then the manager told me something Lily said to another wee girl." Ainsley's throat works. "She said, 'I don't see Daddy. Mummy doesn't like him.'"

Ainsley lets out a helpless little sound. "So I had to stand there and explain that I'm not keeping Lily from her father. It's the other way around. Danny—her da—he's just . . . chosen not to be part of her life."

My jaw tightens. Chosen? Fucking *chosen* not to see his own kid?

I think of Isla. Of Sunday nights and how quiet the van feels on the drive back from Sophie's. Too quiet.

And this guy just . . . walked away?

"He's a fool," I say. "Choosing not to be in his kid's life? I can't understand that."

Ainsley looks at me for a long moment, then she drops her gaze, twisting the tissue in her hands. "God, listen to me. Dumping all this on you when you've got work to finish."

"Ainsley." I wait until she meets my eyes again. "You're doing brilliantly."

She huffs quietly.

"You've moved to a new town. You're opening a business.

You're raising a wee girl on your own." I shrug. "That's not nothing. That's bloody impressive."

Her lips press together. Like she wants to argue but can't quite find the words.

"Lily will settle," I add. "She's just rattled by the change, that's all."

She nods slowly. Takes a sip of tea. Some of the tension eases from her shoulders, though she still looks exhausted.

"Now, tell me about this delivery. What's the situation?"

She sighs. "It's sitting in a depot in Elgin. Ready to go but it won't get here till tomorrow afternoon, which is too late. Elgin is two hours away—I don't have time to go there. And Mum and Dad are off on some dolphin-spotting tour, so I can't exactly call them."

"I'll go."

Ainsley blinks. "What?"

"I'll drive to Elgin, pick the order up, bring it back. I can finish up here tonight."

"Struan, no. I can't ask you to do that."

"You're not asking, I'm offering. Look, I've got the van and Isla's having a sleepover tonight, so I'm not picking her up till tomorrow. Just give me the address and order number so they'll release it to me."

She stares at me. "It's a four-hour round trip."

"Aye, I can count."

"But you've already done so much. The refurb, the furniture, the—" She stops and shakes her head. "This is too much."

"It's really not."

She hesitates. "I'll pay you for the extra hours," she says finally. "And for petrol."

"Don't be daft. We're neighbours. This is just me being neighbourly."

She folds her arms. Still sniffling, but stubborn as ever. "I hate owing anyone, Struan."

"Fine." I hold up my hands in surrender. "I'll add a bit to the invoice for the petrol, but forget the extra hours."

She opens her mouth, then closes it again. Then, quietly: "Okay, deal. Thank you, Struan."

"Save it for when I actually get back with the stuff, aye?"

She almost smiles.

Almost.

CHAPTER SEVENTEEN

AINSLEY

The Lily Room hums with life.

An hour into opening day, and the salon is buzzing. Mum drifts between clients with a bottle of prosecco, topping up glasses and accepting compliments like she built the place herself. Lily works the room in her *Frozen* costume, chatting to anyone who'll listen, while Da moves beside her, passing out nibbles.

"The rose gold is so glam," someone says behind me.

"What a difference from the old place," another voice agrees.

I smile to myself as I section off Blair's damp hair. Every anxious moment, every decision I overthought, every wobble along the way—worth it.

Not that I can take credit for the physical work, of course. That was all Struan and his da.

I'm running on caffeine, adrenaline, and not nearly enough sleep, but I'm in my element. Yesterday's chaos—the missing products, the tears I'm still mortified about—already feels distant. Like a bad dream that dissolved the moment the first clients walked in.

"Right," I say, meeting Blair's eyes in the mirror. "We're doing a butterfly fringe, is that right?"

"Yes! Exactly. I've not had my hair cut for months, so it's practically grown out."

"And we'll add some new layers throughout for body, aye?"

Blair nods. "Perfect."

I pick up my scissors and get to work, muscle memory taking over as I work through the cut. Nearby, Sheila's busy with a client who's followed her from the old salon. Ruby, meanwhile, is talking a curious local through our treatment menu while keeping an eye on the timer for Mrs Galbraith, who's sitting under the hood dryer looking thoroughly pampered.

The waiting bench is full, a mix of pre-booked appointments and walk-ins. All the work, the stress, the risk . . . it's paying off.

I glance up at the mirror and catch Mum watching me from across the room, her smile so proud it makes my cheeks warm. I duck my head and focus on Blair's layers, blending the shorter pieces around her face to frame her features.

As I work, a woman waiting her turn gets up from the bench and drifts over. She peers over my shoulder with undisguised curiosity. She's soon joined by another. Then another. By the time I'm blow-drying Blair's hair—smoothing the round brush through each section, coaxing out volume and shine—there's a small audience.

"What a lovely cut," someone murmurs.

"Look at that shape."

"I want mine done like that."

Blair catches my eye in the mirror and grins. "I feel like a movie star," she whispers.

I lean close, lowering my voice. "Sorry about the performance cut." I switch off the dryer and reach for the styling serum. "It's on the house."

"Don't even think about it. I'm paying full price. End of discussion."

Something warm flickers through me, but I keep my focus on the cut, working the product through Blair's ends before fluffing the layers with my fingers to add movement.

I step back to study the finished result. The butterfly fringe falls perfectly—soft and wispy, longer at the edges to blend into the face-framing layers. The rest swings just past her shoulders, full of body and shine. When I hold up the hand mirror to show her the back, Blair lets out a soft gasp.

"Oh my God. I love it."

"It suits you," I say. The shape flatters her bone structure beautifully. It makes her look effortlessly polished.

Blair stands and gives me a quick hug. "Thank you! This place is amazing. *You're* amazing. You're going to be booked solid."

As I walk her over to the till, I sneak a look around—at the clients waiting on the bench, at Sheila gossiping cheerfully as she seats her next appointment. For the first time in weeks, I let myself properly breathe.

My own salon.

The dream is no longer just a dream. It's real.

◆ ◆ ◆

"Eat something before you keel over."

Mum appears at my elbow with a plate of nibbles. I've just finished ringing up a client, a lovely woman called Alison who's already booked her next appointment.

"I'm fine."

"You've not stopped for lunch." She shoves the plate towards me. "Go on. At least a mouthful."

I pop one of the bite-sized mac-and-cheese balls into my mouth to appease her. It's mid-afternoon now, and the opening has drawn a steady stream of folk. There hasn't been a quiet moment.

Ruby's holding her own at the wash station, handling a constant flow of clients with impressive composure for someone so new. Sheila's in her element, working through her client list with the easy efficiency of someone who's been doing this for decades.

Already I'm mentally noting what's working and what I'll tweak before we reopen on Tuesday. But honestly? Everything has gone pretty damn smoothly so far. Better than I dared hope.

The door opens. I look up, and in walks Struan's mum, Helen, followed by Isla and Struan. He's in a checked shirt, sleeves rolled to the elbows, hair pulled into a loose half-ponytail. He looks . . . like himself. Which apparently is enough to make my stomach flip.

Stop it, I tell myself firmly. *Yes, he saved the day yesterday by driving a four-hour round trip to the depot in Elgin. Yes, he listened—really listened—when you fell apart. And yes, maybe— just maybe—there's a little more to him than you first thought. But that doesn't mean your body should start reacting on its own when he walks into a room.*

Helen beams, her gaze sweeping the salon. "Oh, it all came together beautifully! When I popped in on Monday with the lads' lunch, the floor was all ripped up. But look at this place now!" She clasps her hands together. "It's stunning, Ainsley."

"Thank you," I say. "Walker Builds did a brilliant job with the refurb."

Struan's lips lift into that easy smile of his. The one that used to irritate me. Which probably still should, only it doesn't. Not really.

Mum swoops in with a glass of fizz for Helen. "In for a wee nosy, are you?"

Helen laughs. "Booked in, actually. Long overdue." She lifts a hand to her hair—silver threading through the same thick curls her son and granddaughter inherited.

"You won't regret it," Mum says proudly. "Ainsley's magic with hair."

And just like that, the two of them start chatting away like old friends, rather than two people who only met for the first time at knitting club a couple of weeks ago. They seem to get on well, which is . . . interesting.

A swish of blue fabric barrels into view. "Isla!" Lily twirls for her with maximum drama. "I'm Elsa! See my braid? It's got glitter."

"Wow!" Isla's eyes light up.

"How about Ruby gives you a wee up-do too?" I suggest.

"Yes, please!"

Struan glances at the clients on the bench. "You sure it's okay to squeeze her in? Looks busy."

"Of course. It's the least I can do after everything yesterday."

He waves it off. "Ach, that was nothing."

But it wasn't nothing. Not to me.

"Ruby!" I call across the salon. "Can you fit in a braid for Isla?"

"Absolutely." Ruby smiles at Isla. "Want some glitter in yours too?"

Isla nods eagerly, and Ruby leads her towards a chair. Lily goes with them, offering unsolicited advice about the best glitter colours.

Struan watches them, something soft in his expression, then turns back to me. "Great to see the place up and running. And you look happy. Suits you."

I don't know how to respond to that. So instead I say, "I'd better go get your mum started. Helen? If I can drag you away from my mum, do you want to come this way?"

Seating her for an initial consultation, I run my fingers through her hair—something I always do with new clients to feel the texture before washing. Like her son's, Helen's hair is a thick mix of curls and waves. Beautiful when cut right. A nightmare when it's not.

"Gorgeous texture," I tell her. "When was your last trim?"

"Oh, months ago. Maybe longer." Helen grimaces. "I kept meaning to get it done, but you know how it is."

I do know. I also know that whoever cut it last didn't understand curl patterns because the shape's all wrong—too blunt at the ends, no layering to let the spirals spring properly.

"Let's get you washed first," I say. "I'll do a nourishing treatment to bring out the shine, then we'll reshape these curls."

At the basin, I wet Helen's hair and work in the shampoo, massaging her scalp. She lets out a contented sigh.

"Oh, that's lovely. Maggie never did head massages."

I smile. "It's the best part, isn't it?"

As I rinse and apply the conditioner, a familiar deep burr carries over the noise of the salon. I glance up.

Struan's leaning against the counter, casual as anything, chatting with two pensioners waiting for Sheila. I can't hear what he's saying, but whatever it is has them animated—leaning in, laughing, gossiping away.

Helen chuckles. "That lad could blether for Scotland, so he could."

I squeeze the excess water from her hair. "I've noticed that about him."

"He's a people person," Helen says fondly. "Always has been. Which is why it's surprising he's still single."

Keeping my expression neutral, I wrap a towel around her head. "That's you rinsed. Let's get these curls trimmed."

Back at the chair, I section Helen's hair and begin the cut, working with the curl pattern rather than against it. She talks enough for both of us—small-town gossip, local events, stories about her daughter, Erin, in London. I can see where her son gets it from.

During a lull, Helen catches my eye in the mirror. "Do you do gents' hair too?"

"Aye, we actually had a couple of men in this morning."

She twirls a freshly cut curl, admiring it. "You should cut Struan's next time. You've clearly got the knack for this kind of hair."

My pulse skips. The thought of running my fingers through his curls feels . . . different. Too intimate. Which is ridiculous—I touch strangers' hair all day. But still.

"I'm not sure your son's looking for a cut," I say lightly.

"Maybe not. But I'll mention it." She waves across the salon. "Struan! What about getting a few inches off? It's been ages since you had it done properly."

He excuses himself from the pensioners and ambles over. "And lose my man bun?" He presses a hand to his chest in mock horror. "Mum, how could you?"

Helen looks at me in the mirror. "What do you think?"

I glance at him. Amusement flickers in those golden-brown eyes.

"I think," I say carefully, "he suits it the way it is."

Struan's grin widens. "See, Mum? Straight from an expert."

Helen hums, her gaze still on me.

I ignore the prickle at the back of my neck and keep cutting.

CHAPTER EIGHTEEN

STRUAN

It's late on Sunday night.

I sit on the back step, guitar across my lap, idly strumming. A joint hangs from my lips. I take a slow drag, the tip glowing, then let the smoke drift from the side of my mouth.

I don't smoke often. Just now and again, when the house feels too quiet. Tonight's one of those nights.

With the sleepover on Friday, it felt like I barely picked Isla up before I was dropping her off back in Bannock. And when I got home, the silence just . . . got to me. No chatter. No cartoon jingles from the telly. Only the hum of the fridge and the creak of the pipes.

The house was so quiet I nearly texted Sophie for an update. Which is tragic, considering I'd seen my kid just forty minutes earlier.

No need to feel sorry for yourself, Walker. You can cope with a shorter weekend every so often.

I keep strumming, my fingers wandering without much thought. Nothing fancy. Just the same few chords, over and over, the rhythm steady enough to lose myself in. A dog barks some-where nearby before falling quiet again. Then—

"For fuck's sake!"

Standing, I peer over the fence. Ainsley's at her bins, wrestling with a cardboard box that refuses to fit.

Grumbling, she throws it to the ground, jumps on it, tries again—and swears again. "Just bloody go in, will you!"

"Having trouble there?" I say. When she doesn't respond, I try again, louder. "Want some help?"

She jumps, a hand flying to her chest. "Bloody hell!" She pulls earphones from her ears. "Struan. You scared me."

"Sorry, didn't mean to. You all right there?"

"Fine." She gives the box one last shove before giving up and leaving it sticking out of the bin. Her gaze flicks to the joint. "Oh. Having a herbal remedy, are we?"

"Aye. Want a puff?"

"I've not had one in years."

"Go on. I won't tell."

"What the hell. Child-free night." She places her hands on the fence between our gardens.

"Here," I say, setting down my guitar. "Let me help you over."

"I can manage." She swings first one leg over, then the other, and gives me a satisfied look. "See? No builder assistance required."

Chuckling, I sit back down and gesture for her to join me. She does, only there's not much room on the step, so our shoulders brush.

I offer her the joint. She takes it, her lips closing around it, cheeks hollowing as she inhales.

Something stirs low in my gut.

Coughing lightly, she hands it back. "God, that's stronger than I remember."

"Aye, well." I shrug. "Lily at your mum and dad's?"

"Mm-hmm. She was there for dinner so I could try to make the house a bit more homely. She fell asleep on the sofa so they're keeping her overnight. And Isla? Back at her mum's place?"

"Aye. Dropped her there this afternoon."

I take another drag then look up at the stars. Maybe it's the joint loosening my tongue, or maybe it's just the quiet and the dark, but the words slip out before I can stop them. "Sunday evenings are my least favourite part of the week."

"Must be hard," Ainsley says after a beat. "Saying goodbye to your kid every week."

"Aye." Another drag. I watch the smoke drift up into the night. "You'd think I'd be used to it by now."

"How long have you and Isla's mum been doing the week-day–weekend split? If you don't mind me asking."

"Pretty much since she was weaned."

"So you and her were never . . . ?"

"Together? Nah, not really. Isla wasn't planned. We did give things a shot when Soph was expecting, but we're better as friends."

"Still, you've made it work between you."

"Aye. We do our best." I glance at the joint. "Not much left, I'm afraid. You can finish it."

As I pass it over, our fingers brush. Brief. Warm. Nice.

"Lily was a surprise too," Ainsley admits after a moment. "But unlike you and Isla's mum, it didn't end well."

And then, for the second time in three days, Ainsley opens up to me. She starts off hesitant, but once she gets going, the words come easier. She tells me about her ex—the cycle of taking him back, convincing herself this time would be different, only to be let down again. Then the final straw: the double hit of walking in on him with her best friend.

My jaw tightens but I say nothing. Just listen. Still, part of me wouldn't mind finding this Danny guy and teaching him just how hard a builder's fist can land.

"It's my fault, really," Ainsley says. "I should have realised so much sooner he wasn't cut out for family life."

"*What?*" I can't hold my tongue any longer. "Don't you dare blame yourself. Your ex and your ex-best friend? Those two arse-holes are the only ones to blame. Aye?"

She gives me a wobbly smile and for a horrible moment I think she might cry. Don't know if I could cope with that. Not when we're sitting this close. No way I'd be able to resist pulling her into my arms to comfort her.

But she pulls herself together, and a wee edge creeps into her voice. "And to think I used to give that prick and that cow free haircuts. And bloody good ones at that."

I can't hold back a laugh.

"All right, no more regurgitating the past," she says. "Let's change the subject to safer territory. Like . . ." Her gaze drops to the guitar beside me. "Can you only play folksy stuff on that thing? Or do you know any modern tunes?"

"You mocking my repertoire?"

"Maybe a little."

I lift the guitar and lay it on my lap. "Name your genre."

"Hmm . . . how about something moody? Lewis Capaldi?"

I strum a few over-dramatic, heartbreaky chords, letting my head fall back as I half sing, half groan a handful of lines from "Someone You Loved".

She laughs, the sound bright and unexpected. It does something to my chest that I try not to examine too closely.

"Okay, now how about Paolo Nutini?"

I slide into the bouncy "New Shoes" chords, singing the chorus in my best impression of him.

She claps. "Not bad! All right, now surprise me."

I switch to a lighter, poppier rhythm and do a bit of Sabrina Carpenter's "Espresso".

"Wow! Didn't see that one coming. I take it back. You've got range, Struan."

"Aye, well, that's my whole set list," I say with a wink at her.

She smiles and hugs her knees to her chest. The tension that usually tightens her shoulders has melted away, and in the soft light from the kitchen window, she looks younger. Softer. "I never learned to play. Always wanted to."

"It's never too late. I'll teach you a chord."

"Really?"

"Why not?"

I pass her the guitar, and she settles it awkwardly across her lap. "I have no idea what I'm doing."

"That's the spirit." I nudge her playfully. "Right, we'll start with G. It's an easy one. Handy too."

I reach over and guide her fingers to the right strings, my thigh brushing hers. Her hands are so much smaller and softer than mine.

"Try that."

She attempts a strum but produces only a muffled thunk. "God. That sounded terrible."

I press her fingers down a wee bit firmer. "Try again."

This time the chord rings out—wobbly, but recognisable.

"I did it!" She grins triumphantly.

"Natural talent."

I don't move my hand. Neither does she.

Christ, we're close. I can feel the warmth of her, hear the quick catch of her breath. One shift, one wrong move, and the spell will break.

Our eyes meet. Her gaze flicks to my mouth—just for a heartbeat, but I see it. And then? Then she leans in and kisses me.

It's soft at first—tentative, testing—and for a split second I'm too stunned to react. Then her lips move over mine, and the shock turns into pure instinct.

I kiss her back.

The guitar shifts between us, strings humming, but I barely notice. My hands find her hair—God, it's soft and thick, like velvet between my fingers. I drag my tongue along the seam of her lips, slow and coaxing.

She opens for me, so I taste her. Warm, sweet, dizzying.

A small sound slips out of her—part surprise, part need. It hits me straight in the gut.

With every slick sweep of her tongue against mine, every breath shared between us, I grow harder. Her fingers curl into the front of my shirt like she's trying to anchor herself.

The guitar slips off her lap and clatters to the ground, snapping the moment. We break apart, both breathing hard. Her lips are flushed, her eyes wide and shining. A strand of hair falls across her face. I brush it back without thinking.

"Your guitar," she manages.

"Doesn't matter," I say roughly, not even sparing it a glance. Right now there's only her.

I lean in again and she meets me halfway, nothing tentative about it this time. Her mouth is hot and hungry against mine. Our tongues tangle, and then before I know what I'm doing, I've got an arm around her waist and am hauling her over me so she's straddling my lap right here on the step.

My cock throbs under the sudden pressure. It takes everything in me not to buck up into her straight away. But then she shifts experimentally, making this soft little whimper into our kiss, and that's it for me. I grab her arse and pull her closer, flush against me.

Another moan, then she starts moving with purpose, grinding down slow and sure.

Fuck me.

"Struan—"

My name in her voice, breathless and wanting, punches the air out of me. I grip her arse, guiding her rhythm, and she buries her face in my neck. Her breath comes out in these desperate little sounds—half-moan, half-whimper—that go straight to my dick.

Her breath hitches. She grinds down even harder, pressing into me like she's chasing something just out of reach. The way she moves—so confident now—makes me shudder right through.

Then suddenly she's clinging to me, fingers digging into my shoulders, her whole body tightening. For a second I don't realise what's happening, then it hits me. She's shaking, gasping, coming apart right on my lap.

I hold her, stunned, heartbeat hammering. Jesus Christ. Didn't think that would happen.

Hot as fuck.

She stills, and for a while the only movement between us is the rise and fall of our chests and the twitching of my cock. It's desperate for that perfect, maddening friction to start up again.

But then she's pressing a hand flat against my chest and

pulling away from me. "Sorry—" Her voice is shaky, her head bowed. "Struan, I . . . I don't know what came over me."

"Ainsley—"

"This was a mistake."

The words hit like cold water. I open my mouth to respond but she's already scrambling off my lap, cheeks flaming in the light from the kitchen.

"Ainsley, wait!"

"Goodnight." She's at the fence before I can move, and then she's over it and disappearing through her back door without so much as a glance back.

I sit on my step, heart hammering, my guitar forgotten on the ground. I'm left with just the taste of her on my lips—and a cock that's not settling down anytime soon.

Fucking hell. Can't believe that just happened.

CHAPTER NINETEEN

AINSLEY

I shut the back door, lock it, and lean back against it, palms pressed to my burning cheeks.

Oh my God. Oh my *God*.

I just came on Struan Walker's lap.

I'm still thrumming all over, nerves buzzing with the after-shocks. A shaky laugh escapes me—half disbelief, half pure mortification.

What the hell was that? One minute I was strumming a wobbly G chord, the next I was grinding against him like my life depended on it. Dignity? Nowhere to be found.

Okay. Breathe. Think.

It was just a release. That's all. The last few weeks have been chaos—the move, getting the salon up and running, Lily's tantrums. My body's been running on caffeine and cortisol for God knows how long. Throw in a bit of weed, something I haven't touched in years, plus Struan's hand guiding mine on the guitar, and . . . well, any warm-blooded woman would've reacted the way I did. Perfectly explainable. Completely physiological.

I push off from the door, fill a glass at the tap, and gulp half of it down. It does nothing to wash away the taste of Struan—or the memory of him that still clings to me everywhere else.

I close my eyes and take a few steadying breaths.

No use.

My head's already replaying it—his grip on my arse, the solid weight of him beneath me, his erection pressed tight against me, the way he'd met every roll of my body as if he couldn't help himself.

My stomach flips.

I left him sitting there. With a *massive* hard-on straining against his jeans.

"Oh, for fuck's sake," I mutter, tipping the rest of the water into the sink. Enough. Bed.

Upstairs, I plug in my phone and go through the motions—wash my face, brush my teeth, slap on moisturiser—all on autopilot. Every few seconds, another flash: the look on his face when I moved against him. The way his fingers dug into my arse, pulling me closer, harder, the pressure building—

My body hums with the echo of it.

When I unhook my bra, my nipples are still embarrassingly hard. Nothing to do with the cold: the radiator's humming away. I tug off my knickers, then pause, staring.

Soaked. Of course they are.

I shove them and the rest of my clothes into the wash basket then pull on my PJs—the unsexy flannel ones, as if that'll somehow reset my brain.

I plump my pillows. Crawl under the duvet. It's late, I'm exhausted, and I really, *really* need to sleep.

But now I'm thinking about his bed. On the other side of this wall.

Is he in it? Is he lying there right now, still hard, replaying what happened? That erection of his definitely needed seeing to. There's no way he's just gone to sleep.

A vivid image flashes in my head—Struan sprawled across his rumpled sheets, tawny curls tousled and damp, his hand wrapped tight around his hard cock. Pumping up and down, slow at first, then faster—gripping harder, hips arching into his fist.

Maybe he'd bite his lip to muffle a groan. Maybe he'd tense just before he came, every muscle drawn tight beneath sweat-soaked skin . . .

The ache between my legs, barely dulled from earlier, spikes hot and insistent, as if the memory alone is enough to pull me under all over again.

No, stop it, Ainsley!

I squeeze my eyes shut and roll onto my stomach, but the throb at my core only intensifies. Bloody hell. This is ridiculous. I literally came fifteen minutes ago.

For what feels like hours, I toss and turn, eventually giving up and glaring at the ceiling.

For God's sake, Ainsley. You have a business to run. You do not have time to be lusting after your joiner-slash-neighbour.

But no matter how much I berate myself, the heat keeps rushing back.

His hands. His mouth. The way he'd looked at me like I was the only thing in the world worth seeing.

My phone buzzes on my bedside table. Who the hell is contacting me at 12:58 a.m.?

Of course. Struan.

STRUAN

You still awake?

I can't stop thinking about this evening

My pulse goes funny. I type out *me neither* then delete it.
Instead:

AINSLEY

I think we got a bit carried away

The dots appear almost immediately.

STRUAN

Maybe. But I'm glad we did

Butterflies. Actual traitorous butterflies doing loop-the-loops
in my stomach.

Then reality barges in.

Lily still adjusting to our new life. The salon barely off the
ground. My heart still held together with tape.

I can't be going down this road right now. Not with anyone,
and *certainly* not with Struan Walker, who has charm written
into his DNA and a reputation that precedes him.

AINSLEY

It can't happen again, Struan

It was a mistake

Harsh, but necessary. I need to remind *myself* as much as him
that I can't let this happen.

STRUAN

I disagree. Tonight wasn't just impulse

Short. Certain.

My throat goes dry.

STRUAN

Whatever this is between us, it's been
building since you fell into my lap at soft play

I snort despite my racing heart.

AINSLEY

You're imagining it

STRUAN

No, I'm not. The looks. The banter. The way
we are around each other. Deny it all you
want, Ainsley, but there's something there

And damn him, he's right.

I feel it every time he walks into a room. Every time he flashes
that easy grin or passes close enough that I catch his warm, earthy
scent.

AINSLEY

Okay, fine. So we're attracted to each other.
Doesn't mean acting on it is a good idea

STRUAN

Why not?

AINSLEY

Because we're neighbours. We've got kids.
Things could get messy fast

STRUAN

I'm not saying we have to rush into anything

AINSLEY

So what ARE you saying?

STRUAN

We could date? Take it slow. Just two adults
getting to know each other

He's asking me out?

My heart skips, and for one reckless moment I let myself imagine it. Dinner somewhere nice. His golden-brown eyes crinkling at the corners as he laughs at something I've said. Conversation that isn't about renovation timelines or Lily's meltdowns. His hand reaching across the table to take mine.

Then common sense kicks in, hard.

Of course he's asking me out. He's *Struan Walker*. This is what men like him do: dinner first, a bit of charm, then knickers on the floor.

Nope. Not happening. I've learnt my lesson.

AINSLEY

Struan, I don't have the headspace for
anything remotely romantic right now

Can we just forget it happened? And this
conversation too, for that matter

Let's never talk about it again

The dots blink, vanish, then reappear.

STRUAN

Is that what you really want, Ainsley?

No. *Yes.*

AINSLEY

It is

STRUAN

Then I'll respect your wishes. But if you ever change your mind . . . you know where to find me

I stare at the message, something heavy and tight settling in my stomach. Then I turn the phone facedown, pull the duvet over my head, and squeeze my eyes shut.

I've made my intentions clear. Drawn a line. Which is a good thing.

So why doesn't it feel good?

CHAPTER TWENTY

AINSLEY

"Honestly, Ainsley, you're a lifesaver."

Shona from the post office beams at her reflection, turning her head side to side. Gone is the Irn-Bru orange she walked in with two hours ago, the unfortunate aftermath of a home dye kit and an online tutorial that apparently left out a few crucial steps. In its place, a warm auburn that actually suits her skin tone.

"Always happy to help," I chirp, unclipping the cape from her shoulders.

At the till Shona taps her card then slides a folded note across the counter. "A wee thank you."

It's a healthy tip. "That's very kind, but you really don't have to."

"I really do. For saving me from looking like a traffic cone at my niece's wedding."

"Well, thank you." As tricky as a DIY hair disaster is to fix, it's not exactly bad for business.

Once she's left, I tidy up my station—sweeping clippings, wiping down the shelf—while doing a quick scan of the salon.

Ruby's midway through a graduated bob, the shape coming

together nicely. At the basins Sheila's rinsing one client's hair while another waits nearby with foils. The three of them chatter away happily.

Everything is humming along smoothly.

I've got ten minutes before my next appointment. Just enough time for a breather.

Outside, I draw in a lungful of cool harbour air. The salt air, the smell of fish from the boats, the cry of gulls overhead. Not sure I'll ever get used to having this on my doorstep.

A familiar flash of white catches my eye. The Walker Builds van slows and pulls into a space a few cars along.

Of course it does.

Since Sunday night I've been doing my best to avoid Struan. Checking the coast is clear before pulling my bins out. Hurrying between my front door and car to avoid awkward encounters. But I was never going to be able to avoid him for long.

He climbs out of the van, sunlight catching the loose curls escaping his usual messy bun. I turn and quickly retreat back inside.

What's he doing here? The salon work's finished.

I busy myself tidying things at the counter that don't really need tidied. Then, a prickle at the back of my neck, I glance up just as Struan walks past the window.

His gaze catches mine, and he smiles. Not a big grin. Just that casual, infuriating curve of his mouth.

And then—he's gone. He walks on past.

Oh. He's not here to see me. Must be on another job. It is the town centre, I suppose. Plenty of places he could be going.

"That man is well fit."

I turn to find Ruby and her client—Emma, a girl in her early twenties who works at the soft play—both gazing dreamily at the window.

"All the mums at soft play fancy him." Emma sighs and turns back to the mirror. "The staff too." The way she says it leaves no doubt that this includes her.

Something flickers inside me. Not jealousy. Definitely not jealousy. Just irritation. General, non-specific irritation that has nothing to do with the fact that apparently every woman in Ardmara fancies Struan Walker—and I said no to a date with him.

"Heading to the back for a quick break," I mutter to Sheila and Ruby before escaping to the kitchenette.

I click on the kettle, more out of habit than any real desire for tea. As it boils, voices drift through from the salon, not exactly quiet and impossible to tune out. Struan, unfortunately, remains the subject of conversation.

"Ardmara's very own Casanova, that one," Sheila offers with a chuckle.

I roll my eyes. Harmless banter. Part and parcel of salon life. Still grates, though.

"Well, about that . . ." one of her clients says in a tone that suggests she has *big gossip*.

"Aye?" Sheila says eagerly.

I pop a teabag into a mug, ears pricking despite myself.

"I heard something interesting at the Ferryman's Rest the other day. You know Lindsey McVey? She was Lindsey Wallace before the divorce."

The blonde from the beach. The woman whose house Struan was so keen to visit alone.

"Aye, I know her," Sheila confirms.

"Well, apparently Lindsey invited Struan round to give her a quote for a new bathroom—only a quote wasn't the only thing she was after." She drops her voice to a stage whisper that I can still hear perfectly well in the back. "She all but put it on a platter for him."

I *knew* it. Knew that was why Struan was so determined to go to that appointment without his da.

Not that it matters. He's a free agent. I told him I wanted to forget what happened on his step, didn't I?

My jaw tightens anyway.

"Bold move," Ruby says, sounding impressed.

"Anyway," the storyteller continues, clearly enjoying her moment, "he turned her down. Said he was flattered but wasn't interested. Quite the gentleman about it, apparently."

That's *not* how I was expecting the story to go.

Sheila lets out a low whistle. "Didn't think he was the sort to turn down an offer like that."

"Poor woman," Ruby murmurs. "I'd be mortified."

I pour my tea and perch at the breakfast bar, spoon circling idly. The chatter moves on to something else, but not my thoughts. I'm still thinking about Struan.

He turned her down. Why?

My phone buzzes. "Mum" flashes on the screen.

"Hi, Mum," I say, answering. "Everything okay?"

"No." Her voice is high and shaky. "It's your father, Ainsley. He's fallen off a ladder. He landed on his arm and—oh, Ainsley, he's in so much pain. Gone so pale. And—"

"Mum, have you called an ambulance?"

"Yes, but it was going to take them too long to get here, so our neighbour, Billy, is driving us to Inverness. I'm in the back with your da, and—oh, Ainsley, I'm so worried about him."

My chest tightens. "Mum, deep breaths, okay?" I force myself to do the same. "Everything is going to be fine. I'm going to head through now." I grab my bag and my coat. "You stay strong for Da, okay? I'll see you at the hospital."

"Okay," Mum says shakily. Then: "Oh, your da's saying you don't have to drive—"

"I'm coming through, Mum. I'll see you there."

I end the call and pull on my coat. What the hell was Da doing up a set of ladders? And how many times do Mum and I have to tell him not to attempt stuff like that himself?

Later, I tell myself. Answers can wait. All that matters is making sure he's okay.

I head through to the salon. Sheila takes one look at my face and says, "Ainsley? What's happened?"

"It's my da. He's had a bad fall, and my mum's in bits. They're on their way to the hospital in Inverness, and I need to go too."

"Oh my God," Ruby says.

"Sheila, can you call my remaining clients? Ask them to reschedule?"

Sheila's already ushering me to the door. "Don't you worry about that. Ruby and I will cover everything. You go see your da."

"But you were supposed to finish early—"

"Never mind that! We'll manage. Family first."

"Thank you."

Out on the pavement, I break into a fast walk and try Blair on my phone. Lily finishes at three. If Blair can collect her—

No answer.

I try again.

Come on, Blair. Pick up.

Nothing.

I'll have to bring Lily with me. An hour and twenty minutes

in the car each way, plus however long we're at the hospital. She'll be exhausted and confused and asking questions I don't have answers to—

I round the corner at speed and slam straight into something solid.

The impact jolts through me, and I stumble back, gasping. Strong fingers catch my upper arm.

"Whoa, easy—"

I look up into golden-brown eyes.

Struan's.

"What's wrong?" No sign of the easy smile. He's studying my face, concern sharpening his features.

"My da—he fell off a ladder. He's on his way to the hospital in Inverness. My mum's with him but she's panicking. She's hopeless in situations like this."

"Right." His voice is calm, and his hand stays steady on my arm, warm and solid. "What do you need?"

I take a breath. Then another.

"I need to get Lily from nursery, then get to Inverness."

"I'll pick up Lily. I can look after her till you're back."

"What? No, you're working, I can't—"

"It's fine." No hesitation. No fuss. "What time does she finish?"

"Three, but—"

"I'll get her at three. You go."

I stare at him. My brain's still catching up, trying to find the objection, the reason this won't work.

But there isn't one.

I trust him with her. The realisation lands quietly, settling somewhere beneath the panic.

"Struan, I—" My throat tightens. "Thank you."

"It's fine." His brow creases. "But are you sure you're okay to drive? You're shaking."

I look down. He's right. My hands are trembling.

"I'll be fine."

"Text me when you get there."

"I will."

I fumble for my house key. "Here. Lily might be happier at home, with her things. Books, colouring stuff, Mr Flops—whatever keeps her busy."

"Got it. Go."

I hold his gaze for one more second—steady, reassuring—then hurry towards my car.

CHAPTER TWENTY-ONE

STRUAN

I'm sitting cross-legged on Lily's bedroom floor, surrounded by a sea of Barbies, tiny shoes, and enough plastic paraphernalia to stock a small toy shop. My knees are protesting—I'm a six-foot-three bloke, not exactly built for sitting like a pretzel—but Lily's in charge here and she knows it.

In my hand is "Stwuan Barbie", the doll Isla and Lily renamed at the beach barbecue because apparently the resemblance to me is uncanny. Without the outfit I was wearing that day, I don't see it myself, but Lily is adamant the doll is Stwuan Barbie. She's also adamant that Stwuan Barbie is a girl, not a boy.

She carefully manoeuvres a tiny rucksack onto the doll's shoulders, her tongue poking out in concentration. Then she picks up another doll—a slightly battered Elsa from *Frozen*, her blonde braid fraying at the ends—and holds her up.

"This is Stwuan Barbie's mummy," she informs me.

"Right. Course she is."

"Okay." Lily's voice goes serious, like a director about to call action. "Pretend you shake the bag off and say you're staying home today. You're not going to school."

I make my Barbie shrug off the rucksack. "I'm staying home today," I say, pitching my voice high and squeaky. "No school."

Lily instantly switches to her "adult" voice—deeper, slower, dripping with maternal patience. "But you *have* to go. School is where you learn important stuff like reading and counting and how to share."

"Well, okay then," I say.

Lily's face falls. "No! Pretend you didn't say that. Instead, you stamp your foot and say, 'No, not going,' and then I say, 'I'm going to count to three, Stwuan Barbie,' and then you say, 'Okay, fine, I'll go to school.'"

I nod. "Got it."

I try again. Lily watches me with narrowed eyes, then nods, apparently satisfied with my performance.

It's not lost on me that she's acting out her own morning routine—through a plastic doll named after me. Working things out in miniature. That's what play's for, I suppose.

We carry on, Lily running the show with an iron fist wrapped in pink sparkles. Now the class has a new pet pony—a plastic thing with an improbably glittery mane—and the teacher (played by Lily, naturally) has chosen Stwuan Barbie to take it home for the night.

"You have to be very careful with Sparkle," Lily says sternly, handing me the pony. "She gets scared if you brush her hair too fast."

"I'll be gentle," I promise, arranging the tiny reins with more care than I've given most actual tasks today.

It's been ages since Isla wanted to play dolls with me like this. She's moved on to books and facts and card games and chess—which is brilliant, don't get me wrong. I've no wish to turn back the clock and be at this stage again every weekend. But as a one-off? Revisiting something Isla and I used to do together but don't anymore?

Aye. It's kinda nice.

My phone buzzes on the floor beside me. I glance at the screen. Ainsley.

"Right," I say, setting Sparkle down carefully, "I'm going to get this, okay?"

Lily fixes me with a look so stern it's comical on her wee face. "Don't be long. The school's closing soon."

"Aye aye, teacher."

I push myself to my feet and step out onto the landing, pulling the door almost closed behind me.

Ainsley texted about half an hour ago to say she'd made it to Raigmore. She promised to call the moment she found out the state of things.

I swipe to answer. "Hey. How's your da?"

"Better than we thought, thank God." Her voice is tired but relieved. "No surgery needed after all—just a fracture and a nasty cut that required stitching. They're putting the cast on now and will probably keep him overnight for observation, just to be safe. But all going well, he'll get out tomorrow."

"That's good news. Proper relief, that."

"Aye." A pause. "How's Lily been?"

I glance through the gap in the door. Lily's brushing the toy pony's hair with a tiny brush, murmuring something to it in a soothing voice.

"We've been playing Barbies for almost two hours," I say. "She's keeping me right."

Ainsley laughs softly, the sound light and warm. "You're playing Barbies with her? That's . . . actually very sweet."

I grin and rub the back of my neck. "Sweet, aye?"

"Aye. Sweet."

From her tone, I reckon she's smiling. I certainly am.

"And also, did you say two hours? You deserve a medal. Lily can be bossy at the best of times, but when it comes to her dolls, she's next level."

"Och, I don't mind. She's a proper wee Spielberg in the making. Got the whole thing scripted down to the last line." I pause. "Oh, I hope you don't mind, but when I picked Lily up, she asked where her grandparents were. I just told her Grandad wasn't feeling well and Gran was looking after him."

"That's exactly what I'd have said. Thanks for handling it. I owe you for this, Struan."

"Seriously, it's no bother."

"It might be late before I get back. Blair said she could pop over and sort Lily's tea and bedtime—"

"Och, don't be daft," I cut in. "No need to get Blair out when I'm already here and have a free evening."

A bit of a lie, that last bit. I was meant to play at the Ferryman's Rest tonight with Rab and Ellie, but I messaged them earlier to cancel. Figured Ainsley wouldn't be home any time soon, and I wasn't about to palm Lily off on someone else.

"You sure?"

"Aye, I'm sure. Lily and I are just fine."

Through the gap in the door, I watch Lily settle the toy pony into a makeshift bed made of tissues.

"Okay," Ainsley says quietly. "Thank you. Really."

"Stop thanking me. Focus on your da, aye? Everything's just grand at this end."

After ending the call, I head back into Lily's bedroom. "Right. How's Sparkle getting along?"

"She had a bad dream so Stwuan Barbie has to sing her a song." She looks at me expectantly.

"A song?" I lower myself back onto the floor. "What kind of songs do ponies like?"

Lily considers this. "A lullaby. But make it up. Sparkle doesn't like normal songs."

"A made-up lullaby for a toy pony. Got it."

I pick up Stwuan Barbie and clear my throat dramatically. Then, in the softest falsetto I can manage, I start singing absolute nonsense about glittery manes and magical meadows while Lily watches me with solemn approval.

CHAPTER TWENTY-TWO

AINSLEY

The headlights sweep across the front of the house as I pull into the drive. I let the engine idle for a moment before switching it off.

I tip my head back against the headrest and let out a long, slow breath. No surgery. No life-altering damage. Just a cast, a hospital bed for the night, and several weeks of healing.

Da's going to be fine.

According to the dashboard clock, it's 10:45 p.m. Struan's had Lily since three. That's nearly eight hours with my daughter.

I open the car door and step out into the cool night air. A faint breeze carries the salt-and-seaweed tang of the harbour.

On the drive back, my thoughts kept drifting to Struan. The way he offered to collect Lily without hesitation, like it was the most natural thing in the world. The salon gossip—how quickly I assumed the worst of him, and how wrong I was. The four-hour round trip to Elgin. And the way he listens to me without trying to fix me or smooth things over.

I was so sure I had him pegged. Charming smile. Easy flirtation. A reputation that preceded him.

Just like Danny.

Only, that doesn't quite fit anymore. Not neatly anyway. Struan's shown a kind of care and quiet decency I didn't expect.

I push the thought aside as I open the front door and step inside.

The hall is dim, lit only by the glow spilling from the living room. I slip off my shoes then pad towards the light. And stop in my tracks.

Struan's stretched out on the sofa, mouth slightly open, fast asleep. Curled against him is Lily, a blanket tucked around her, Mr Flops held close, one small hand resting against Struan's chest.

On the TV Igglepiggle prances across a moonlit garden, his cheerful song murmuring from the speakers.

I stand there for a moment, taking it in. The steady rhythm of their breathing. Lily's wee body heavy with sleep.

I swallow then cross to the sofa and crouch beside it. "Hey," I murmur, reaching out to touch Struan's shoulder.

He stirs, a soft grunt escaping him. His eyes blink open—unfocused at first, then finding me. He rubs a hand over his face.

God, he looks adorable waking up. All rumpled and—

Stop it, Ainsley.

"Sorry." He carefully sits up, his voice rough with sleep. "I *did* get her down in her own bed. But she came back down a wee while ago. Put *In the Night Garden* on to settle her, and . . . well, guess we both conked out."

"You've been amazing, Struan," I say quietly. "Thank you so much."

He waves off my gratitude. "Ach, don't be daft. Happy to help." He glances down at Lily, who's still dead to the world. "I'll take her up."

"Oh, I can—"

But he's already scooping Lily into his arms, one hand supporting her head. She stirs, makes a small sound of protest, then burrows closer into his chest and goes still again.

And just like that, my body reacts in a way I very much did not authorise.

It's just because you're tired, I tell myself. *It's been a long day.*

But I know that's not the whole truth.

I follow Struan up the stairs. In Lily's room he lowers Lily onto her bed, eases his arm out from beneath her, then steps back to give me space.

I tug the duvet up around her shoulders, smooth her hair back from her forehead, and lean down to press a gentle kiss there. "Night, baby."

As we quietly head back down the stairs, voices drift in from the street—two of them, tipsy and cheerful, belting out a very enthusiastic rendition of "Caledonia". I smile faintly. Must be on their way home from the pub.

I pause.

Wait, doesn't Struan usually play at the pub on Thursdays?

In the living room, Struan runs a hand through his curls, still clearly half-asleep. "She didn't even stir when we put her down," he says. "Out like a light."

"Aye." I hesitate, then: "Struan, something just occurred to me. Weren't you supposed to play at the pub this evening?"

He shrugs then reaches for his hoodie, which is draped over the arm of the sofa. "Aye, but I told Ellie and Rab I'd sit this one out."

I stare at him.

He must catch the look on my face because he adds, "They can still play without me. It's not the first time one of us has had to pull out of a gig. Just means an adapted set, that's all." Another easy shrug, like it's nothing. Like cancelling his evening plans to babysit his neighbour's four-year-old is just what you do.

"You cancelled," I say slowly, "to help me? And my family?"

"It's not a big deal, Ainsley."

Except it is. All those assumptions I made about him. The walls I built, brick by brick, to keep men like him safely on the other side. And here he is, dismantling them without even trying. Just by being . . . this. Kind. Dependable. *Good.*

"Well," he says, moving towards the door and pulling on his hoodie. "Goodnight, Ainsley."

"Wait!"

He turns, brows lifting.

My heart is hammering. This is impulsive. Probably a terrible idea. But the words are already forming, rising up from somewhere beneath all the caution and the fear and the carefully maintained distance.

"I've changed my mind."

"Aye? About what?"

"I'd like that date." My voice is steadier than I feel. "If it's still on offer."

For a moment he just looks at me. Then his hands come up, palms out. "Ainsley, you don't have to go on a date with me as a way of paying me back for this evening. I meant what I said before—"

"I know. But I'd still like that date."

His eyes don't leave me. He searches my face, looking for . . . what? Obligation? Gratitude dressed up as interest?

Whatever he finds must satisfy him because he breaks into a slow smile. Not the easy grin he deploys like a weapon, but something softer. Warmer.

"Well, then. A date it is."

There's a flutter in my chest. Nerves. Excitement. A complicated tangle of both.

"I'll let you get some sleep," he says. "I'll text you tomorrow. We can sort the details then."

I nod, not quite trusting my voice.

He opens my front door then pauses on the threshold, glancing back. The outside light catches his eyes, turning them to amber. "Goodnight, Ainsley."

I swallow. "Goodnight, Struan."

CHAPTER TWENTY-THREE

STRUAN

The Grays' house is exactly the kind of place people commission custom oak pieces for. High ceilings, ornate cornicing, a fireplace that deserves more than an off-the-shelf mantelpiece.

Da's set up by the bay window, the new mantel shelf laid across a pair of trestles. He's sanding the edges smooth while I work along the chimney breast with a tape measure and pencil, marking out fixing points and checking my levels so everything lines up when we're ready to mount the wood.

The radio crackles in the background, last night's rugby being picked apart by the presenters.

"Bloody defence was a shambles," Da mutters, not looking up.

"Mmm."

"And don't get me started on that try they disallowed. It was in, clear as day."

"Aye." I'm not really listening. My mind's elsewhere—specifically, on a certain dark-haired lass with green eyes and a smile she doesn't hand out to just anyone.

There's a buzz under my skin that won't settle. Excitement—

and aye, a bit of nerves. Not like me, but this isn't just any date. Ainsley made me work hard for it, and now that she's giving me a chance, I don't want to fuck it up.

I check the time on my phone. An hour to go.

Christ. Time's crawling today.

"Remember, I'll need to head off in a bit," I say. "I'll be back around three."

Da glances up. "What's this for again?"

"Dentist." I keep my voice casual. "Plus a few errands. The bank, that sort of stuff."

Lying doesn't come naturally to me. But Ainsley wants to keep things quiet for now, and I get it, especially after everything she went through with her ex. The last thing she needs is the Ardmara rumour mill cranking into life.

"I'll make up the time later."

Handy thing about working on an empty house when the owners are away on holiday: you can be flexible with the hours.

Da eyes me for a second longer then shrugs. "Fine. Just make sure you lock up and set the alarm when you're done tonight."

Mum would never have left it there—she'd have badgered me until I cracked. Da's different that way. He knows when to let something drop.

We fall back into comfortable silence. Just the steady rasp of sandpaper, the murmur of the radio, the scratch of pencil on plaster as I mark another fixing point.

My phone buzzes. I wipe my hands on my jeans and check the screen.

AINSLEY

This place you picked, is it nice or fancy nice?
Trying to decide what to wear

We're going for lunch at a sprawling hotel and golf estate called the Glen Garve Resort. It's near Bannock. I've driven past it umpteen times over the years on my way to Sophie's but I've never once been inside.

From the website the restaurant looks like the kind of place where everything's laid out just so and you're never quite sure which fork to use. I'm normally more pub lunches and Sunday roasts, but Ainsley's special. Deserves to be treated right.

Plus, it's far enough away from Ardmara that we shouldn't bump into anyone we know.

STRUAN

I'd say fancy nice. But don't feel you have to dress up. You'll look great whatever you wear

AINSLEY

Good answer, Mr Walker ☺

We've been messaging on and off all weekend. Started with me checking on her da—he's home now and mending well—then turned into date planning, followed by general nonsense that's had me grinning at my phone like an eejit.

STRUAN

I aim to please

AINSLEY

That's good to know

Christ. Is she flirting? That feels like flirting.

"You're in a good mood."

I look up to find Da watching me while he wipes down the mantel shelf to clear away the worst of the wood shavings.

"Ach." I slide the phone back into my pocket. "Just a bit of banter with the lads."

He hums but leaves it there and returns his attention to the task in hand.

"All right," I say a few minutes later, "I've marked everything up for fitting." I pick up a pair of cast-iron brackets the Grays found at a salvage yard—ornate curls and Victorian flourishes buried under decades of paint and rust. Once cleaned up, they'll look spot-on with the oak mantel shelf. "I'll sort these outside."

"Aye, fine. Goggles, Struan."

"Of course."

Outside, the mid-morning air is cool and sharp, noticeably colder than it was a week ago. Autumn making itself known.

I fit the wire-brush head to the drill, pull on my goggles, and brace a bracket against a pile of offcuts. I get to work, flecks of rust and old paint spitting into the air. Dirty, noisy, mindless. My hands keep moving but my thoughts slip elsewhere.

Right. I need to leave myself enough time to shower and make myself presentable. I even bought new clothes for today—a proper shirt, dark trousers, shoes rather than my usual work boots.

I picture Ainsley across the table from me. Relaxed and less guarded for once. That spark in her eyes when she teases me. And her laugh—the real one, not the polite one she uses out of habit.

Maybe, if the moment's right, I'll reach across the table and take her hand. Maybe I'll even—

A bird explodes out of the hedge beside me.

I jolt, just enough for the spinning wire brush to catch the loose strands of my hair.

A sharp *zzzip!* rips across my scalp.

CHAPTER TWENTY-FOUR

AINSLEY

My shower is, for once, blissfully unhurried.

No small fists banging on the bathroom door. No cries of "Mummy, I need a wee!" No clock ticking down the minutes until nursery drop-off. Just me, the steam, and the steady drum of hot water against my shoulders.

I tip my head back and let the spray rinse through my hair. Bliss.

Lily's at nursery. The salon's closed. I have an entire morning to luxuriate in getting ready—I'd almost forgotten what that felt like. I squeeze a generous dollop of conditioning mask into my palm and work it through from roots to ends, taking my time, actually *enjoying* the process for once.

Monday lunchtime might not be most people's choice for a first date, but it made the most sense with my schedule. And really, a daytime date is probably for the best.

Daylight feels safer than candlelight. Less chance of things slipping into something . . . more.

And by "more", I mean intimacy. Which is absolutely, categorically not on the cards today. This is strictly a no-nooky date—

a chance to get to know Struan better, in a civilised setting, with cutlery and conversation and zero risk of me losing my head.

Technically, nooky has already occurred. Well, sort of. In the form of me dry-humping him on his back step like a woman possessed.

But that was different. That was the weed, and the late hour, and his stupid sexy guitar playing, and the way the stars had looked scattered across the sky like someone had flung a handful of glitter at the universe. Today there'll be none of that. No twinkly-star aphrodisiac. No shared joint to blur the lines. This time, I will not get carried away.

I'm only just settling into my new life here. I can't risk getting swept up in something that burns too bright, too fast.

I lather the soap between my palms, working it into a rich foam.

The thing is, the human brain—especially mine—has a spectacular talent for sabotage. Because as I rub the suds along my arms and over my shoulders, my thoughts slide right back to that night on the steps. The way Struan's hands gripped me, steady and sure. The hardness of him beneath me. The slickness of my knickers inside my jeans as I moved on his lap, chasing something I hadn't meant to chase—

I drag the soap across my chest and hiss softly, startled by how sensitive I've become. The warmth of the water, the slick slide of my palms—it's far too easy to imagine hands other than my own.

"For fuck's sake," I mutter, and twist the dial hard.

The shock of cold water hits like a slap. I gasp, shoulders hunching, but I force myself to stay under the icy spray.

There will be none of that, Ainsley. No daydreams. No detours. And absolutely no nooky with Struan Walker.

Except my mind, apparently, is in a rebellious mood today.

Because now it's conjuring something far too vivid. Struan's van pulled over on some quiet stretch of road, the windows fogged, the whole vehicle rocking gently in time with—

Ding-dong.

My heart hammers. For one ridiculous second guilt shoots through me, as if the universe has just caught me in the act of thinking something indecent.

Who the hell is at my door?

I reach out the shower and grab my phone from the shelf. No messages. Struan isn't due for another forty minutes.

The doorbell chimes again.

"All right, all right," I mutter, hastily rinsing the last of the conditioning mask from my hair. I twist off the water, wrap my hair in a towel, and shrug into my robe, yanking the belt tight as I pad downstairs. My feet leave damp prints on the carpet.

I pull the front door open, and it's as if my stray thoughts have conjured him out of thin air.

Struan. In his work clothes. Wearing a baseball cap.

For a moment I can only stare. Then a gust of cold air sneaks through the doorway and brushes my bare legs, and I'm abruptly, mortifyingly aware that I'm naked beneath this robe. Nothing but terry cloth between me and the Scottish autumn. Oh, and Struan.

His gaze dips—briefly—to where my neckline gapes slightly, showing more cleavage than I'd like.

I tug the robe tighter. "Struan, you're early! *Really* early."

He has the decency to look contrite. "Aye, well, the thing is . . ." He rubs the back of his neck, sheepish in a way I haven't seen before. "Had a bit of an accident at work. And, er, I was wondering if you could help me."

My eyes do a quick scan, head to toe and back again. He's standing. He's upright. No visible blood.

"You're not hurt, are you?"

"Not exactly." A wry twist of his mouth. "Just my pride, maybe."

I frown, not following. And then he reaches up and pulls off the cap.

I inhale sharply. "Oh, dear God."

The man bun is gone. His hair—those gorgeous, tawny curls I've been trying very hard not to think about running my fingers through—is . . . well, *massacred* is the word that springs to mind. It's shorter at the crown by several inches, ragged in patches, with uneven tufts sticking out at angles that defy gravity.

"What happened?"

"Wire-brush drill head. I was buffing some old brackets and I caught my hair. Killed the power fast, but it snarled a chunk— well, more than just a chunk." He attempts a self-deprecating laugh that doesn't quite land. "Da tried to free it. Ended up cutting me loose with scissors."

"Struan Walker, you absolute *eejit*! You could've scalped yourself. Or lost an eye!"

"Aye, well." He gives a small shrug. "Lesson learnt. Sorry to interrupt you while you're getting ready, and I hate to ask, but . . . any chance you could give it a tidy before we head to the restaurant?"

The request shouldn't make me pause. I'm a hairdresser. Cutting hair is literally what I do. And yet, just like when his mum suggested I give him a trim at the salon opening, the idea of touching *his* hair feels oddly intimate.

He must catch my hesitation because he starts to ramble. "It's just, I've never been to the Glen Garve Resort before, but it's not the kind of place you wear a cap in. I don't want to turn up looking like I've been attacked by a strimmer, but if it's too much trouble—"

"Struan." I cut him off before he can spiral further. "Of course I can sort it."

So much for my indulgent getting-ready session. Hello, noble rescue mission.

"I always keep a pair of scissors at home," I add. "For cutting Lily's hair." And for when Mum springs one of her many "Can you just trim my fringe, dear?" moments on me.

His shoulders drop with relief. "You're a lifesaver."

"Don't thank me yet. I haven't seen the full extent of the damage."

"Fair point." He runs a hand through what's left of his curls, a gesture that would normally be casual and attractive but only highlights the chaos. "I don't want to get your place messy, so why don't we do it at mine? Does it need to be wet first?"

"Preferably."

"Right, then." He's already backing down the drive, that familiar easy energy returning now we've agreed a plan to deal with his hair. "I'll grab a quick shower and see you in ten?"

"Sounds good."

I close the door, my brain already—unhelpfully—conjuring images of him naked in the shower.

CHAPTER TWENTY-FIVE

AINSLEY

Ten minutes later, I'm standing on Struan's doorstep with my scissors case tucked under one arm, hair still damp and twisted into a clip.

Footsteps sound from inside, then the door opens.

He's fresh from the shower, wearing grey joggers and an old, well-worn T-shirt. Despite the fact his damp hair is settling into what can only be described as the world's worst mullet, he looks . . . good. Because apparently Struan Walker just can't help but look good.

His eyes skim over me, and there's warmth there. "Wow, Ainsley. You look lovely."

I scoff. "Hardly." My hair's half-dry, my face is bare, and my jeans-and-sweater combo is nothing special. "This isn't what I'm wearing later," I say, gesturing at my outfit. "Figured I'd keep my nice clothes for the restaurant—and spare them from being covered in your tawny locks."

"Fair." He glances down at himself. "Same idea here."

That's when I notice his bare feet—another unexpectedly distracting detail. Who knew feet could be attractive? When I drag my gaze back up, it catches—briefly, mortifyingly—on what grey joggers are famous for *not* hiding.

I yank my eyes to his face.

For God's sake, Ainsley.

"Come on in," he says, stepping back.

As I brush past him, I catch his scent—clean soap, a hint of aftershave, and something else. Warm. Earthy. Distinctly Struan.

The hall is the mirror image of my own, but where mine is still a work in progress, his feels settled. Calm, neutral walls. A few framed photos—mostly of Isla, one of the two of them together on a beach somewhere, wind whipping their matching curls. And mounted on the wall, a decorative guitar made from repurposed metal, all curves and copper patina. Art piece and personality statement in one.

"I meant what I said, you know. You really do look lovely."

I turn to him, and he nods at my forest-green sweater. "That colour suits you. It's the exact shade of your eyes."

Butterflies take flight in my stomach. I clear my throat. "Thank you. Er, are we doing the cut in the kitchen?"

"Aye, please."

I walk ahead, and I'm certain—*certain*—I can feel his eyes on me, a prickling awareness that trails up my spine. I resist the urge to look back.

The kitchen is bright and warm, sunlight spilling through the window and pooling across wooden worktops. I run my hand along the edge, admiring the grain, the smooth finish.

"These are gorgeous," I say. "You make them yourself?"

Struan nods. "Aye. Bit of timber from a job last year. Client changed their mind about it at the last minute, and I didn't want to see it go to waste." He pulls out a chair. "Here do?"

"Perfect. You got a towel? You know, to save your top."

He looks down. "This thing? It's as old as the hills. Honestly, don't worry. Go for it."

Even sitting, Struan is tall—so tall that the crown of his head reaches almost to my chin. I set my scissors case on the worktop, unzip it, and pull out my comb and clips. Then I slide my fingers into his hair, testing its weight and texture.

A spark shoots through me, and I'm not the only one. Struan *shivers* under my touch—actually shivers. And when he speaks, his voice comes out low and rough. "So . . . what's the verdict on the hair?"

Good idea. Focus on the practical.

"When I even it out, I'll need to take about three inches off in places." I comb through the damp strands, assessing the damage. "You'll still have more length than most guys—enough for the curls to sit properly—but it'll be a while before you can manage another man bun."

I sigh. Actually sigh. Out loud.

"You sound heartbroken," he teases.

"Maybe a little," I admit as I separate out a section and secure it with a clip. "It was growing on me. You, on the other hand, are taking the news well."

"Aye, well, figured it was doomed the second it happened." He shrugs, the movement shifting beneath my hands. "But hair grows, as they say."

"Just as well or I'd be out of a job."

He laughs, the sound deep and rich.

I start cutting, and for a while there's only the rhythmic *snip* of the scissors. Curls drift to the floor. In the faint reflection of the window, I catch him watching me, his gaze soft, thoughtful.

"You've got talent, you know," he says. "Transforming folk the way you do. I saw what you did for my mum's hair. Half of

Ardmara's walking around with better hairstyles thanks to you."

"Aye, well, you're one to talk." I trim another curl, evening out the layers, then gesture around the kitchen with my comb. "These worktops. The bench at the salon. You make the most beautiful things. *That's* talent."

"Ach." He ducks his head slightly, actually modest for once. "It's just wood and nails."

"Don't sell yourself short, Walker."

He doesn't respond, but in the window I spot the pleased curve of his mouth.

I step to the side, reaching for a clip I discarded earlier, and as I lean over—

My right boob betrays me. It doesn't just brush his cheek. It *whacks* across it. Full contact. Unmistakable.

"Oh my God, sorry!" I blurt, the words tumbling out far too fast as heat floods my face.

I never invade a client's space like that. Ever. It must be the chair. Or the angle. Or Struan Walker's fault for looking too damn attractive and completely distracting me.

Struan turns to me, his mouth already twisted into a wicked grin. "Don't worry about it. There are far worse ways to get hit in the face than by a boob."

His eyes dance with mischief. And then—because apparently he can't help himself—his gaze flicks down.

"Oi!" I swat him lightly on the shoulder. "Eyes and head facing the window." I cup his stubbled chin and turn him back to the front. "No moving when I've got scissors near your ear."

He chuckles, and then very unsubtly shifts in his seat. Oh, for the love of—

Do not look down, Ainsley.

I look down.

And holy hell, he's getting hard. Like, right now. In real time. I can literally see the front of his joggers lifting.

My breath stutters. Jesus Christ!

I force my eyes back to his hair, heart hammering. I mean, my boob *did* just whack him in the face. What man wouldn't react?

What *really* worries me is the delighted thrill that zings through me. Because I shouldn't be pleased by his reaction. Not at all.

Get it together, Ainsley. No nooky, remember? Focus!

I try. I really do. Except when I touch his hair again, there's a *twitch* down there. I can't *help* but notice it in my peripheral vision. And it draws my gaze like a bloody magnet.

Oh God. Those grey joggers really don't hide anything. He's got a full hard-on now, and I swear I can see the entire outline of it.

And Struan? He doesn't even try to hide it. He just sits there, perfectly calm, like erections are a normal part of kitchen haircuts. Doesn't cover himself or apologise.

The confidence of that does something low and wicked to my insides.

Focus, Ainsley. Distraction. Now.

"So," I say, my voice coming out slightly strangled, "tell me about this job. The one that nearly cost you your scalp."

He launches into it easily—a Victorian house, the oak mantelpiece he and his da were working on. I keep cutting, letting the rhythm of the scissors and the sound of his voice steady me.

After a while, out of the corner of my eye, I do a discreet dick-status check.

Thank Christ. Things seem to be settling down a little. Mission accomplished.

"This morning I was buffing these cast-iron brackets," he goes on. "Beautiful old things, covered in rust. That's what I was working on when the drill got a bit too friendly with my hair."

I wince, trimming another curl near his nape. For one insane moment, I want to lean down and press my lips to that spot—the vulnerable dip where his hairline meets golden skin.

"You were lucky, you know," I manage instead. "That could've gone much worse."

My fingers sweep through his newly evened hair. The worst of the accidental mullet is gone, leaving the shape clean and deliberate. And damn him, he was gorgeous with long hair, but the shorter cut is good on him too. Sharpens his jaw. Draws attention to the strong lines of his neck, the breadth of his shoulders.

"Usually I am careful, but I was daydreaming and a bird startled me."

"What were you daydreaming about?" I ask as I trim an errant lock.

"You."

My pulse stutters.

He turns to me, forcing me to stop cutting, and his eyes meet mine.

Then his gaze drifts lower, to my lips, which I can't seem to stop wetting. When his eyes lift again, the golden flecks in his irises are barely visible, his pupils dark and wide.

Dear God. That's a man who knows exactly what he wants.

The air hums between us, charged and waiting.

He doesn't move. Just watches me. Patient. Sure.

"Fuck it," I whisper.

I drop the scissors onto the worktop, and then my hands are in his hair, my mouth on his. Our lips fuse together and I melt into him, his hands anchoring me at the waist. Our mouths part and his tongue slides against mine—slick, teasing, tasting of mint and something so utterly *him* it's dizzying.

Last time I blamed the joint for how wild he made me feel. But this, right here—this is all Struan. No haze but the one he puts in my head.

And judging by the way his grip tightens—I mean *really* tightens—on my hips as he pulls me closer, he feels it too.

He kisses me harder, and then suddenly I'm lifted and shifted onto his lap. Not straddling him, just perched sideways like some 1950s pin-up. But his erection is insistent against my thigh, and my brain short-circuits at the feeling of him, hot and hard through those joggers.

I nip his lower lip between my teeth, and he groans—low in his throat, a sound that goes straight to my core. There's a deep ache building between my legs now, throbbing with every kiss.

I break away just long enough to shift, flinging one leg over so I'm straddling him properly, my centre settling against the thick, hot line of his cock. The contact is so good I whimper.

His hands find their way under my sweater—callused palms searing against my bare back—and I arch into him with a gasp. My fingers tangle in his new, shorter hair.

I start to move. Rocking gently against him. And he groans again, the sound so desperate I swear I could come just from hearing it.

So much for not getting carried away on the first date. We've not even made it to the date yet.

But the tide's got me now, pulling hard and certain, and I don't want to fight it.

He kisses me again. It's messy, hungry, all tongues and teeth and need.

Then suddenly he pulls back.

His lips are puffy and red. His chest rises fast beneath me. "How far do you want to take this?" He searches my face, earnest and raw. Then, gripping my arse in both hands, he drags me along the length of his cock—slow, devastating friction that hits me right where I need it. "Do you want to do what we did the other night? Or . . ."

"Or?" I rasp back, barely breathing.

He kisses along my neck, nuzzling the skin just below my ear before inhaling deeply. "Or do you want to go further?"

I told myself I wouldn't do this. Not today. I told myself today was about getting to know him better. About conversation and keeping things sensible.

But sensible flew out the window the moment my boob hit his face.

"Further," I gasp. And then, just so there's no room for confusion: "I want our clothes off this time."

His nostrils flare. And then he stands, lifting me with him like it's the easiest thing he's done all week. My legs wrap around his waist automatically.

He walks us out of the kitchen, his erection still snug against me, right where I'm throbbing.

"Where are we going?" I manage, breathless, already half-drunk on anticipation.

"My bedroom." He kisses me hard enough to steal what little remains of my composure. "I've fantasised about you naked in my bed since the day I met you. And now it's fucking happening."

Oh God. A shiver rips down my spine. This side of Struan—demanding, hungry—is new.

And I like it.

He carries me up the stairs, alternating between kissing me and nuzzling my neck, murmuring things against my skin that I can't quite catch but feel everywhere. Every upward step grinds his cock against me—thick, perfect pressure that makes me moan into his mouth.

I can feel myself getting wetter with every step. If we make it to the bedroom without me spontaneously orgasming, it'll be a miracle.

Somehow, I manage it.

By the time we reach his room, I'm vibrating with want. Struan lowers me onto the bed with surprising care, as though I'm made of something breakable. Then he straightens, looking down at me with dark eyes and dark intent, raw and almost worshipful emotion flickering there.

I return the favour by drinking him in. The way he stands over me, broad and golden in the late-morning light, hair damp and curling softly at his temples, those battered grey joggers hanging low on lean hips, his erection straining against the fabric like it's seconds from ripping through.

Jesus Christ.

I want more. Desperately.

"Off," I say, tugging at the hem of his ancient T-shirt with both hands.

Struan chuckles and peels it off in one fluid motion, tossing it behind him without looking.

My mouth waters. No exaggeration.

Aye, I've seen his chest before—that time in the courtyard behind the salon. But now I get to *stare*. As much as I want.

It's a perfect landscape: broad shoulders tapering to a narrow waist, muscles carved by years of honest work. A dusting of golden hair across his chest. A wave tattoo curling around his bicep.

My fingers can't help themselves. Sitting up on the bed, I

reach out and trace the line between his pecs, then drag my nails lightly through his soft hair.

He sucks in a sharp breath, eyes dropping to where my hand roams shamelessly over him.

"You know," he murmurs, voice rougher than sandpaper, "the way you touched me earlier—when you were cutting my hair—nearly did me in." He leans down until our eyes are level, his eyes molten gold. "You standing behind me all bossy and focused . . . Christ, Ainsley."

Heat flushes my cheeks—and lower too—but I can't stop smiling like an idiot. Never, and I mean *never*, in my life have I felt so wanted by a man.

His gaze drops pointedly to my sweater, and he traces a finger along the hem where it meets my jeans. "As lovely as you look in that, I wouldn't mind seeing it come off now." His eyes flick back up to mine. A question and desire all at once.

I gulp, nerves kicking in hard. Because I'm wearing my sensible bra—nude, practical, the kind you wear when you're absolutely not expecting anyone to see it. Not exactly the lacy, enticing number I might have chosen if I'd known this morning would end with me in Struan Walker's bedroom.

But the way he's looking at me . . . like I'm already the most beautiful thing he's ever seen . . .

I tilt my chin, toss my hair back, and draw my arms across my body, slipping free of my sweater.

The air hits my skin. Goosebumps race across every inch of me—not just from the chill, but from the way he looks at me. His eyes track over my bra like it's the sexiest thing he's ever seen.

Before I can lose my nerve, I reach behind me, unhook the clasp, and toss it aside.

He *stares*. Like boobs haven't existed until this moment. Like mine are some kind of miracle he wasn't expecting.

And then, grinning wickedly, he addresses them. "Well, now. Aren't you two bonny as anything?"

I laugh—a wild, reckless sound—but it dies in my throat when he reaches out and traces his knuckles over one peaked nipple. A barely-there touch that steals the laughter right out of me.

Then his head dips, and his mouth closes over the other nipple—heat and hunger in every slow pull—while his big hand cradles and palms the first. Pleasure sparks through every nerve ending as his tongue circles and sucks, his scruff dragging deliciously across my sensitive skin.

I catch sight of us in the mirror across from his bed: Struan suckling my breast like a starving man, my hands tangled in his hair, my own expression utterly undone and desperate for more.

Dear God. This was *not* part of my plan for today. But nothing could drag me away from him now.

He guides me back down onto the bed and leans over me, moving to my other breast, lavishing it with the same slow, reverent attention—his tongue swirling, lips teasing, stubble scraping in a way that makes me shiver. At the same time, he raises his knee between my legs, and—*oh!*—the pressure sends a jolt of pleasure straight through me.

I grind against his knee. Shamelessly. My jeans are still on, but it hardly matters. My whole body is tuned to him, and between my legs I'm throbbing, achy and desperate.

Struan finally lets my nipple go with a soft *pop* and glances down at my denim-clad hips. "Would you like me to eat you out, Ainsley?"

His crude words, said in that low, raspy voice, are enough to make my toes curl.

I nod desperately, not even pretending to play it cool. "Yes, please."

He grins wickedly. "So polite, Miss Reid."

He shifts me further up the bed and kneels between my legs, hands working at the button of my jeans. I brace myself on my elbows, watching his fingers, deft and sure, as he pops the button and drags down the zip.

I lift my hips to help him slide my jeans—and then my knickers—down and off.

Suddenly I'm completely naked, with Struan Walker kneeling between my thighs and looking at me like I'm the answer to every question he's ever had about happiness.

Vulnerability crashes over me. I'm *exposed*. The light is unforgiving and there's nowhere to hide.

But then Struan glances up at me, and his expression shifts. Softens.

"You're lovely," he says. "And I'm crazy about you. But if you want to slow down or even stop, that's more than okay."

That tenderness—the total lack of pressure—is what makes me certain about this.

"No," I say firmly. "I want this."

Something flares in his eyes. He kisses my mouth, hungry but somehow still gentle, and then trails kisses down my body. Over my ribs. Across my stomach. And lower still.

When he settles between my thighs again, he looks up at me—face haloed by those tawny curls, eyes full of absolute mischief—and I feel more naked than ever. "Do you always wax it all away?"

Heat rushes to my cheeks. And literally everywhere else. "Aye . . . usually."

"Mmm." He turns back to look at me—at *all* of me—and spreads me open with two callused fingers.

"I can see everything." There's a reverent gravel in his voice. "You're so pink, and so fucking wet. Is this really all for me, Ainsley?"

I make a sound. Something between a whimper and a moan that just about passes for *yes*.

The first brush of his tongue is slow and deliberate—a long lick up through slick folds that has me gasping out loud. He moans into me like I'm the best thing he's tasted all year.

And then he does it again. And again. Each pass firmer than the last until I'm trembling beneath him.

He takes his time exploring every inch, sucking gently on my clit until stars spark behind my eyelids, then flattening his tongue wide before flicking just right, exactly how I need it. Goosebumps pebble across my skin. Pleasure builds tight as a fist inside me.

Struan pauses sometimes just to murmur things against me: "God, you taste incredible . . . so sweet . . . could stay here forever licking your perfect wee cunt."

Each filthy compliment only makes things worse—by which I mean better, of course.

I'm shameless, hips tilting up for more as his stubble scorches delicate skin. My fingers find his hair—those newly shortened curls—and grip hard.

Then a finger slides inside me. A thick press that has me keening. And soon another joins it while his mouth works over my clit. He thrusts them slow at first, then harder, reading my every shiver and gasp.

I realise with delirious clarity that, as he devours me, he's grinding into the mattress beneath us, desperate for friction against his cock. Somehow that knowledge pushes me right to the edge.

"Struan—" I gasp, my voice breaking. "I'm going to—"

"Aye," he growls against me, the vibration making me shudder. "Come for me, Ainsley. Let me feel it."

His fingers curl inside me, hitting a spot that makes my vision blur, while his tongue flicks fast and relentless over my clit.

And then . . . and then . . .

CHAPTER TWENTY-SIX

STRUAN

Never when I woke up this morning did I picture my day turning out like this.

Me, flat on my stomach between Ainsley Reid's thighs, two fingers buried inside her while my tongue works her clit like it's the only thing I was put on this earth to do. She's so hot and tight around me, and Christ, she tastes unreal—salt and sweetness and something uniquely *her* that I already know I'll be thinking about for weeks.

I've imagined this. God, have I imagined it—hand wrapped round my cock in the shower, or lying in bed after a restless night, picturing her legs thrown over my shoulders, her breathy moans.

But the reality? No dirty daydream I've ever had comes close to having her here, writhing beneath me, her thighs trembling against my ears, every sound she makes wrecking me from the inside out.

My cock is so hard it's almost painful. Every pulse of her pleasure has me grinding down into the mattress, and I don't care how pathetic that probably looks. Not when she's making *those* sounds.

"Struan—" Her voice breaks. "I'm going to—"

"Aye. Come for me, Ainsley. Let me feel it."

I curl my fingers up, finding that perfect spot inside her, and her body clamps down around me in hard, frantic waves. She lets out this wild, broken cry—pure need and pleasure—and it goes straight to my cock like a live wire. Jesus, I'm leaking pre-cum into my boxers like it's my first time with a woman.

If this is what it's like making Ainsley Reid fall apart, I never want to stop.

She finally collapses back onto the bed, utterly spent. Flushed cheeks. Messy hair. Bare skin glowing. A beautiful disaster, and she's in my bed.

For a second, I wonder if that's it. If we're done. Because she looks properly wrecked, and maybe I should be a gentleman about this. Lie here with her in my arms and count myself lucky.

But Christ, I'm greedy. All I can think about is having more of her.

Then Ainsley lifts her head just enough to find me between her legs. Her green eyes are hooded, dark with heat, and she crooks a finger at me—the universal sign for *come here*.

I crawl up the bed towards her, and before I can settle beside her, she's pushing me—none too gently—onto my back.

"Let's get these off, Mr Walker," she murmurs, fingers hooking into my waistband.

She makes quick work of my joggers, dragging them down over my hips with a determined wee tug. My boxers are all that's left—straining, barely holding me back. When her palm skims over the bulge in them, I suck in a sharp breath through my teeth. Bloody hell.

Then she pulls my boxers down too, and my cock springs free—eager, shameless, ready for whatever she wants to do with it.

She studies me for a moment, head tilted, and I've no idea what she's thinking.

Then she smiles. And it hits me right in the gut.

"My turn now," she says.

Three words. Just three wee words, and somehow they make me harder.

She wraps one small hand around my cock and pumps slowly—once, twice—her thumb swiping over the head to spread the pre-cum down the shaft. My hips jerk before I can stop them, and I let out a groan that sounds embarrassingly desperate even to my own ears.

Then she shifts lower . . . and takes me into her mouth.

Hot. Wet. Perfect.

Every rational thought leaves my body in a rush. Releasing me with a *pop*, she licks up one side, then down the other, then she swirls that devilish tongue right under the head before sinking down onto me again, slow enough to make my eyes roll back in my skull.

"Fuck . . . Ainsley . . ."

My hands clench uselessly at the sheets. Every muscle in my abdomen draws tight as a bowstring. She hums—a smug little sound that vibrates through every inch of me—and starts bobbing up and down in a rhythm that's both torturous and brilliant.

Her hand works what she can't fit in her mouth. When she looks up at me from under those lashes, it's nearly game over. Then her other hand cups my balls with this careful, perfect pressure that makes my vision blur.

Christ. I'm not going to last.

Here's the thing: I'm not usually the type to worry about stamina. I've had plenty of practice over the years, and I know how to pace myself, how to hold back, how to make sure the woman I'm with has a good time before I let go.

But with Ainsley? All that hard-won control is crumbling like wet sand.

Just when I think I'll lose it far too soon, she pulls off and wipes her mouth with the back of one hand. A wicked smile curves those kiss-swollen lips.

"Condom?" she asks, sure of herself in a way that makes every nerve ending in my body stand at attention.

"Aye—in there." I gesture towards the bedside table while trying not to combust entirely from anticipation.

She pulls open the drawer, finds one, and tears the packet open, her eyes fixed on mine. It shouldn't be as hot as it is, but apparently everything Ainsley does is hot now.

She rolls the condom down my cock with fingers that linger just long enough to drive me mad. And then she climbs astride me—gorgeous hair spilling everywhere, tits heaving above me—and wraps her fingers around me, guiding me to her entrance.

The first slide is heaven.

Hot. Tight. Perfect.

I groan as she sinks down onto me, inch by inch, until our hips are flush and I'm buried so deep inside her I swear I can feel her heartbeat.

For a second, neither of us moves. The moment's too big for anything but breathing each other in.

Then Ainsley leans forwards so we're chest to chest, and she starts moving in slow circles that nearly end me.

She sets the rhythm. Takes what she wants at the pace she likes. All I can do is hold on to those lush hips for dear life while trying not to embarrass myself.

Her hair brushes across my cheek with every thrust forwards.

When our eyes meet, it's electric—all want and wonder and something else I'm not ready to name.

She rides me harder. Faster. Little gasps spilling from her lips. My hands grip tighter at her waist, and when I roll my hips up to meet hers, we both cry out together in a tangled mess of pleasure.

I've had good sex before. Course I have. But nothing's ever hit like this. I don't know what's different about her, but whatever it is, I'm hooked.

It builds fast between us: fire licking low in my belly until there's nothing left but white-hot need.

"Ainsley," I groan—a warning maybe, or just a plea—but she only leans down so our foreheads touch, staring right into me as heat surges up my spine.

My balls tighten. That sharp, impossible pressure building—

"Ainsley—"

And then I'm gone.

Coming hard, hips jerking up into her as she clenches around me, pulling every last drop from me. She cries out too, her whole body tightening, trembling, her pussy spasming around me, milking me through it until we're both shaking, breath punched out of us in broken, desperate gasps.

When at last it ebbs, she collapses against my chest, and we just lie there. Clinging to each other. Panting.

The house is quiet. The bed's warm. And Ainsley's soft and sated in my arms.

I could stay like this forever.

◆ ◆ ◆

We're a glorious tangle of limbs when Ainsley finally lifts her head from my chest. She squints at the clock on the wall, then lets out a groan.

"Shit, Struan. We're going to miss our lunch booking."

For a solid five seconds, I just stare at her in confusion.

Lunch? Right. Plans. That thing people do when they aren't too busy losing every brain cell to the woman beside them.

Honestly, after what just happened, I barely remember my own name. I completely forgot we were supposed to be at the Glen Garve Resort approximately—I glance at the clock—five minutes ago.

"Ah." I make an apologetic face. "We've already missed it. We're due there right now, and it's a bit of a drive. Plus, we're completely naked."

She rolls off me and I immediately miss her warmth. "I hope you're planning to call and grovel," she says, arching a brow, "and not just leave them hanging."

"Aye, course. Maybe I should ask if we can reschedule for next week?"

She narrows her eyes in mock suspicion. "Is this your way of locking in a second date?"

"Might be," I say, all casual-like.

"Well, then." A little smirk plays at her lips. "Yes to another date . . . but only if you go phone them now." She nudges me with her foot under the covers like she's shooing out an unruly dog, but there's this secret delight in her eyes.

I grin wickedly as I swing my legs out of bed and stand, noticing how her gaze drops—very blatantly—to my cock. Soft now, aye, but she's looking at it like she's replaying exactly what we just did. A tiny, satisfied smile tugs at her mouth.

Christ, I could die happy right now.

"You think they'll accept 'Sorry, I was shagging the hot single mum next door' as an excuse?" I ask, stretching my arms above my head.

She snorts then reaches over and slaps my bare arse. "Just hurry up and go!"

I'm halfway to the door when she adds, low and teasing, "And Struan? When you get back, if you fancy it, maybe we could go another round?"

I turn to look at her. She's propped up on one elbow, the sheets pooled at her waist, hair a wild tangle, looking like every fantasy I've ever had made flesh.

Jesus Christ.

If that isn't motivation to sprint stark-bollock naked downstairs to grab my phone, I don't know what is.

CHAPTER TWENTY-SEVEN

AINSLEY

I give Struan's bare arse a satisfying slap. "Just hurry up and go!"

He grins at me then heads for the bedroom door. The muscles in his back shift as he walks. The arse I just smacked flexes with each step like it's putting on a show just for me.

"And Struan?" I call after him. "When you get back, if you fancy it, maybe we could go another round?"

He looks back at me, his grin full of promise.

Then he's gone, footsteps thudding down the stairs.

I flop back against the pillows with a sigh, staring at the ceiling. My body's still humming, warm and loose and thoroughly satisfied. The sheets smell like him. Like *us*.

So much for taking things slow. Still, I can't bring myself to regret it.

I close my eyes, letting myself sink into this feeling—this rare, perfect contentment—while I wait for him to come back.

Downstairs the front door opens.

Then—a shriek.

"Struan!" A woman's voice, high and startled. "What are you

doing here? Your da said you were at the dentist! And why are you *naked*?"

I sit bolt upright.

"Sorry for being naked in my own house, Mum!" Struan retorts. "What are *you* doing here, more to the point? And, er . . . hello, Mrs Reid."

Mrs Reid.

The words hit me like a bucket of ice water. *Mum.*

No. No, no, no, no, no.

I'm out of the bed before my brain catches up, scrambling for my clothes like the house is on fire. My sweater's inside out. My jeans are a crumpled, tangled mess on the floor. I grab them, shove one foot in, hop on the other, nearly crash into the wardrobe, and catch myself on Struan's chest of drawers.

"Fuck," I whisper. "Fuck, fuck, fuck, fuck, *fuck*."

Downstairs the conversation continues with horrifying clarity.

"Pauline and I were chatting away at knitting club just now," Helen explains, her tone cheerful despite the circumstances. "I was asking her about the new place she's moved into, and she said it's lovely but the kitchen's a bit dated—she'd like to do it up at some point. So, naturally, I told her how brilliant you and your da are at jobs like that, and how gorgeous your own kitchen turned out. Then I said, actually, I've got a key to Struan's place, why don't we pop in so you can see it for yourself? I was sure you wouldn't mind."

"Aye, well, normally I wouldn't have minded at all," Struan says, "but as you can see—"

"Yes, yes." My mother's voice. And she sounds—God help me—*amused*. "It's not the best time. I'll see the kitchen another day." A pause. "Still, someone's been eating their porridge, eh?"

I freeze, one arm halfway through my sweater.

Is my mother—is she *admiring* Struan while he stands down there starkers?

I'm going to die. Right here, in Struan Walker's bedroom, tangled in my own clothes, I am going to die of mortification.

"You know what, Helen?" Mum continues brightly. "I've got a key for my daughter's place next door. Why don't we grab a cuppa through there?"

A flicker of relief cuts through the panic. They're leaving. Thank God, they're leaving.

"Good idea," Helen agrees. "But hang on, Struan, your *hair*! Oh, I love the new look!"

"*Mum!*" Struan's voice pitches higher. "I'm standing here completely naked, cupping my bits. Maybe don't look too closely, eh? You can admire my haircut another time."

Despite everything—despite the absolute catastrophe unfolding below me—a grin tugs at my lips. I can picture it perfectly: Struan with his hands strategically placed and these two women carrying on a conversation with him like this is all perfectly ordinary.

Focus, Ainsley. This is not funny.

Well . . . maybe it's a wee bit funny.

I pull my sweater the rest of the way on and start hunting for my bra.

"Actually, you know what," Mum says, "maybe I should give Ainsley a quick call before barging into her place. Give me a moment . . ."

My blood turns to ice.

And then, from my back pocket, a quacking sound erupts. The ringtone Lily picked for me because she thought it was hilarious.

Quack quack quack quack quack—

I yank the phone out and jab at the screen to quiet it.

Silence.

Then, Mum's voice: "Ainsley? Are you . . . upstairs?"

I stand frozen, phone clutched in my hand, heart hammering so hard I can feel it in my throat.

Think. Think, think, think.

But I've got nothing. No escape route. No clever excuse. I'm standing in my neighbour's bedroom with sex-mussed hair and my bra still missing, and my mother is downstairs with his mother, and they both know exactly what's been happening. There's no way they can't. Struan's naked—it's a bit of a giveaway.

Slowly, like a condemned woman walking to the gallows, I step out onto the landing and peer down the stairs.

There's Struan, stark naked, hands cupped in front of himself. And there, beside him, are Helen and my mum, both looking up at me with expressions of pure, undisguised glee.

"Er . . ." My voice comes out strangled. "Hi, Mum. Hi, Helen."

The mums exchange a look—one of those loaded looks that says more than a whole afternoon's gossip.

"Well!" Helen clasps her hands together. "We'll . . . leave you to it."

"Aye," Mum agrees. "We'll pop to the Lighthouse Café for a cuppa instead. Give you two some space."

"Right." Struan clears his throat. "Just . . . maybe keep this to yourselves, aye? It's early days and—"

"Of course, of course," Helen says, waving a hand. "Not a word."

"Lips sealed," Mum adds, miming a zip across her mouth.

They leave, pulling the door shut behind them with a decisive click. And then—because apparently they think a wooden door is soundproof—their voices drift back, clear as anything.

"Looks like we won't need to play matchmaker after all!" Helen exclaims.

"I *knew* there was something brewing between them," Mum replies. "Did you see her face? Flushed as anything—"

Their voices fade as they move away.

Struan turns and looks up at me, an amused smile playing at his lips. Like this is *funny*. Like our mothers didn't just catch us post-sex. Like the entire situation isn't an absolute nightmare.

"Well," he says, "that was—"

"Oh God. Oh God, oh God, oh God."

His smile falters. "Hey, what's wrong?"

My skin is cooling now, and as the mortification of being discovered by our mums fades, reality creeps in.

This isn't just between us anymore.

Struan starts up the stairs towards me, no longer bothering to cover himself, far too at ease for a man whose mother was here moments ago. Normally, I'd find the view—and the *movement*—distracting, but panic claws at my chest, shame burning through every nerve.

When he reaches me, he pulls me into a hug, wrapping those strong arms around me and pressing me against his bare chest.

No, no, no, no. Our mums know, and that means—

Skin. Heat. So much of him, everywhere, when what I need is space to breathe.

I stand rigid in his arms, my heart hammering against his ribs. Can he feel it? Can he feel how fast I'm spiralling?

"Hey," he murmurs into my hair. "It's okay. What's wrong?"

"Could you . . . put some clothes on?" The words come out sharp.

He pulls back, eyebrows lifting. "Oh. Shit, sorry. Of course."

He strolls into the bedroom, grabs his boxers from the floor, and pulls them on. He gives himself a quick absent-minded tug, like he's making sure everything's sitting right, then turns back to me with an easy smile.

"What's up? It's just our mums. Bit embarrassing, aye, but—"

"Just our mums?" I can hear my voice climbing. "Struan, they *saw* us. They know."

"Aye, but . . ." He shrugs, still looking faintly bemused. "So what? They're our mums. They're hardly going to judge us for—"

"Our mums love nothing better than gossiping at knitting club. You do realise that, right?" I'm pacing now, my hands twisting together. "How long do you think it'll be before they let slip? I mean, what do you think they're going to discuss at the Lighthouse Café? And their voices—God, their voices aren't exactly *quiet*. I wouldn't be surprised if word's spreading through the whole town in the next half hour."

"Ainsley." He steps towards me, reaching out. "Come on, you're overthinking this—"

"Don't." I jerk back before he can touch me. "Just . . . don't."

He stops, confusion creasing his features. "I don't understand. Why is this such a big deal?"

Why is this such a big deal?

The question lands like a slap.

He doesn't get it. Then again, he didn't live through those weeks after everything with Danny came out—the whispers in the corner shop, the pitying glances at nursery drop-off, the way conversations stopped the moment I showed up anywhere. Struan didn't feel the weight of an entire village knowing your deepest humiliation, picking over the bones of your failed relationship like it was entertainment.

I wanted things to be different here. Slow. Private. *Controlled.* I wanted to be the one who decided when and how and who knew what.

And now that's gone. Ripped away before we've even had our first date.

"I wanted . . ." My voice cracks. I swallow hard and try again. "I wanted to take things slowly. To have time to figure out what this is before everyone else got involved. To have some *control* over—"

"Hey." He reaches for me again, and this time his hands find my shoulders. Even through my sweater, his palms are warm. "Ainsley, it's going to be fine. I'll talk to Mum, make sure she keeps quiet—"

"You heard them!" I pull away, and something in his expression flickers—hurt, maybe, or confusion. "I bet they're already out there gossiping. And even if they *try* to keep quiet, it's bound to slip out."

"Then . . . so what?" He spreads his hands, genuinely baffled. "We're two single adults. We've not done anything wrong."

He really, truly doesn't get it. And maybe that's not his fault. But right now, standing here with my pulse racing and my chest tight, I can't explain it. Can't find the words to make him see.

All I know is that I need to get out. I need space. I need to *think.*

"I have to go."

"What? Ainsley, wait—"

But I'm already moving, hurrying down the stairs then out the front door and into the bright, unforgiving daylight.

The air hits my face, cool and sharp. I gulp it down but it doesn't help. My chest won't loosen, my thoughts keep spiralling.

I just want to be home. In my own space. Where I can close the door and shut out the world and try to make sense of this mess.

But my home is *right there*—literally next door, a low hedge away from Struan's. That's not far enough.

I go inside only to grab my car keys then head out again and into my car.

"Ainsley!" Struan's voice. I see him emerging from his doorway, joggers and T-shirt now on. He raises a hand to stop me. "Ainsley, wait! Can we just talk about—"

I turn the key in the ignition. The engine coughs to life.

"Ainsley!"

I pull away, not looking back, not slowing down, just driving.

I don't know where I'm going.

I just know I can't stay.

CHAPTER TWENTY-EIGHT

STRUAN

The phone rings out. Again.

I stare at the screen like it's personally betrayed me, then hit redial.

Pick up. Come on, Ainsley. Just pick up.

Nothing.

I'm pacing the length of my living room, phone pressed to my ear, listening to the hollow drone of the ringtone. Four rings. Five. Then her voicemail kicks in. "You've reached Ainsley Reid. Leave a message."

Beep.

"Ainsley, it's me. Struan." I drag a hand through my hair—my newly short hair—and try to sound calm. Reassuring. "Please come back. Or at least let me know you're okay, aye? I just . . . I want to know you're all right."

I hang up and collapse onto the sofa.

Immediately my leg starts bouncing. Nope. Sitting still isn't happening. Not right now.

I stand again. Need to keep busy. Need to do something. Anything.

The kitchen. Right. There's still hair all over the floor.

I head through, grab the dustpan, and sweep up the clippings. It doesn't take long—a minute, maybe two—and then I'm back to having absolutely nothing to do to occupy myself.

Hmm . . . the kettle. Tea. Don't really fancy one, but it'll keep my hands busy for a few moments.

I fill the kettle and click it on, then lean against the worktop and stare at my phone, willing it to light up.

It does.

My heart lurches—for a second. But it's not Ainsley's name on the screen.

I stare at the message. At that bloody winking emoji. At the way she's written "ANYTHING" in capitals like she deserves a medal for basic discretion.

Shit.

The way she says it—so pleased with herself—tells me everything I need to know. She's *dying* to tell someone.

Ainsley was right. Our mums aren't going to be able to keep this to themselves.

No wonder Ainsley panicked. After what she went through with her ex, of course she's more sensitive to tongues wagging. I should have realised that. *Idiot.*

The kettle clicks off. I pour water over a teabag and watch the colour bleed into the mug.

Of all the days our mothers could have picked to pop round for an impromptu kitchen viewing. Seriously, just my fucking luck.

I ditch the teabag, add milk, stir, then leave the mug on the worktop and go back to pacing again. Not in the mood for it.

It's long gone cold when my phone pings again.

I read it twice. Three times.

Space.

I want to call her. Want to text back something that'll fix this, make it right. But that's the opposite of what she's asking for.

I set the phone down carefully.

It's fine, I tell myself. *She just needs time. It's fine.*

Except it isn't fine.

◆   ◆   ◆

When I walk into the Grays' living room, Da glances up from checking a spirit level.

"Hair looks much better," he says. "More practical having it short anyway. Less likely to end up in a drill."

"Aye."

"Did you manage to get to the dentist? And do your other errands?"

"What?" I blink at him. "Oh. Aye, yes."

I'm about to get stuck back in when Da hums then says, "You know I'm not one to gossip, lad, but your mum's already told me about finding you and Ainsley together."

I go very still.

She promised not to tell anyone. It's been less than an hour. Less. Than. An. Hour.

"Did she now?"

"Mm-hmm." Da's tone is casual as you like. "Seemed quite pleased about it."

Shaking my head, I step out into the hall, pull out my phone, and call Mum.

She answers on the second ring, voice bright and cheerful. "Hello, love! How's your afternoon going? Pauline and I were just saying—"

"Mum." I cut her off. "Ainsley's gone."

"Gone? What do you mean, gone?"

"I mean, she drove off. Because she was upset. About you walking in on us."

"Oh." The cheer drains from her voice. "Oh dear. I didn't realise she'd—I mean, we left right away, gave you both your privacy—"

"Mum, you promised not to tell anyone."

"What? I didn't—"

"You told Da."

A pause. Then: "Well, I had to tell your *father*, Struan. He's your father!"

I pinch the bridge of my nose. "Mum—"

"I haven't breathed a word to another soul. I promise."

I sigh. "Okay. Well, please don't. Ainsley's private. She doesn't want the whole town knowing her business."

"Of course, love. My lips are sealed."

We say our goodbyes, and I hang up.

◆ ◆ ◆

I stay late at the Grays' to make up for the hours I missed earlier, so it's dark by the time I get home.

Ainsley's back. Her car is in her drive, and lights glow warm behind her curtains.

I sit in the van for a wee while, keys in hand, staring at those lit windows. Part of me wants to march over there, knock on her door, and . . . what? Apologise? Explain? Kiss her until she forgets why she was upset in the first place?

Space, I remind myself. *She asked for space.*

So instead I head inside. The house greets me with silence.

I make myself pasta with pesto—easy, mindless, something I can do on autopilot while my brain churns through everything else.

Memories from earlier keep replaying in my head. Not the sex—though, Christ, that was incredible—but everything after. The way Ainsley looked at me when we were tangled together in my sheets, soft and open in a way I hadn't seen before. Like she was finally letting me in.

Then our mums appeared, and all of that vanished. Shutters slamming down. Walls going back up.

Fuck.

I swear I've never wanted anyone the way I want her, and she's just on the other side of the wall. But I can't go to her.

The pasta tastes like cardboard. I eat it anyway.

Then, through the wall, muffled but unmistakable: Lily crying. No, not just crying, proper wailing. A full-throated tantrum.

I hesitate.

She asked for space, the sensible part of my brain reminds me.

But the crying continues—escalates, in fact—punctuated by thumps and snippets of Ainsley's voice, strained and pleading.

Before I can talk myself out of it, I'm out my front door and approaching hers. At it, though, I hesitate again. Is this a terrible idea?

I push aside my doubts and knock.

After a short wait Ainsley answers, looking like she's been through a war. Hair dishevelled. Cheeks flushed. Eyes glassy with exhaustion. Lily's sobs spill from the living room.

"Struan." She blinks. "What are you—"

"I heard Lily." I keep my voice gentle. "Thought maybe you could use a hand."

Something crosses her face, too fast to read. "I'm fine. And I don't need help with my own daughter."

"I wasn't saying you did, I just—"

"I told you I needed space, Struan. I couldn't have been any clearer." She takes a deep breath in, and then out. "Goodnight."

She doesn't slam the door. Just closes it on me, gently but firmly.

◆ ◆ ◆

Back in my own house, the silence presses in from all sides.

I wash my pasta bowl. Wipe down the worktops. Tidy things that don't need tidying. Anything to keep my hands busy while my head refuses to quiet down.

When my phone rings, it's Sophie's name that flashes on the screen.

"Hey, Soph."

"Hi, Struan. So, I'm looking ahead to the October holidays— wanting to get Isla booked into a few activities to keep her busy. There's this company called Bannock Adventures that runs a Paddle 'n' Play course. A few of her friends are doing it, and I thought she'd love it. What do you think? She'd get to try paddle-boarding and—"

"Water sports?" I say. "Really, Soph? Don't you think you're stepping on my toes a bit?"

I mean, for fuck's sake, *I'm* the surfer.

Silence on the other end. When Sophie speaks again, her tone is careful, measured. "Oh. Well, honestly, Struan, I thought you'd be pleased at the idea of Isla getting out on the water. I wasn't meaning to start an argument. The course is run by these two guys called Ally and Aidan. I think you'd get on well with them. They're your kind of people."

"They sound like prats."

The words are out before I can stop them, petty and ridiculous and based on absolutely nothing except two alliterative names.

A long pause. "Really, Struan? *They sound like prats?* What's with you tonight?"

She's right. I'm being a complete arse and I know it. But the frustration's been building all day with nowhere to go, and Sophie's getting the brunt of it.

I should stop. I really should. But I don't.

"Last weekend I got a day less with my daughter because you wanted to organise a sleepover for her, and now you want two random men to teach her how to get on a board instead of me. Can't you see how that might tick me off a bit?"

"The sleepover?" Sophie's voice rises with disbelief. "This is about the *sleepover*? Struan, *you* were the one who didn't want Isla missing out on things! That's why we *agreed* she'd have her own sleepover at my place."

I take a long breath. Let it out slowly.

"Shit, Soph. I'm sorry. You're right. I'm being a dick."

And here's the thing about Sophie—instead of agreeing, instead of telling me exactly where I can shove my bad attitude, she says, "What's wrong, Struan?"

Christ. That's almost worse.

"It's . . . nothing."

"It's clearly not nothing."

Aye, it's the woman next door. But Sophie and I don't discuss my relationships—mainly because they tend to be pretty casual—and besides, the whole reason Ainsley got upset was because our mums found out. I'm hardly going to go spreading the news further.

"You're right, it's not nothing, but I can't talk about it. Not yet. It hasn't got anything to do with the sleepover or the paddleboarding anyway. The paddleboarding sounds great. Sign Isla up, please. I'll transfer you the money. And I'm sorry for being a dick."

"You're worrying me, Struan. This isn't like you."

Jesus. I snap at her, and her response is concern? I really don't deserve this woman as my co-parent.

I force a laugh. "Please don't worry. I'm fine. You just caught me at a bad time, that's all. And again, I'm sorry. I shouldn't have spoken to you like that."

"Hmm." She isn't convinced. "Do I need to phone your mum and da? Ask them to check in on you?"

"What? No, *please* don't do that. That'd be too embarrassing. Honestly, I'm fine. Sorry again."

We finish up the call—me feeling thoroughly ashamed of myself—then the house settles back into silence.

I grab my guitar and drop onto the sofa, positioning it across my lap. Usually, this helps. The familiar weight of it, the smooth curve of the body against me. I can lose myself for hours in chord progressions and half-written melodies.

I play a few notes—something slow, easy—but my heart's not in it.

I try again. A different song. Something upbeat this time.

Nope.

The notes fall flat, lifeless. Just sounds with no feeling behind them.

After a few more attempts, I give up and set the guitar aside.

I sit in the quiet and stare at the wall that separates my house from hers.

Just a few inches of plaster and brick. But right now it feels like an ocean.

CHAPTER TWENTY-NINE

STRUAN

The Pit is heaving.

Every screech, every thud of small bodies hitting foam, every parent's weary "Be careful!" bounces off the walls and rattles around my skull like loose change in a tumble dryer. Sunday soft play wasn't part of the original plan, but the rain's been hammering down since yesterday morning with no sign of letting up, and there's only so much kids' TV a man can take before he starts losing the will to live.

"So let me get this straight." Douglas leans back in his plastic chair, arms folded, looking far too pleased with himself for a man trapped in the Pit on a Sunday. "You shagged your client. Who also happens to be your neighbour."

"Wait a minute—" I start, but Lachlan cuts me off.

"Bold move, Struan. Very bold."

Blair's mouth twitches, like she's trying not to laugh.

"It wasn't like that." I take a sip of truly horrific coffee. "She's not my client anymore. Nothing happened while I was working for her."

That's technically true. The dry-humping-on-my-back-step incident occurred after hours. And in my own garden. So . . . aye.

"Flora said your mum walked in on you naked," Lachlan says, one eyebrow raised.

Bloody Flora. Don't know whether it was my mum or Ainsley's who couldn't hold their tongue. Either way, Flora— Lachlan's neighbour—found out, and naturally she mentioned it to Lachlan. So here we are.

I suppose it's just a bit of banter. A bit of good-natured teasing. Only it really fucking stings.

Of course, I'm hardly going to say that to them. So instead I smile sheepishly and say, "Aye, well, *that* bit is true."

At this, Blair can't contain her laughter. It bursts out, and she holds Lachlan's shoulder to keep from doubling over. He looks at her with this soft expression that twists something in my chest.

Because that's what I want.

Not the casual hook-ups I've been coasting on for years. Not the empty house that greets me every Sunday night after I've dropped Isla home.

I want someone who stays. Someone like—

I shut that thought down hard and drain the rest of my coffee.

"Da!" Isla appears at my elbow, face rosy from the climbing frame.

"All right, princess? Having fun?"

She gives me a small smile. She's been a bit off this weekend. Turns out she overheard the call Sophie and I had earlier in the week. The one where I was a complete dick.

Yesterday she offered to cancel her paddleboarding course because she didn't want it to upset me. I felt about two inches tall.

"Can I sit here for a minute?" she asks.

"Course you can." I pat the chair beside me, and she swings herself onto it. "So, what's the chat from the soft-play frame?"

"Logan says there's a secret tunnel at the top, but I couldn't find it."

"Oh, aye? Well, maybe it's *really* secret. Or maybe Logan's just winding you up. You've been coming here for years. Pretty sure there's not a secret tunnel you don't know about."

Her eyes narrow. "I knew it!" She jumps down from the chair and charges off.

Wouldn't like to be in Logan's shoes when my girl finds him.

I watch her till she disappears from sight then glance down at my mug. Empty. Could go get another, even though the stuff here is more punishment than pleasure.

I decide to wait. If the others start their teasing again, *then* I'll go.

"Well," Douglas says, nudging my arm, "look who just walked in."

I glance towards the entrance, and my heart does something stupid.

Ainsley. Holding Lily's hand and scanning the room with a guarded expression. Her gaze sweeps to our table, lands on me for half a second, then darts away again.

She picks a table on the far side of the soft play. As far from us as physically possible.

Lily, though, spots me. She points, tugging at Ainsley's arm, and I can practically hear her voice from here: *Stwuan! Stwuan is over there!*

But Ainsley shakes her head, bends down to say something, and Lily reluctantly climbs into the seat beside her.

"Ouch," Douglas murmurs.

"Shut up."

Blair's already on her feet. "I'll go say hello. You"—she points at me—"stay here."

"Wasn't planning on going anywhere."

She gives me a look that says she doesn't believe me, then heads across the café.

I try to focus on what Douglas is saying—something about how bloody awful it was when the twins had their stomach bug—but my eyes keep drifting back to Ainsley's table. She's half-turned away from us, shoulders tight, and every few seconds she glances around the room like she's checking whether people are staring.

They're not. Nobody's looking.

Well, except me. I'm staring. Can't help it.

Blair returns after a few minutes and rests her hands on the back of her chair, a sympathetic grimace on her face.

"So?" I try to sound casual. "What's the verdict?"

"Lily's desperate to come over and see you. But Ainsley . . ." Blair hesitates. "She says things went a bit too fast. She needs to put on the brakes."

"Right." I nod, like this is perfectly reasonable information that doesn't feel like a kick to the ribs. "Well, at least someone's happy to see me."

I mean it as a joke, but it comes out flat.

Blair reaches across the table and squeezes my hand. "Give her time, Struan. She's been through a lot."

Didn't think I'd miss the teasing, but I reckon the sympathy is worse. Lachlan and Douglas both just look awkward.

"Aye. I know," I say.

Blair heads back to Ainsley's table, and I try—really try—to engage with Douglas and Lachlan. But my gaze keeps sliding sideways. I can't help it. It's like there's a magnet in my skull, and Ainsley's the only thing made of metal.

"You're doing it again," Lachlan says.

"Doing what?"

"Staring."

"I'm not—"

"STWUAN!"

A small body barrels into my legs. I look down to find Lily beaming up at me, arms already raised in the universal "pick me up" gesture.

I glance over at Ainsley's table. She's watching, lips pressed thin, but she doesn't immediately rush over to retrieve her daughter. So I figure I've got a minute.

"Hey, Lily." I lift her onto my lap. "How's things?"

"I went down the big slide all by myself!"

"Did you now? That one's too big for me."

Lily giggles, settling against my chest like she belongs there. And something in me softens, even as I'm aware of Ainsley's gaze burning into the side of my head.

"When are we going to play Barbies again?" she asks.

"Well . . ."

"I liked it when you played Barbies with me. It was really fun."

"Aye, it was."

"Wait." Isla appears beside us. "Da, you played Barbies with Lily?" She looks between me and Lily, something tight and unsettled in her face.

"He did!" Lily says happily. "And he did all the voices, and then he read me bedtime stories and got me to sleep."

"You got Lily to sleep?" Isla's brow furrows.

"Aye." I keep my voice light. "Just as a favour to Lily's mum. She had an emergency."

"Stwuan is my Ardmara daddy," Lily announces, patting my chest.

Isla folds her arms. "No, he's not. He's *my* daddy."

"He can be my Ardmara daddy and your home daddy."

"That's not how it works, Lily!"

"But he likes me," Lily says, with the supreme confidence of a four-year-old who's never been contradicted. "Lots and lots and lots."

"Girls—"

"No, he likes *me* lots!" Isla's face crumples. "He's *my* da!"

Wow, this is going sideways fast. Lily's lower lip wobbles.

"Okay, okay." I hold up a hand. "Girls, let's just—"

But it's too late. Isla—my sweet, well-behaved Isla—steps forwards and says right into Lily's face, "He's MINE!"

Lily bursts into tears. Isla's eyes fill too.

Jesus. What the fuck is going on?

Heads turn, the low hum of conversation dipping as people glance over at the commotion. Finn and the twins gape from the climbing frame because Isla *never* misbehaves. She's the good one. The sensible one.

Ainsley materialises beside us, cheeks flushed. Hating the attention, naturally.

"Lily, we're leaving." Her voice is tight, controlled. "Now."

"Hey," I say quietly, reaching out to touch her arm. "It's fine, it's just—"

She jerks away like I've burned her.

"But Mummy—"

"*Now*, Lily."

The sharpness in Ainsley's tone freezes Lily mid-protest. Her eyes go wide.

Ainsley scoops Lily up and heads for the exit without looking back. Lily buries her face in her mother's shoulder, her small body shaking with hiccuped sobs.

Isla's crying now too, silent tears tracking down her cheeks.

"Hey." I squeeze her arm. "Hey, princess. It's okay."

"I was mean," she whispers. "I was really mean to Lily."

"Aye, well. We'll sort it. Don't worry."

But my chest feels hollow as I watch Ainsley disappear through the door.

"Boys," Blair says to Lachlan and Douglas, "can you look after Isla for a minute? Struan, come with me."

She heads off after Ainsley, and I don't need to be told twice. I hug Isla then follow Blair, out of soft play and out of the leisure centre itself.

Outside, the rain's still hammering down. Ainsley's halfway across the car park, both her and Lily getting soaked.

"Ainsley, wait!" Blair says.

She doesn't stop, but Blair indicates to me to stay put, jogs after her, and says something to her I can't hear. Somehow—God knows how—she convinces Ainsley to come back. Blair takes Lily back inside, leaving Ainsley and me standing under the overhang, rain sheeting down inches from our feet.

She looks tired. Pale and drawn, shadows under her eyes. Her hair's going frizzy in the damp, and she keeps her arms wrapped tight around herself.

"I'm sorry," I say. "About the girls. That was—Isla should know better."

"It's not her fault."

"No, but—" I rake a hand through my hair. "Look, she's

been a bit unsettled this week. Sophie and I had a disagreement, and Isla overheard it." I pause, then admit: "Actually, it was less of a disagreement and more of me acting like a bit of an arse."

Ainsley doesn't smile. Doesn't soften.

"The kids arguing like that?" she says. "It only proves that *this*"—she gestures between us—"was a mistake."

"It didn't feel like a mistake to me," I say. "And kids argue. It happens."

"It happened because of *us*, Struan. And I can't—I *won't* let anything upset Lily. She's my priority. My *only* priority."

"Look, Ainsley—" I step towards her, but she *shrinks* back. Wraps her arms even tighter around herself.

Shit. If I keep pushing, she'll only bolt. I want to point out that one small spat doesn't mean we're doomed. That kids are resilient, that they bounce back, that this doesn't have to be the end of anything.

But I'm not going to make her see that by arguing with her. So instead I say, "I don't think we're a mistake. But I can't ignore the fact you're scared and Lily's upset."

She doesn't respond. Just stands there, rain misting around us.

"I like you, Ainsley. A lot. And I'm not chasing a fling here. You're . . ." I swallow. "Well, I think there's something here. Something worth exploring. Slowly and carefully, if that's what you need. But if you don't want to take things any further with me, I'll accept that."

"I don't," she says quickly. "I just want to be neighbours. That's all."

Well, fuck. That wasn't what I wanted to hear.

"All right," I say. My voice sounds strange to my own ears.

Steady, when nothing inside me feels steady at all. "If that's your final decision, I'll respect it." I manage a small smile.

She nods once, then turns and heads back inside for Lily.

Aye, I'll respect it.

But fuck, it hurts.

◆ ◆ ◆

The house is quiet.

Too quiet, really, given Isla's sitting across from me at the kitchen table. She's been subdued since we got back, and she's pushing her pasta around her plate more than eating it.

I've tried the usual tricks—silly voices, daft jokes, that face she normally can't resist laughing at. Nothing's landing tonight.

"Da?"

I look up from my own barely touched plate. "Aye?"

"Are you going to get me into trouble?"

I blink. "What?"

"For being mean to Lily." She's staring at her fork, not meeting my eyes. "I wasn't very nice. You should be cross with me."

The words catch me off-guard. My wee girl, asking to be told off. Wanting it, even.

"Hey." I reach across and cover her hand with mine. "No. It's okay, Isla. I don't want you getting upset about that. I get it. I understand why you reacted the way you did."

She finally looks up, eyes red-rimmed. "But I *shouted* at her. Right in her face."

"Aye. And that wasn't great. But you know what? Sometimes even grown-ups feel jealous and do daft things." I pause, trying to

232

find the right words. "When I found out Mei was moving in with you and your mum, I felt a wee bit jealous."

"You did?"

"Aye. Because I love spending time with you, and I didn't like the idea of someone else getting to spend more time with you than I do." I squeeze her hand. "But here's the thing, the people you love can have other people in their lives too. Just because I looked after Lily for a night doesn't mean I love you any less. And just because Mei lives with you now doesn't mean you love me any less. Right?"

"Of course it doesn't." She says it fiercely, as if the very idea offends her. Then she's out of her chair and throwing her arms around me, squeezing tight. "I love you, Da."

"Love you too, princess. More than anything." I hug her back, breathing her in. "Right, are you going to eat any more of your food, or are you not hungry?"

"Not hungry."

"Aye, me neither. You go off and play and I'll tidy up here, all right?"

She scampers off and I put some music on, clear the plates, and fill the basin.

I'm humming away to myself and drying off the last dish when Isla reappears.

"Da, I wrote a letter to Lily. To say sorry for shouting. And I drew her a picture."

"Oh?" I'm proud, of course, that my seven-year-old took it upon herself to apologise. She's mature beyond her years, my Isla. But I don't think Ainsley wants to see any more of us today.

"Well done. Maybe we can give it to Lily another time?"

"I already put it through their door."

I don't let my smile drop, but inwardly I'm thinking, *Shit, Ainsley's going to see that letter.*

She'll probably think that I put Isla up to it. That I'm trying to worm my way back in through the kids. That I can't respect her boundaries.

"Oh, right. I didn't hear you going out. That was a really nice thing to do."

Isla beams.

I dry my hands on the tea towel, thinking. I *could* leave it. Let the letter speak for itself. But if Ainsley thinks I orchestrated it— if she thinks I'm playing games—

"Give me two minutes," I tell Isla. "I just need to write a quick note."

I find a scrap of paper and a pen, and scribble:

Just so you know, Isla wrote that note herself. She didn't tell me about it until after she'd posted it. S.

Short. Factual. Nothing that could be misread.

I slip it through Ainsley's letterbox.

Back inside, I check the time. "All right, princess, we better get you back to Bannock, eh?"

CHAPTER THIRTY

AINSLEY

Tuesday

A hairdryer whirs. Scissors snip. The till drawer slides open with a satisfying *clack* that's becoming pleasantly familiar.

Three weeks in, and the salon is *busy*. The appointment book is filling up. Word is spreading. I'm not just surviving—I'm building something.

This is what I wanted. What I worked for.

I should be proud. Content.

And I am. Obviously, I am.

As I work on Mrs Patterson's hair, I catch sight of my reflection in the mirror. Smile in place. Posture confident. The picture of a woman who has her shit together.

So why does something feel . . . off?

I push the thought aside and reach for my thinning shears.

◆ ◆ ◆

The Ferryman's Rest is a lot quieter on a Wednesday than a Thursday. Means Blair and I can have a proper catch-up without our conversation being drowned out by a certain folk band.

"Cheers," Blair says, raising her glass to mine.

"Cheers." I take a sip of the white wine, letting the crisp tartness settle on my tongue.

We chat about nothing for a while—Finn's new obsession with dinosaur facts, Lily's ongoing Barbie empire, the weather turning properly autumnal. Easy, comfortable stuff.

Then Blair tilts her head, that gentle curiosity in her eyes that I've learned means she's about to ask something I won't want to answer.

"So," she says. "Struan."

I set my glass down. "Aye? What about him?"

"I just wondered if—"

"Nothing's happening there. And I'd really appreciate it if people stopped asking."

Blair's eyebrows lift. "Oh. Sorry. Of course."

Guilt pricks at me. She's only being a friend. It's not her fault I'm . . . whatever I am.

"Sorry," I say, softer. "I didn't mean to be prickly. It's just, at the moment my priorities are Lily and the salon. I don't have the headspace for anything else."

"Understood." Blair smiles, no trace of offence. "Subject closed."

We both take a sip of our drinks.

Blair's phone pings. She glances at it then smiles to herself— one of those small, private smiles.

"Lachlan," she says, almost apologetic. "He's sent over a cute photo." She turns the screen towards me. "My boys."

Finn's tucked against Lachlan on the sofa, Gus sprawled on the floor beside them, all three of them looking half-asleep and utterly content.

A knot twists in my chest. I ignore it.

"Cute," I say lightly. I drain the last of my wine. "Right, next round's on me."

I stand and head for the bar before Blair can say anything else.

◆ ◆ ◆

Thursday

"Time for your bedtime story, Lily," I say, pushing open her bedroom door.

I stop short. Because there, taped to the wall above her wee desk—slightly wonky, obviously Lily's handiwork—is Isla's drawing. The apology picture. Now pride of place in her room.

"You put it up," I say, pointing to it.

Lily looks up from arranging Mr Flops on her pillow. "Yep. I like it."

"You know, you don't *have* to display it. If it reminds you of what happened."

"It's fine." She shrugs. "Friends fight sometimes. But then they're friends again. Can we see Isla this weekend?"

My stomach tightens. "We'll see about that."

"But—"

"Bedtime story," I say firmly, settling onto the edge of her bed. "Go on, pick one from your bookcase."

◆ ◆ ◆

Friday

I shiver as I pull the recycling bin out onto the street. The evening air has a bite to it now. Autumn's settling in.

Headlights sweep across me, then Struan's van pulls into his drive. Back from picking up Isla for the weekend, no doubt.

As he kills the engine, he glances over and our eyes meet through the van window. He smiles—quick, familiar.

I turn and head for the house at a pace that's definitely not running away. Nope, it's just cold and late, and I have things to do.

I'm inside before he even steps out of the van. I close the door behind me and lean back against it, breath leaving me in a tight rush.

Just the cold, I tell myself. *Just the cold.*

◆ ◆ ◆

Saturday

I'm in the kitchenette, on my phone, nursing the dregs of a lukewarm tea. The hum of the salon drifts through the door.

I'm scrolling through emails—a supplier confirmation, a booking enquiry, the usual—when a text notification slides onto the screen. A name I haven't seen in months.

Rachel.

My thumb freezes mid-scroll.

I read it twice. Three times.

Rachel. My ex-best friend. The woman who slept with my boyfriend—the father of my daughter—behind my back. *That* Rachel is texting me for . . . what? Sympathy? Comfort?

And she doesn't even apologise! Not a single "sorry for what I did". She actually wrote "what he did to you", like she wasn't right there with him, doing it too.

My pulse races.

Of course Danny cheated on her. Because that's what men like Danny do. The charming ones. The flirty ones. The ones who make you feel oh so special, when in their eyes you're really not special at all.

For one stupid half-second, my thumb hovers over the keyboard. Old habit. Old instinct. We were best friends once. Used to share everything.

But then I catch myself.

Why should I comfort her? Why should I offer anything to the woman who helped tear my life apart and never once said sorry?

No. I have to protect myself. Prioritise my own peace.

I tap through to her contact. Press "block".

I set the phone down and pick up my tea. It's gone completely cold, but I drink it anyway.

◆ ◆ ◆

Sunday

"Can we get a Ken doll?"

I blink at Lily over the pile of Barbies between us. "A Ken doll? Since when do you want a boy doll?"

"Because Barbie needs a boyfriend, Mummy." She says it like I'm being thick. "*Obviously.*"

"Why does Barbie *need* a—"

"Stwuan Barbie can't be her boyfriend," Lily continues, steamrollering right over me. "She's not *really* a boy. I want a real boy to be Barbie's boyfriend. Someone who gives her cuddles and kisses."

A lump forms in my throat. "Er . . . right. Well, maybe. For now, let's find Barbie a nice outfit, shall we?"

"Okay!" Lily happily dives into her drawer of tiny clothes.

I try to help, holding up a sparkly pink dress which she rejects in favour of something with more sequins. But my mind drifts.

Cuddles and kisses. Where did *that* come from?

◆ ◆ ◆

Sunday (later)

Lily is finally asleep.

It took three stories, two glasses of milk, and a lengthy negotiation over whether Mr Flops needed his own pillow (he did, apparently). But she's out now, breathing soft and steady, one arm flung over her rabbit.

I should probably try to have a bit of me time—watch some grown-up TV, maybe—but I honestly don't have the energy for it. So I get myself ready for bed. I'm just pulling back my duvet when I hear it.

A guitar.

A slow, wistful tune drifts through the night air. Acoustic. Gentle. Familiar.

My chest tightens.

I step out onto the landing almost without deciding to. Peer through the gap in the curtains into the dark.

Struan is on his back step, head bent over his guitar, fingers moving softly over the strings. The light from his kitchen window casts him in warm gold, picking out the tawny curls, the slope of his shoulders, the quiet confidence of his hands.

Heat flickers through me—sharp and unwelcome. I remember the last time I watched him play. The kiss. His lap. My body giving in far, far too easily.

I clamp down on it. *No.*

But the music keeps playing. Something slow and aching, the kind of melody that curls under your skin and finds all the places you've been trying to protect.

I step back. Pull the curtains fully closed. Head back into my bedroom and switch off the light.

I'm just tired. That's all. It's been a long week.

I climb into bed and lie there, staring at the ceiling, waiting for sleep.

It doesn't come.

CHAPTER THIRTY-ONE

AINSLEY

The kettle clicks off, steam curling up towards the ceiling while Mum rattles through her kitchen cupboard for mugs.

Da's through in the living room, keeping Lily busy. He's still got his cast on, but he'll be fine with her for a few minutes.

"So," I say, leaning against the worktop, "a funny thing happened a couple of days ago. Rachel texted me."

Mum's hand stills above a mug, a teabag pinched between her fingers. "Rachel? As in—"

"The very same."

"What on earth did she want?"

"Sympathy, I think. Danny cheated on her too." I can't quite keep the bitter edge from my voice. "She thought I'd *understand.*"

Mum clicks her tongue. "Maybe this is mean of me, but I can't say I'm very sorry to hear that. There's a certain poetic justice in it, isn't there?"

I don't comment. Don't need to.

Mum finishes pouring the water, then glances at me with a look I know all too well. "Anyway," she says casually, "Struan—"

"Nope." I hold up a hand. "There's nothing going on between us—*as I've already told you.*"

Mum sighs. A heavy, theatrical sigh that could win awards.

"What was that noise for?" I fold my arms. "Also, Mum, I *still* can't believe you gossiped about me behind my back. You *know* how humiliated I was after Danny. You know how awful it was, with everyone knowing everything. And yet you and Struan's mum went blabbering away anyway."

She sets down the teaspoon and turns to face me properly, her expression softening. "I am sorry about that. Truly I am. And if I'd known how it would turn out, I'd never have done it."

"How it would turn out?"

"Yes. You pushing Struan away before you even gave him a proper chance. That's the last thing I wanted." She reaches out and squeezes my arm. "If Helen and I couldn't stop blabbing, it's only because we were both so excited. Helen was over the moon at the thought of you and her son together. And me? Well, I was too. After what happened with Danny . . ." She pauses, lines deepening around her mouth. "I'd never seen you so small, Ainsley. I hated seeing you like that. I thought that maybe, just maybe, Struan might help you put all that behind you. Besides"—her voice lifts—"that lad is quite the catch."

"Mum!" I gape at her. "Listen to you. You're *still* interfering. You just can't help yourself!"

"What? I'm only pointing out the truth. He's charming, handsome, and so good with Lily. You told me about how he played Barbies with her on the day your da had his fall. Says a lot about his character, if you ask me."

I open my mouth to argue, but she's already leaning closer, voice dropping conspiratorially.

"And, well . . ." She glances towards the living room, where

Da and Lily's laughter drifts through. "The body on that lad! I love your da very much, but even at his best he never had muscles like that. Honestly, they were all on show when Helen opened Struan's front door that time." Her eyebrows perform an act of pure mischief. "And, well, let's just say I caught a glimpse of something else before Struan rushed to cover himself up. All very respectable."

Heat floods my cheeks. Oh my God. Is my mother really talking about Struan's *dick*?

"*Mum!*" I practically choke. "You did *not* just say that."

"What?" She laughs, utterly unbothered. "I'm just saying he's the full package, that one." A wicked pause. "And he has a very nice package too."

"MUM!" My soul attempts a swift exit.

She only chuckles harder, the absolute menace. But then the humour drains away, something more serious settling over her.

"But seriously, Ainsley? Helen . . . she's worried her boy is lonely."

I pause, the mug I've just picked up frozen halfway to my lips. "*Lonely?*"

The word doesn't compute. This *is* Struan Walker we're talking about? The man with the charming grin and a bit of cheeky banter for anyone who passes. Who plays guitar at the Ferryman's Rest each Thursday and is surrounded by admirers afterwards, like he's some kind of rock star. The guy who's so quietly confident it's like he's never experienced anxiety in his life.

"I doubt that very much."

"Well, it's what Helen thinks. He loves the weekend, when he's got Isla. But during the week, when it's just him, she thinks he gets a bit . . ." Mum searches for the word. "Down."

Down?

Are we talking about the same person?

And yet . . .

Something tugs at the back of my mind. The guitar I heard last night. That slow, aching melody. It wasn't the first time I caught him playing outside on a Sunday night. And the last time—before things got out of hand and I came on his lap—he said that Sunday evenings were his least favourite part of the week.

He *did* seem a bit lonely then.

"Anyway," Mum continues, "if you don't think Struan is the right person for you, or you don't want *anyone* right now, I get that. After what you went through, it'd be completely under-standable if you wanted to forget about dating for . . . well, however long you need. Only"—she meets my eyes—"I'm your mum and I want to see you happy. You deserve someone so much better than Danny was. And Helen? She wants to see Struan settle down with someone too."

I start to object but she holds up a hand.

"And if that's not with each other, that's okay! Of course it's okay. But Struan is a popular man around town. Just be aware that he might, well, get snapped up." She shrugs. "And, again, that's fine. If he's not the one for you, that's no issue.

"But if a part of you *does* have feelings for him . . ." Her tone grows gentler. "Please don't let your fears get in the way of giving him a proper shot. Anyway, that's all I wanted to say on the matter. I won't meddle or interfere anymore. I promise."

"Thank you!" I say, perhaps a little too emphatically. "I'm going to keep you to that promise."

But internally—annoyingly, inconveniently—I have to admit she's given me a thing or two to think about.

Not that I'm about to admit that out loud.

I'm back at the house, and it's just me here. Lily's staying with my parents tonight, which means I can have a decent sleep and get to the salon early tomorrow without the nursery drop-off dance. A rare gift.

All I want is to change into something comfortable, collapse on the sofa, and let some mindless TV wash over me until my eyes get heavy.

But in my bedroom, reaching for my pyjamas, I catch a glimpse of myself in the mirror. And pause.

My fringe sits perfectly, not a hair out of place. My make-up—soft glam, natural but polished—still looks fresh despite the full day.

This is the image I present to the world. Professional. Put-together. A woman who's got it all figured out. Even if that's far from how I feel inside.

I think about what Mum said earlier. About Struan being lonely. I scoffed at the idea because it was absurd. And yet . . .

What if it's the same for him? What if his carefree demeanour, his easy smile, his cheeky banter—what if they aren't the full picture? What if there's something underneath all that charm that he doesn't let people see?

My heart gives a quiet pang.

The sad song he played on his guitar last night. That said it all, didn't it? Maybe music is Struan's way of communicating how he's really feeling. If so, last night he wasn't feeling carefree.

Bloody hell. This is what happens when I get time to myself. Time to *think*.

But what if I *am* making a terrible mistake?

I stare at my reflection. The woman there is more uncertain than she was a moment ago.

Fuck it.

The TV can wait. The comfy clothes can wait. I should go talk to him. I've been putting it off and putting it off, and it's getting ridiculous. We're adults. We can have a conversation.

Just talk. Talk and see how things go.

The idea terrifies me. But he only lives next door. I can be there in thirty seconds. Just walk over, knock, and—

Before I can talk myself out of it, I'm heading downstairs and out the front door.

The evening air hits my face, cool and bracing. His house is right there, separated from mine by nothing but a low hedge.

But his van isn't in the drive. And there are no lights on inside.

I knock anyway. Wait. Knock again.

Nothing.

I stand there for a moment, arms wrapped around myself against the chill. Maybe this is a sign. Maybe avoiding Struan is the right call. Maybe the universe is trying to tell me something.

I catch myself. Because I've not *really* tried, have I? One unanswered door and I'm ready to give up?

Back inside, I grab my phone and type out a quick message.

AINSLEY

> Hey. Are you around? Was hoping we could talk

Send.

I watch the screen. The message sits there, unread.

I try the TV. Some property programme where couples argue about square footage and kitchen tiles. I couldn't tell you a single thing about it because I keep checking my phone every thirty seconds like a teenager waiting for a text back from a crush.

Which is ridiculous. I'm a grown woman with a business and a child and absolutely no time for this sort of nonsense.

I check my phone again.

Still nothing.

I go to the window and peer out. His lights are still off. No van.

Where the hell is he?

Eventually, restless and irritated with myself, I call Mum.

"Hi, love," she says. "Everything okay? Lily's fine. She's just brushing her teeth."

"Can I say goodnight to her?"

A shuffle, then Lily's voice, bright and chatty despite the late hour: "Mummy! Granny let me have extra bubbles in my bath!"

"Did she now? That sounds lovely, baby. You be good for Granny and Grandpa, okay? I love you."

"Love you too, Mummy. Night night!"

More shuffling, then Mum's back. "She's off to bed now. Your da's going to read her a story—one-handed, bless him."

"Thanks, Mum. For having her."

"Of course." A pause. Then, with that annoying maternal instinct: "Was there anything else you were calling about?"

I take a breath. "I've been thinking," I say slowly, "about what you said earlier. About Struan."

I can practically *hear* her perking up on the other end.

"And I've been thinking . . . maybe I *should* give him a chance."

"Oh, Ainsley!" At the joy in her voice, I half expect confetti to burst out of my phone speaker. "That's wonderful! I knew you'd come round. I just knew it."

"Mum—"

"Sorry, sorry. Not meddling. I'll behave. Go on."

"The thing is, I went to speak to him but he's not in. I messaged him and he's not replying. And I know there's nothing I can do about that, but now that I've decided I want to talk to him, I feel all restless and I can't focus on anything else."

"Give me a few minutes," Mum says. "I'll see if I can help."

She hangs up before I can protest.

I pace the living room. Check my phone. Pace some more.

When it rings again, I answer before the first ring finishes.

"Had a word with Helen," Mum says. "Seems he's gone out for dinner. To a place called the Glen Garve Resort. Heard of it?"

My stomach drops.

The Glen Garve Resort.

That's where Struan was supposed to take *me*. On the date we never made it to.

"Ainsley? You still there?"

"Yes," I manage, my voice coming out strange. "Thanks, Mum. I'll . . . I'll sort it from here."

I hang up before she can ask questions.

He's at the Glen Garve Resort. For dinner.

That's not the kind of place you go alone. It's fancy. Romantic. The kind of place you take someone you're trying to impress.

A date. He's on a date.

My hands shake slightly as I try calling him. It rings and rings, then goes to voicemail.

I try again. Same result.

Fuck.

I'm pacing now, properly pacing, wearing a track in the carpet.

I remember what Mum said about Struan being a catch. I

remember Lindsey McVey, the blonde jogger, and the bathroom quote she turned into a proposition. I remember the crowd of women around Struan after his gig at the Ferryman's Rest, all twirling hair and flirty smiles.

Has he already moved on? Has he gone on a date with someone else?

And if he has . . . do I have any right to feel upset about that?

I told him—*insisted*, in fact—that I wanted us to be neighbours and nothing more. I shut him down. Multiple times. I practically slammed the door in his face.

So why does my chest feel like someone's reached inside and squeezed?

Jealousy. That's what this is. Hot and ugly and completely irrational.

I have no claim on him. None at all.

But God, this is just my luck, isn't it? I finally decide that maybe Struan and I *could* work, and I've left it too late.

Fine. I'll talk to him in the morning. What else can I do?

But then a worse thought surfaces, cold and unwelcome.

Is Struan the kind of guy who'd sleep with a woman on a first date?

Of course he is. Hell, *we* didn't even make it to our first date because we were too busy fucking in his bedroom.

Which means tomorrow morning might be too late.

By then, he might have already—

No. *No.*

I stop pacing. Stand very still in the middle of my living room.

There's only one thing for it. If I can't get through to him on the phone, I'll have to go speak to him in person. At the Glen Garve Resort. Tonight.

The thought is absolutely terrifying.

But I've let fear control me for too long. Fear of being hurt. Fear of being humiliated. Fear of trusting someone again only to have it blow up in my face.

And where has that fear got me? Alone in my house on a Monday night, pacing holes in the carpet while the man I might actually have feelings for is out with someone else.

No. Now is the time for action.

I head upstairs to my bedroom and throw open the wardrobe. My fingers move past comfortable jumpers and practical work clothes until they land on something else entirely.

This one.

I pull it out. The dress I picked for our first date.

Green velvet. Long-sleeved, above the knee, hugs every curve. The kind of dress that makes me feel like I'm calling the shots.

The Glen Garve Resort is a fancy place. I need to look like I belong there.

A flash of hesitation. Christ, am I really doing this?

But then I lay the dress on my bed—the bed Struan built, with his own hands, because I couldn't manage the bloody flat pack—and sit down at my make-up table.

I study my reflection. The woman looking back is scared. But also determined.

If I'm going to walk into that restaurant and potentially make a complete fool of myself, I'm damn well going to look incredible while doing it.

I reach for my make-up bag.

CHAPTER THIRTY-TWO

AINSLEY

The Glen Garve Resort rises out of the darkness like something from a fairy tale, all honey-coloured stone and turrets and windows glowing warm against the October night. It's the kind of place that whispers *old money* and *you don't belong here* in equal measure.

I park the car and sit for a moment, hands still gripping the steering wheel.

What am I doing?

This is insane. A terrible, terrible idea. I'm about to walk into a fancy restaurant, uninvited, and interrupt a man's dinner. A man who is almost certainly on a date with someone else. A man I told, in no uncertain terms, that I wanted nothing further to do with romantically.

My reflection stares back at me from the rear-view mirror. Green velvet dress. Make-up done to perfection. Hair styled within an inch of its life.

I look like a woman who knows what she wants. It's a shame my insides feel like jelly.

Just get out of the car, Ainsley. You've come this far.

The night air wraps around me as I step out—crisp, carrying the faint scent of wood smoke from somewhere. My heels click against the paving slabs as I walk towards the entrance, and with every step, a little voice in my head whispers, *Turn back, turn back, this is a terrible idea.*

I ignore it. I've spent too long listening to that voice.

Inside, the lobby is all polished hardwood and crystal chandeliers, the kind of elegance that makes you stand up straighter. A fire crackles in a grand stone hearth, and from somewhere deeper in the building come the soft notes of a piano.

At the doorway to the restaurant stands the maître d'. Immaculate suit, practised smile.

"Good evening, madam. Welcome to the Glen Garve Resort. Do you have a booking with us tonight?"

"I'm meeting someone," I say, with far more confidence than I feel. "They should already be here."

"Of course, madam. And may I take the name of—"

But I'm already walking past him, heels tapping purposefully as I head into the restaurant.

Act like you belong. That's the trick, right?

"Madam?" he calls after me, a note of polite alarm in his voice.

I don't stop. Don't look back. This is a posh establishment and I look the part—he's not about to chase me down and cause a scene. That would be terribly undignified.

The restaurant opens up before me: white tablecloths, gleaming cutlery, the soft flicker of candlelight. Couples lean towards each other over expensive wine. A pianist plays something gentle in the corner. Through tall windows, the glen stretches into darkness, the hills just visible against the night sky.

I scan the room, heart hammering against my ribs.

Where is he? Where—

My eyes land on a man at a table near the window. For a split second, I dismiss him—too polished, too put-together—and I'm about to move on when something makes me look again.

My breath catches. Because it *is* Struan. Only he's . . . different. Very different.

Gone are the usual crumpled checked shirt and worn jeans. Tonight he's wearing dark tailored trousers, a crisp white button-down, and a blazer that makes his shoulders look impossibly broad. His hair—still shorter than I'm used to, thanks to my emergency rescue mission with the scissors—curls just above his collar, and even from here, I can see the way the candlelight catches in those golden-brown eyes.

He looks *good*. The kind of good that makes my stomach flip and my mouth go dry.

And he's sitting across from a woman.

They're leaning close over the white linen, laughing quietly at something. Empty dessert plates sit between them. The candlelight paints them both in soft, romantic gold.

My heart drops straight through the floor.

The woman is gorgeous, of course. Dark-blonde hair falling to her shoulders, pretty features, a relaxed smile. She looks comfortable with him. Familiar.

For one horrible, lurching moment, I'm back in my old village. Walking in on Danny and Rachel tangled together. The shock of it. The humiliation. The way my world tilted sideways and never quite righted itself.

My chest tightens. My vision blurs at the edges.

No.

I force myself to breathe. Force the panic back down.

This isn't like that. Because I'm not with Struan. He has every right to be here with another woman. *I* told him I didn't want this. *I* pushed him away. Multiple times. I practically slammed the door in his face.

So what right do I have to feel this way?

None. Absolutely none.

And yet here I am. In a velvet dress. In a restaurant I wasn't invited to. About to do something monumentally stupid.

For a moment, I consider turning around. Walking back out. Driving home and pretending this never happened.

But then I think about all the times I've let fear make my decisions for me.

No. I need to say my piece. I owe him that. I owe *myself* that.

If he's moved on, fine. But I'm not leaving without trying.

I straighten my spine, smooth down my dress, and walk towards their table.

Struan is mid-sentence when he looks up. Whatever he was saying dies on his lips. His mouth parts, and he stares.

His gaze travels down, taking in the dress, the heels, all of it. Something shifts in his expression. Something warm and surprised and—unless I'm imagining it—a little bit awestruck.

That look gives me a bolt of courage I desperately need.

"I know how this looks," I say. "And I know you're clearly on a date—sorry—but I have to say this before I lose my nerve and run out of here and spend the rest of my life wondering what if."

"Er, Ainsley—" Struan starts.

"Shh!" I hold up a hand. "There are things I need to say, and I *will* say them."

I glance at the woman—she's watching me with an expression I can't quite read—and give her a quick, apologetic smile before turning back to Struan.

"Right." I take a breath. My heart is pounding so hard I'm

amazed the whole restaurant can't hear it. "I pushed you away, and I'm sorry about that. I really am. But I was scared, Struan. Properly scared. The last time I let myself trust someone, it ended with my best friend in bed with my boyfriend and the whole village whispering about me like I was some tragic cautionary tale."

"Ainsley—"

"I'm not finished!" I say, loud enough for a couple at the next table to glance over. I lower my voice. "The point is, I was so terrified of getting hurt again that I convinced myself it was safer to push you away. Easier. But it wasn't easier. It was bloody miserable, actually. Because you . . ." I swallow hard. "You make me feel safe. You make me feel *seen*. Not the polished version I show everyone else, but the actual me. The one who throws instruction manuals out of windows and can't assemble flat-pack furniture and sometimes cries in salon kitchenettes."

Struan opens his mouth again.

"Still not finished!" I'm on a roll now, the words tumbling out faster than I can control them. "And you're wonderful with Lily. That night you looked after her when Da was in hospital, playing Barbies and reading her stories and just . . . being there. You didn't have to do any of that. But you did. Because that's who you are. You're kind and patient and you make terrible jokes, and you—you built my bed, for God's sake!"

A small smile tugs at the corner of his mouth, but he stays quiet this time.

"My heart wasn't broken. It was more like . . . under renovation. Or something. God, that sounded better in my head." I wince. "The point is, I want this. I want *you*. I want to try—properly, slow and steady, without me panicking and running away."

I pause, suddenly aware that I've been talking for what feels like an eternity. Struan is watching me with soft eyes.

"Only," I add, my voice smaller now, "it seems I might be too late. You've already moved on." I gesture at the woman across from him.

Then I turn to her directly, because she deserves an apology for having to sit through . . . whatever this is.

"I'm so sorry about this, by the way. I'm honestly not meaning to embarrass you or cause a scene. I just . . . there were things I had to say. And I've said them. So." I give a helpless little shrug. "Sorry. Again."

The woman looks at me. And then, to my utter confusion, she *smiles*. Warmly. Kindly. Like I've done something charming rather than completely unhinged.

"You must be Ainsley." She holds out her hand.

I take it, bewildered. "Er . . . hi?"

"I'm Sophie."

"Sophie?"

"Isla's mum."

The words take a moment to land. And then my face catches fire.

Oh God. Oh no. I've just confessed my feelings in front of the mother of his child.

I want to crawl under a table and never come out again.

Struan, the bastard, is grinning at me.

"I *was* trying to tell you," he says, "but you weren't letting me get a word in edgeways. And then you started saying such nice things about me that I didn't want to interrupt. It was doing wonders for my ego, listening to all that."

"Struan!" I choke out, horrified.

He just grins wider and winks. "Anyway, Soph and I are, of course, not on a date. I thought I owed her an apology dinner after being a bit of a dick on the phone the other day."

"We were actually just talking about Isla," Sophie adds. "Trying to clear the air a bit. Struan sometimes bottles things up—he's a man, after all." She shoots him a teasing look. "But I never want him feeling pushed out of Isla's life. So we're making some changes. Over the school holidays, he's taking some time off work to take her to a paddleboarding course I signed her up for. And to give her a few extra lessons himself, apparently."

Struan nods. "Aye, that's right. Looking forward to it. A bit of time with my girl."

Sophie's gaze flicks over me, giving me a once-over. "You're gorgeous, by the way. Struan has good taste."

"Oi!" Struan jokingly protests. "You're a taken woman."

His attention shifts back to me, and his voice softens. "Sophie's right, though. You're a knockout."

My face is still burning, but something in my chest is starting to loosen.

"And you . . ." I manage, taking in his sharp clothes. "You fairly got dressed up for a meeting with Sophie."

He glances down at himself like he's only just noticed. "What, this? Honestly, I bought it for the date you and I were supposed to go on here. I didn't get to wear it then, so . . ." He shrugs, sheepish. "Seemed a shame to waste it."

"Well, it looks . . . very good on you." I swallow. "And, er, it's the same story with me, actually. This is the outfit I was planning to wear on that date we never quite made it to."

Struan's eyes darken slightly, travelling over me again in a way that makes my skin warm. "Aye? Fuck, Ainsley. You look incredible. I wouldn't have been able to resist you if I'd seen you like this."

I scoff, though my heart is racing. "You didn't exactly resist me in my casual clothes. That's why we missed the date in the first place."

He laughs—that warm, rumbling sound that does things to my insides. "That's true."

Sophie raises her eyebrows with interest. Then she stands. "It's been lovely to meet you, Ainsley. But I think I'm maybe intruding on what should be a private conversation between you two." She looks at Struan. "I'll see you on Friday?"

"What?" Struan blinks. "Oh, aye, right. Friday. See you then."

Sophie catches my eye and winks—a small, conspiratorial thing—before slipping away.

Struan gestures to the vacated chair. "Join me?"

I do. The candle flickers between us. Beyond the window, the glen stretches into darkness.

"I'm still trying to get my breathing back to normal," I admit. "I honestly thought I'd lost my chance. I thought you'd moved on."

Struan reaches across the table and takes my hand. His hand is warm and calloused and fits around mine like it belongs there.

"I haven't looked at anyone else since the day you fell into my lap at soft play."

Heat creeps up my cheeks. "Well. We made it to the Glen Garve Resort in the end. Only, it's not quite how I imagined our first date going."

He chuckles, his thumb stroking across my knuckles. "No, me neither. Still, I'm sitting across from you, and you look incredible. That's something. But this isn't our first date, Ainsley. This is just . . . a preview. Trust me." His fingers tighten around mine. "Our first date for real is going to blow you away."

"Oh, aye?"

"Aye." He grins, slow and devastating. "By the end of our first *proper* date, you'll be mine."

My breath catches. "Bold claim."

"Not a claim, Ainsley." He holds my gaze, steady and sure. "A promise."

EPILOGUE
STRUAN

Spring

The gate is coming together nicely. Sturdy oak slats, brass hinges I salvaged from an old wardrobe on a job last month, and a latch simple enough that wee fingers can work it.

The spring sun is warm on my back, and somewhere in the garden behind me, a blackbird is going absolutely mental with its singing.

"I'm helping," Lily announces beside me, giving the gatepost an enthusiastic whack with her plastic hammer.

"Aye, you are. Couldn't do it without you."

She beams up at me, all round cheeks and pigtails, then delivers another blow that wouldn't dent a marshmallow. "This is *very* hard work, Stwuan."

"The hardest," I agree.

Next up is the middle hinge, the fiddly bit that needs both hands and a level of concentration that's hard to maintain when a four-year-old is tapping everything within reach. I catch Isla's eye across the garden.

She's lying on the picnic blanket with a book, but a twitch of her mouth tells me she gets it. That's my girl.

"Lily!" She sets down the book. "Come see what I've just spotted. I think it might be a fairy house."

Lily's plastic hammer clatters to the ground. "A *fairy house*?" And then she's off, toy toolbox abandoned at my feet.

I get on with the work in peace and am just tightening the last screw when I hear Ainsley's back door open, followed by the soft pad of bare feet on patio stones.

I turn, and the sight of her knocks the breath out of me, as it always does. She's in a floaty green dress that matches her eyes, and the breeze keeps lifting bits of her hair, making them dance around her cheeks. She's backlit by afternoon sun, and all I can do is stare.

She catches me at it and rolls her eyes, but a smile tugs at her lips.

"You've got sawdust everywhere," she says, stepping close and brushing at my shoulders.

"Occupational hazard."

She peers past me at the gate, then runs her fingers along the smooth edge of the top slat. "It's beautiful. You do good work, Mr Walker."

"Aye, well. It'll make it easier for the girls to go back and forth." I give her a wink. "And it'll make it easier for me too."

Ainsley arches one perfect brow. "Oh?" she says in a low voice. "You don't normally have any difficulty finding your way to my bed."

God, I love this woman.

"Ainsley Reid." I press a hand to my chest in mock horror. "There are children present."

But then I reach for her, my fingers curling around her waist, pulling her flush against me. She comes willingly—no resistance, no walls, just Ainsley, soft and warm and *mine*. When I kiss her, she tastes like the tea she's been drinking and something sweeter underneath.

"Stwuan and Mummy are *kissing*!" Lily's shriek carries across the garden like a foghorn.

I don't pull away. Not yet.

"Aye." Isla's voice is flat, unimpressed. "They do it *all the time* now."

"That's because they love each other," Lily says, with the absolute certainty only a four-year-old can muster. "Just like I love Mr Flops."

I chuckle into the kiss, and Ainsley's shoulders shake as she tries to hold back a giggle.

When I finally pull back, I find both girls watching us—Lily with delighted fascination, Isla with theatrical long-suffering patience.

I clear my throat. "Right." I try the gate. It opens and closes easily. "There you go, girls. What do you think?"

They test it out, Lily going first. She gives a nod of approval.

"It's perfect, Stwuan! But you need a password to go through."

"A password?" I say.

"It's fairy sparkles," Lily whispers. "But don't tell anyone. Only us four know."

"Okay, Lily," Isla says. "Fairy sparkles!"

Lily beams and unlatches the gate for her.

Ainsley and I watch the girls play, the gate swinging gently on its hinges between our two gardens.

"I suppose this means you're stuck with us now," Ainsley says after a bit.

I loop an arm around her and pull her closer to me. "Aye. Suits me just fine."

Not ready to let Struan and Ainsley go just yet? Subscribers to our free email newsletter can download a bonus epilogue in which they finally go on that first date. (Will they manage to keep their hands off each other this time? Spoiler alert: nope!)

And the *Scottish Single Dads* series wraps up in *Catching Feelings*, Douglas and Ellie's story.

Find out more at amymcgavin.com.

Bonus Epilogue

Next Book